A BODY AT THE TEA ROOMS

DEE MACDONALD

bookouture

Published by Bookouture in 2021

An imprint of Storyfire Ltd.
Carmelite House
50 Victoria Embankment
London EC4Y 0DZ

www.bookouture.com

ISBN: 978-1-80019-412-0
eBook ISBN: 978-1-80019-411-3

CHAPTER ONE

No matter how great a holiday was, it was always good to come home, Kate thought, as she got her first glimpse of the wild Cornish Atlantic coast again at close quarters. It was January and the sea was grey and surly, in contrast to the blue of the Pacific which they'd left behind.

Lower Tinworthy was a Cornish seaside village of houses and cottages scattered on the lush green hillsides above the River Pol. Kate had recently moved to Lavender Cottage, a postcard-worthy building which overlooked the local shops, the ancient bridge across the river, the sandy beach and the sea. She'd fallen in love with the view the first time she'd seen it and, nearly a year later, it still had the power to make her heart lift.

Kate and her travelling companion, Woody Forrest, had been lucky enough to get a lift all the way back from Heathrow from Aaron Hedgefield, a local businessman who'd flown in from Los Angeles on the same flight. He'd rescued them from hours on the National Express coach to Exeter, for which Kate was very thankful!

Now, as Aaron Hedgefield dropped them off outside Lavender Cottage, Kate took a deep breath of damp Cornish air, looked fondly at the old stone building and the little walled garden, and pushed open the green-painted gate.

Barney, her springer spaniel, was, in the meantime, leaping off the ground in his eagerness to welcome her. As Kate fondled his ears and stroked his head, she wondered if he'd had a walk each day whilst she'd been away but, knowing her errant sister Angie and her predilection for the gin bottle, she somehow doubted it. There was no sign of the unreliable sister. Angie had recently inherited some money from her mother-in-law, and had wasted no time in spending the cash. She had just bought The Locker Café near the beach, which she was renaming 'Tea Rooms', which sounded more rustic, although she hadn't decided on a final name yet. She was also hoping to obtain a licence so that it could be a little bar in the evenings. Some of the building required major structural repairs and, in this endeavour, she was accompanied by her dubious but charming new Irish friend, Fergal. They certainly had their work cut out for them. Back to reality, Kate thought.

'I'm desperate for a coffee,' she said to Woody as she unlocked the door. He followed behind with the suitcases and looked around the kitchen.

'Good to be back,' he replied.

They'd met shortly after Kate had arrived in the village and had inadvertently got involved in some murders. Woody was the detective inspector in charge at the time and there had been instant attraction.

Angie, her normally immaculate blonde hair tousled and her face pink, burst in the door half an hour later as they were making coffee. After she gave them both a quick hug, said how pleased she was to see them back home and how tanned they were, she hardly drew breath before adding: 'You're not going to *believe* this!'

'Probably not,' Kate said wearily, rubbing her eyes as she sat down. What *now*, she wondered, had Angie got involved in? She'd only been away for a few weeks…

'It's the tea rooms! We have *gutted* the place,' Angie went on, 'and we discovered this great cellar we didn't know we had.'

Kate shuddered, recalling a bad experience she'd had in a cellar a few months previously.

'You made quick work of that! How big is it?' Woody asked, stirring his coffee. Although he, too, looked tired, he was still a good-looking man, Kate thought. She'd fallen for his Mediterranean looks and, at sixty-two, his dark brown eyes still normally sparkled, although not that much just at the moment.

'Not huge, but we thought it would be good for storage,' Angie continued, 'and we found this big trapdoor in the floor leading down to where smugglers probably hid their loot. It's got metal fittings which had all rusted up and it took us some time to get it open. I thought we could make a feature of it, you know?'

'Sounds intriguing,' Kate said. 'And who knows what interesting artefacts you might find down there.'

'Well, I was just getting to that!' Angie exclaimed. She plonked herself down on the cream sofa next to Kate.

'Here's the coffee,' Woody said, emerging from the kitchen with a mug in each hand.

'Thanks, Woody,' Kate said, 'I really need this. I'm knackered.'

'Are you *listening*?' Angie yelled, her eyes wild with excitement.

'Yes, yes, get on with it,' Kate said shortly, stifling a yawn.

'Do you want to *know* what we found in the cellar?'

'Buried treasure?' Woody suggested with a chuckle.

Angie shook her head in exasperation. 'We found a bricked-up wall down there. We were curious, wondered what might have been behind it. Well, you aren't going to *believe* this…' She paused for maximum effect. 'When we took it apart, we found a *skeleton*!'

'A skeleton?' Woody placed his mug back on the table. 'A *human* skeleton?'

'A *human* skeleton,' Angie confirmed.

'My God!' said Kate, sitting up straighter. 'A genuine skeleton in a cupboard! I don't believe this!'

'Well, you'd better believe it,' Angie said.

'Where is this skeleton?' Woody asked. 'Or have you left it in the wall?'

'We haven't touched it.' Angie shook her head. 'We phoned the police and they came and taped the whole place off. They've taken the body away but we're not allowed to go in there again until they finish their investigation.'

'Any idea how long it had been in there?' Woody asked, plainly fascinated.

'Oh, a long time apparently. Years. And they think it's a man, but it has to be examined properly and all that.'

'Poor Bill Robson!' Woody said to Kate, referring to the detective inspector who'd taken over when Woody had retired from the local police force. Like Woody, Bill had decided to spend the last few years prior to retirement in what he considered to be a Cornish backwater and thought the most he'd have to contend with would be the occasional pub brawl or sheep rustler. He, like Woody, had been greatly mistaken.

'Well,' said Woody. He thought for a moment. 'You don't suppose Polly Lock finished off one of her suitors some years ago?'

Angie giggled. 'No, apparently Polly Lock only owned the place for the past ten years and never bothered to open up the cellar, which is why the door was so rusted up. Before that the building was just a sort of old warehouse place where some of the fishermen left their nets, lobster pots and things like that. I think builders used it to store stuff too, according to Des at The Gull.'

'Very interesting,' said Woody, gazing out of the window. He glanced at Kate.

'I'm hoping it was a smuggler,' Angie said dreamily. 'It would add a bit of atmosphere to the place and get people flocking in. Anyway, we could perhaps cover it up eventually with a glass panel or something in the floor so people could look down and *see* the space in the wall where the smuggler had been hidden for probably hundreds of years. What a *fantastic* tourist attraction it could be!' She sighed happily.

'So how much space was there in this wall?' Kate asked.

'Probably about six feet square and about six feet high. Perhaps we'll get a waxwork pirate made and pop him in there. The possibilities are endless!'

'Don't get excited, Angie. It'll depend on how long the body's been there and, more importantly, *who* it is,' Woody said sternly.

'Well, they're hardly going to be able to find out after a couple of centuries, are they?' Angie muttered. 'And we know for a fact that smugglers were forever roaming this coast. Everybody knows that they had hidden caches where they stored all the contraband.'

'Have the police given you any indication yet of how old the skeleton is?' Kate asked. 'After all, it may *not* be centuries old.'

'Of *course* it will be! I just *know*!'

'Well,' said Woody, 'I'll see what I can find out. But don't go getting too excited until we discover some more.'

Kate could scarcely believe her ears. In the short time she'd lived in this village she'd unwittingly been involved in solving several murders, and here was yet *another* dead body! Even if it *was* hundreds of years old! *If* it was hundreds of years old. Well, at least the killer couldn't still be on the prowl! Or could they?

CHAPTER TWO

Suddenly wide awake, Kate and Woody accompanied Angie back down the lane to the tea rooms, which were situated on the cobbled street alongside the river, about two hundred yards from the beach. It was a long, low building, now painted white and prettified with a thatched roof. Apparently, Polly Lock had done miracles with the place and her cream teas were popular for miles around. She was a popular lady with the men, but surely she wouldn't go so far as to murder one of her suitors?

Bill Robson was standing outside the tea rooms and shouting instructions at his men. He turned round to glare at the three of them as they approached. Kate disliked the man intensely, having had several clashes with him during the past year, so she stood aside with Angie and let Woody do the talking.

Then Fergal, Angie's new beau, appeared from the upstairs flat.

'You couldn't feckin' make it up!' he called by way of a greeting. Then, as an afterthought, 'So, how was California?'

'It was great,' Kate replied, 'and I can scarcely believe it's less than twenty-four hours since we left. It already seems like a lifetime ago. And to come back to *this*...'

Fergal put his arm round Angie. 'Now Angela here's getting all worried about ghosts.'

'I am *not*,' snapped Angie. 'Anyway, a ghost or two wouldn't do any harm in attracting customers to our new business, if we *ever* finish transforming the tea rooms.' She sighed as she waved a hand at the taped-off area.

'Oh, we will, we will,' said Fergal soothingly.

Kate had mixed feelings about Fergal. She could see what Angie liked about him: his blue eyes and black hair, his sense of humour and constant cheerfulness. He'd had a variety of jobs and could turn his hand to almost anything, which was just as well since Angie had big plans for the place. Fergal had been in the building trade and he'd worked in lots of bars seemingly, so he was ideally suited to this project. However, they knew very little about him and sometimes Kate worried that Angie was putting so much trust in him.

Woody returned to join them. 'Nothing we can do here,' he said to Kate. Then, turning to Angie and Fergal, 'We're tired, so we're off now. I'm afraid your skeleton is probably younger than you are, Angie! See you later.' Angie was left staring sadly into space.

As they walked back up the lane, Woody said, 'The body would appear to be that of a man in his twenties, Bill Robson said. And it has most likely been in that cellar for more than ten years because that's when Polly Lock took over the place. The man is wearing some sort of modern-day suit, apparently, so they've checked the records going back thirty years and no one around here appears to have gone missing in that time. It's all a bit of a mystery at the moment.' He hesitated. 'There is an impact wound on his skull so it could be that somebody caved his head in. His suit is still in reasonable condition and they are examining that as we speak.'

'A passing stranger perhaps?' Kate suggested.

'Possible, but unlikely. He must have been known to *someone* here if they took the trouble to kill him and hide the body. I guess that dashes Angie's hopes that he was a smuggler from centuries ago. She'd planned to cash in on that.' He sighed. 'I think she's out of luck.'

'What happens now?' Kate asked, looking back over her shoulder at the tea rooms.

'The whole cellar area has been sealed off and has to remain that way until they've got all the evidence they need. Once they've confirmed the cause of death they'll know for sure if it has to be treated as murder which, plainly, it could be. What *is* it with this place?'

Kate sighed. 'Well, at least Bill Robson can't accuse *me* of having anything to do with it!'

Kate had only just begun to unpack when Angie came rushing back through the door of Lavender Cottage.

'Isn't this exciting!' she gushed. 'I can't wait to find out how old my Locker Man is! I don't believe that he could be younger than I am!'

'Just don't get too excited,' Kate said, folding up some cotton tops. 'He's really only likely to be thirty or forty years old from what I hear.'

Angie glared angrily at Kate. 'Why do you *always* have to bugger up my dreams?'

Kate was appalled. 'What are you talking about? I haven't buggered up anything. I'm only stating a fact. Woody says that, according to Robson, the skeleton has probably been stuck in that wall for no more than thirty years, judging by his clothes, so it is *not* a smuggler from centuries ago.'

'How can they be so sure? They could be wrong.' Angie looked petulant.

'Well, they could tell by the fact that he was wearing a modern-day suit. Didn't you notice what he was wearing?'

'I didn't stay to look for that long,' Angie said. 'I caught sight of the skull gleaming in the torchlight and I legged it out of there as fast as I could. I got quite a shock, you know!'

'After the police have finished I'd just shut that trapdoor again if I were you, and say nothing about it to your customers. It's certainly *not* the kind of publicity you need.'

'It could have been such a crowd-puller,' Angie commented sadly. 'Mind you, if he turns out to have been a bit naughty, like a robber or something, we could still market the place as The Smuggler's Cabin, couldn't we?'

'What's wrong with your original idea? You know, dressing Fergal up as a pirate or something? You might even be able to buy a parrot to sit on his shoulder!'

'You're making fun of me again!' Angie retorted. 'All I want to do is scratch a living out of this place and help visitors enjoy the Tinworthy experience. That's the heading we're going to use on our brochures: The Tinworthy Experience. Cream teas by day, drinks by the sea at night. Fergal's designing them right now.'

'Well, good luck with that,' Kate said, recalling her own Tinworthy experiences. She only hoped those in the future would be a little less eventful.

Woody had popped home to his cottage on the other side of the valley, to ditch his suitcases and pick up his mail. An hour later he was back.

'It's good to be home,' he said, gazing out of Kate's sitting-room window at the river and the sea, before settling himself in the chair alongside the wood burner and stroking the dog's head.

'Shall I open some wine?' Kate suggested, heading through the archway into the large bright kitchen with its Shaker units and French doors to the garden.

'Good idea.' Woody stroked his chin. 'So far,' he said, 'according to what I've been able to wiggle out from Bill Robson, the police only know that Locker Man, as they're now calling him, was in his twenties, had died of a head injury and had been holed up in that cellar for anything from ten to forty years. Bill has checked ownership of The Locker Café, as Polly Lock christened it. But what I didn't know is that Larry Lock, Polly's late husband, had actually owned the place for about twelve years prior. Before that it was known only as "the long cabin", where fishermen kept their nets and lobster pots, and I've a feeling Aaron Hedgefield told me that the family had leased it for a time for storing boat stuff.'

'It must have been owned by somebody originally, surely?' Kate said.

'Well, the building is a couple of hundred years old and it was used for storage by countless people before Larry bought it, half of whom are no longer with us. Polly's going to have to be questioned, of course, because Bill's trying to locate and question everyone still alive who might have used the place. He's got a mammoth task on his hands.'

'Good,' Kate said with some pleasure. 'But what if they don't find anyone?'

'Which is highly likely,' Woody said, refilling her glass. 'But who the hell *is* this guy? And how come no one was reported missing at the time? He couldn't have been a local, so he must have been visiting or just passing through.'

'Well, he must have hung around long enough to have upset *someone*,' Kate remarked. 'Probably a builder, judging by where he was entombed? Could it be that a builder owned it? Who did Larry buy it from?'

'Apparently Larry bought it for a song from the local council, who wanted to get rid of it. They'd planned to knock it down but then someone slapped a Grade Two listing on it and so the council decided to sell. Because of the listing it had to be restored sympathetically – in character and all that – and, when Larry died, it cost Polly a small fortune to convert it.'

Kate thought for a moment. 'Maybe one of my patients will remember something,' she said. 'In fact, I might just call in on Polly for a chat too.'

Woody laid his hand on hers. 'Kate,' he began, 'don't—'

'I know, I know,' Kate interrupted, 'you're going to tell me not to get involved.'

'Well, look at what happened *before*,' Woody said in an exasperated tone. 'You nearly came to grief a couple of times *because* you got involved!'

'But, like it or not, I did help to solve both cases,' Kate protested.

Woody sighed. 'Yes, you did, but if it had gone wrong…' He laced his fingers through hers. 'It's just that I don't want to *lose* you.'

Kate squeezed his hand. 'That's a sweet thing to say, Woody. But this isn't a killing that took place this week, this month, this year even. This is a killing that took place decades ago and we don't even know who the victim *is*! You must admit my life's hardly likely to be in danger if I just ask around a little bit?'

CHAPTER THREE

After getting home only that morning, followed by all the excitement of discovering a body at the tea rooms, Kate found herself feeling hungry but too worn out to fix something, so she suggested going for a meal at their local to Woody, who of course agreed.

The local pub, The Greedy Gull, a short walk down the lane, had been Angie's undoing on several occasions when she'd run out of gin at home. Woody's cottage, on the opposite hillside and appropriately called On the Up, was a ten-minute walk away: down the hill, across the ancient bridge and up the other side.

Then, half a mile or so up the road, was Middle Tinworthy, which housed the medical centre where Kate worked three or four days a week, the school, the church, the village hall, The Tinners' Arms and the large housing estate.

A further three quarters of a mile up the road was Higher Tinworthy. This elevated part of the village housed mainly the wealthy with their large, old houses, along with some modern glass-fronted new-builds, most with distant panoramic sea views. There was no pub in Higher Tinworthy so the residents were obliged to descend either to The Tinners' or The Greedy Gull for alcoholic refreshment.

On this occasion Kate was very glad The Greedy Gull was only a short walk away as they went in search of something to eat after their long trip and the shocking discovery they'd returned to.

'Well, look who's here!' Des Pardoe, the landlord, looked up from his newspaper which was spread out across the countertop in an almost empty pub. 'When did *you* get back then?' He folded the *Racing Times* up carefully and studied them with his long lugubrious face.

'Only about three hours ago,' Kate replied, thinking so much had happened since their return already. As she was warming her hands by the fire she studied the blackboard which proclaimed, in chalk, 'Des's Daily Specials'.

Des, or his wife, had obviously been polishing the horse brasses which decorated the overhead beams and also each side of the inglenook where the huge wood burner was situated. It was a traditional pub but Des, who had an occasional artistic bent, had painted a large gull on the whitewashed walls on either side of the fireplace. Each gull had a fish in its beak, to emphasise the fact that gulls were greedy, as many summer visitors, sitting outside, soon discovered when their pasties were snatched from their hands by fast-diving birds.

'Where *is* everybody?' Woody asked, looking around. 'Have you killed them all off with your dodgy steak and ale pies?' Steak and ale pies were Des's speciality and always topped the menu list.

'Nothin' wrong with my steak 'n' ales,' said Des. 'Mind you, it don't look right havin' suntanned punters in here in bleedin' January.'

'The tans won't last long in this weather,' Kate said sadly. It was a bitterly cold day with an icy wind and she was already missing the Californian sunshine. Then again there was something comforting about coming into a nice, warm, friendly pub on a chilly day.

'I'll have a pint of your best bitter,' Woody said, 'which is about the only thing I've missed. How about you, Kate?'

'Glass of house red, please.'

'So, how was California?' Des asked as he sorted out the drinks.

'Comfortably warm,' Woody replied. 'About seventy during the day.'

'Hollywood, was it? See any stars?' Des asked as he waited for the froth to settle on Woody's beer before he topped up the glass.

'Los Angeles is a big area, Des,' Woody said, 'and Hollywood's only part of it. We drove around it one day so Kate could see how the other half live but, no, we didn't see any movie stars.'

'They were all hidden away in their vast palaces behind security gates,' Kate added as she watched Des pour out her wine.

'Nobody out and about havin' a walk?' Des asked hopefully.

Kate was amused that Des appeared to be somewhat star struck.

'*Nobody* goes out for a walk over there,' Woody said as he downed the first gulp of his beer. 'Everyone drives, everywhere.'

'Funny way of livin',' Des remarked as he turned to serve some locals who'd just come in.

'And another of the reasons why I live over here,' murmured Woody, who'd come to England from California nearly forty years previously, and had never gone back to his homeland to live. He did like to visit every so often, though, as his siblings, and his ninety-two year old mother lived there, and he'd been keen for Kate to meet them. He held up his glass to admire the contents.

'Plus the unparalleled charm of the nurses,' Kate added, with a sparkle in her eye.

Woody snorted. 'Who all fancy themselves as lady detectives.'

'Without whom most of the crimes round here would probably remain unsolved,' Kate said firmly.

Before Woody could reply, Des reappeared at their end of the bar.

'Have you seen your sister yet?' he asked Kate casually.

'Yes, I have, briefly.' She pursed her lips, not wanting to say too much on the matter.

'So what's happenin' down there? I hear there's police millin' around all over the place, and they've found a *body*?'

'We don't know the details yet,' Woody said firmly. 'I guess we'll all know more soon enough.'

'Well, she's been knockin' hell out of them old Locker tea rooms,' Des said. 'Rumour has it she's plannin' on openin' a *bar*.'

'I doubt she'll be much competition to you,' Kate said with feeling. 'She'll be her own best customer.'

'That'll be my loss then,' Des said sadly.

Kate studied Des's menu. 'I'm going to have some of your fish and chips, Des.'

'Same for me,' Woody said, 'which is *another* reason why I live over here.'

'Two fish and chips!' Des hollered into the kitchen where his other half presided over the deep-fat fryer and the microwave. He turned his attention back to his two customers. 'Did you have a good flight back then?'

'Not bad,' Woody said.

'You were snoring for the best part of five thousand miles,' Kate said, 'so speak for yourself!'

'This woman,' Woody informed Des, 'slept all the way back from Heathrow, which is more than I did.'

'What, did you park up there or somethin'?'

'Believe it or not, Des, we got a lift, and from none other than Aaron Hedgefield.'

'Well!' Des looked impressed. 'What was *he* doin' up there?'

'Oh, you know, just flew in after a couple of days looking at Californian vineyards or something.'

They'd met Aaron Hedgefield as they stood waiting at the baggage carousel at Heathrow. Woody had introduced them, and Kate, feeling scruffy and exhausted, had been impressed with the perfectly groomed businessman with the dark blue eyes. It transpired he'd travelled in first class, no less, which explained his debonair appearance. He'd flashed her an expensive smile and asked how they were getting home. Horrified at the thought of *anyone* sitting on a bus for four hours, he had immediately offered them a lift back in his large, luxurious Mercedes. Kate had stretched out in the back and slept all the way home. She'd since learned from Woody that he was the owner of Hedgefield Estates, Hedgefield Engineering, Hedgefield Agricultural Services. 'Hedgefield bloody everything!' he'd added.

'More money than sense,' said Des. 'He's changed, you know. Used to be a nice enough lad, even if he did get into trouble several times. But he's got greedier and greedier. His father was a real gentleman – old Henry Hedgefield. He committed suicide about twenty years back.'

'How awful!' Kate exclaimed.

Des leaned across the bar and tapped his nose. 'Strung himself up in a tree, he did.'

'Well, I didn't know that,' Woody said.

'Before your time. Aaron never got on that well with his father, of course,' Des said, warming to his subject. 'It was Aaron who found him there in the orchard, danglin' from one of them old apple trees – a Brownlees Russet, I think it was. You've never tasted a finer apple. Terrible shock Aaron got.'

Even Woody looked appalled.

'Aaron was heir to the whole kit and caboodle,' Des went on. 'Nice wife he's got; her father farms up at Pelworthy.'

'I have to say we were mighty pleased to see him and his Merc,' Woody admitted.

'He did seem very nice to me,' Kate added.

Des grunted as he turned to serve two hardy-looking souls, kitted out with waterproofs and rucksacks, who had just come into the pub.

'He doesn't sound too enthusiastic,' Kate observed.

'I've never known Des to be enthusiastic about anything much,' Woody said drily.

Des returned once the new arrivals were provided with drinks and menus. 'You wouldn't catch me braving that coast path in January,' he muttered.

'Oh, I don't know,' Kate said. 'I'm planning to take Barney for a good long walk up on the cliffs tomorrow. No doubt we both need it. But tell me more about Aaron Hedgefield, Des.'

'Rumour has it he got in trouble with the police once too often and his dad was despairing of him. Some folks said that was the reason old Henry did himself in.' With that he turned his attention to yet more backpackers who had just come through the door.

'Well,' Kate remarked as they carried their drinks to a table close to the fire, 'isn't *that* interesting?'

'Yes, it certainly is,' Woody said. 'I had no idea he'd ever been in trouble with the law. It's strange that I never heard any rumours when I was in CID in Launceston.'

'It sounds as if it was a long time ago,' Kate said. 'Perhaps it was just a misspent youth because he's *very* respectable now. Maybe the shock of his father's death made him see the error of his ways…' She sipped her drink. 'Interesting about his father hanging himself. We've only been home five minutes and already we've heard of *two* dead bodies! But it's Locker Man who fascinates me! Haven't you any idea who he might have been? I mean, you know the area well, don't you?'

'I've only lived here five years, Kate, and I covered quite a large area, not just Tinworthy. No matter how thorough you are, you can't get to know everyone. All I know is that, when I took over as detective inspector, there were no unsolved murders or mysteries in the area. And I didn't know about Aaron's father either.'

'It must be awful for Aaron to have to live with something like that,' Kate said sadly.

'There's definitely more to Aaron Hedgefield than I'd reckoned,' Woody said. 'He mentioned the possibility of an invitation up to the dizzy heights of the Hedgefield empire, so you'll be able to see how the other half live in Cornwall – if not in Hollywood.'

'Perhaps we'll be able to find out some more about his misspent youth, and whether that was the reason that his father decided to do away with himself.'

'It'll take more than one visit to find out all *you* want to know!' Woody said with a grin. 'Let's just hope he'll need some crew again on that yacht of his this coming summer. I spent a day out at sea with him a couple of years ago, and it was amazing.'

'Two sexy men on a boat!' exclaimed Kate.

Woody raised his right eyebrow and said nothing. She loved the way he did that. It heightened his sex appeal and she began to feel quite fruity.

'On a lighter note,' Kate said, 'do you fancy coming back to the cottage for an hour, or two?'

'Is Angie out?'

'Angie's out.'

'Let's go!' He winked.

CHAPTER FOUR

Kate's first day back at work was predictable.

'Don't you look well!' Sue, the other practice nurse, exclaimed. '*Love* the tan!'

'Did you get married over there?' Denise, the receptionist, asked eagerly. 'Or at least e*ngaged?*'

'No, I did *not*!' Kate replied. When she'd told Denise, back in October, about her forthcoming trip to California with Woody, Denise had immediately decided that she and Woody should head to Las Vegas for one of those 'quickie' weddings, complete with an Elvis Presley lookalike conducting the ceremony.

She looked so disappointed that Kate said consolingly, 'We only went to see his mum, Denise. She lives in LA, which is lovely, and so is she. She's Italian, you know, and the only trouble is she spends most of the day cooking and baking, and I've gained half a stone! We also visited his sister in San Francisco, and I just loved that place! I'd love to go back.'

Denise grinned. 'And get married *next* time?'

'Now why would I do that?' Kate asked.

'Aw, just to please me,' said Denise as she turned to deal with the queue of patients at her desk.

Having divorced her unfaithful husband almost thirty years earlier, Kate had no intention of ever marrying again. She liked her life, her job, her home, her independence. She and Angie got on reasonably well, the only hiccup being Angie's insatiable thirst for gin. Nevertheless, they managed to jog along together at Lavender Cottage with only the occasional row.

Sometimes Kate found it hard to believe that she'd only known Woody for less than a year. She'd unwittingly found herself involved in the nasty incident at the Women's Institute of all places, shortly after her relocation to Cornwall. Her connection to the first case had resulted in her photo in all the local papers. And a journalist had recently referred to her as the Cornish Miss Marple! Now everyone in Tinworthy knew who Kate Palmer was and that she was involved with Woody Forrest, who'd been in charge of the case. But then, in the autumn, she'd become involved yet again in a poisoning case. As a result, she'd become addicted to some super-sleuthing, as well as Woody Forrest. She'd fallen for his American accent, still strong after forty years in the UK, his Mediterranean looks (inherited from his Italian mother), and his calm, considered approach to everything (inherited from his English father).

Woody had won a prestigious scholarship to study criminology at Oxford, after which he joined the Metropolitan Police in London, and decided to stay in the UK. Widowed, with two grown-up daughters and approaching retirement age, Woody had relocated to North Cornwall. He'd come to know the area after years of surfing weekends, hoping for a quiet life. He'd certainly got that well and truly wrong.

Their arrangement suited them both: seeing each other most days, but having their own space when they wanted it. And nothing Denise could say was going to alter that!

In the medical centre Kate went about her duties, without comment, as all around everyone voiced their theories about Locker Man's identity. News travelled fast in a small place like this.

'Your sister must have got the shock of her life when she found that body,' Sue said, with a delighted shiver, as she and Kate stood chatting to Denise at the reception desk later.

'Yes, she did,' Kate agreed.

'But how come Polly Lock never found it then?' Denise asked. 'She must have had that place a good ten years. And Larry had it before that. It's funny *Angie* was the one to find it…'

Kate was aware that Angie could be a suspect in the minds of the villagers who had no idea of how old the body was. After all, she was a newcomer to the village and not everyone knew her very well.

'I don't believe Polly ever used the cellar,' Kate replied. 'She stored all her supplies upstairs. Angie and Fergal are converting the upstairs area into a little flat.'

'Is this Fergal a permanent fixture then?' Sue asked.

Kate shrugged. 'Who knows? But he has to sleep somewhere and I'm certainly not having him as a permanent fixture in Lavender Cottage!' She worried from time to time about Fergal's motives towards her sister, and wondered briefly if he might know more about the body than he was letting on. Then she'd dismiss the idea and think it was totally ridiculous. But…

'I hear he has a great deal of Irish charm,' said Denise, 'and that he's a good looker too. How come I never meet anyone like that? Where did she find him?'

'I think he found her,' Kate replied, deciding not to mention the first occasion when he helped to get Angie to her feet after overdoing the gin in The Greedy Gull, a fact of which Angie was still completely unaware. 'She slipped outside one of the little shops down near the beach and literally landed at his feet.'

They'd been an item ever since. He'd been selling postcards and tourist stuff to the local shops, but sometimes Kate wondered if that was his *real* reason for being in Cornwall. A couple of years back she probably wouldn't have given it a thought, but she was much more suspicious of everyone these days.

'I must try that next time I'm out shopping,' Denise said with a giggle, 'except that, with my luck, I'd probably get picked up by some dirty old man!'

'Well, you could always clean him up,' Sue said as she disappeared into the treatment room.

Kate laughed. 'Who's next on my list, Denise?'

'How about Sadie Thomson?'

'I remember my old man used to store stuff in that place,' Sadie Thomson said as she presented a spotty arm to Kate in the surgery. 'Didn't used to belong to no one, it didn't. No lock on the door or nothin'. Never any trouble in them days, everyone respectin' everyone else's things. That's before all them incomers arrived—' She clapped her hand over her mouth. 'Don't mean *you*, of course, nurse, but some of them…' She shook her head in despair. 'Mind you, Larry Lock owned that place for years and he had a terrible temper, he did. It wouldn't surprise me if he finished off one of Polly's fancy men; wouldn't surprise me at all.'

'Really?' Kate didn't want to sound too interested but couldn't resist asking, 'Polly was popular with the men then, was she?'

'Popular? Somethin' like that. She put it about a bit, did Polly. Anyway, I'm here for some of that ointment.'

'Have you been eating seafood again?' Kate asked as she examined Sadie's array of colourful spots.

'Well, only a couple of them little mussels,' Sadie admitted, 'cos our Tom's been out and—'

'Sadie, a couple of little mussels are seafood,' Kate said, 'and you are allergic to seafood. And this is not the first time we've had this conversation, is it?'

'Well, no, I s'pose not,' Sadie conceded, shifting her bulk from one side of her bottom to the other on the plastic chair. She ran a pudgy finger through her grey, thinning hair.

Kate sighed. 'You know what to do and what not to do.' But she was aware that Sadie, like several other elderly patients, *liked* coming to the surgery. They could see who was coming in and going out, they could exchange gossip and, with a bit of luck, might be able to glean some interesting information from whoever was treating them.

'You still with that detective fellow?' Sadie asked as she stood and picked up her prescription.

'He's retired now,' Kate said shortly.

'What about this new bloke then? Robertson, isn't it?'

'Robson,' Kate corrected. And wouldn't you like to know what I think of *him*, Kate thought as she shepherded Sadie out of the door.

'It isn't bloody fair!' Angie moaned later when Kate got home. 'We can't go ahead with any of our renovations downstairs until they remove the tape, but at least Fergal is getting some work done upstairs.'

'What exactly is upstairs?' Kate asked.

Angie had taken possession of the property while Kate was in California, so she hadn't yet had a chance to see it all. Angie had said to 'wait until we've done some work on it', because she'd wanted her to be surprised, amazed, impressed. Kate was indeed amazed at their findings, but not exactly in the way that Angie had originally intended.

'It's a tiny flat,' Angie went on, 'with just a couple of rooms. The larger one is going to be the sitting room, with a mini kitchen in the corner, and the other will be the bedroom, although we're going to have to store some stuff up there too. And there's a separate loo, which is just big enough to be made into a wet room.'

'Sounds like you're pretty well organised,' Kate remarked. 'So, what's Fergal doing right now?'

'He's trying to work out how to install the shower,' Angie said. 'The main worry will be storage because there's not a lot of room if we're going to be storing bottles and mixers and all that, as well as tea and coffee.'

'Well, perhaps you can store your provisions in some ancient-looking chests down there in the cellar, so your customers can look down at the treasure trove. It's high fashion now to make stuff looked distressed and old.'

Angie thought for a moment. 'Do you know what, Kate? Sometimes, just sometimes, you come up with some cracking ideas!'

The village was agog with gossip for the rest of the day. Who would have thought that Polly Lock's old place could provide such excitement? As always, everyone had a different theory about Locker Man: he'd been brought in by boat from somewhere else; whoever had killed him could have been a builder because the brickwork wasn't at all bad. Maybe Polly Lock had finished off old Lenny Briggs, who used to fancy her at one time and then disappeared, so she probably buried him down there. They'd conveniently forgotten that Lenny had gone to live with a daughter in Swindon. Then there was someone-or-other, back forty years ago, who had run off to sea and never been heard of again, so perhaps that was as far as he got. And so on, and so on. Kate had overheard hushed references to Angie and Fergal as 'them newcomers' and 'things like that didn't happen till they got here'.

If any further incentive was needed to solve this case, the fact that Angie might be a suspect was sufficient for Kate to begin her investigations.

CHAPTER FIVE

'Well,' Woody said a couple of days later, as they set off for a walk along the clifftops with Barney, 'Aaron's not wasted much time after our journey back home with him. He'd remembered seeing your photo in the paper and seemed fascinated by your escapades. We've been invited to dinner on Saturday night.'

'We *have*?' Kate was amazed. 'But I hardly know him, and I don't know her at all.'

'You soon will then,' said Woody. 'I told him I'd check with you and let him know.'

'I should just about have got over my jet lag by then,' Kate said, 'and my social calendar isn't exactly bursting at the seams.' She took in a deep gulp of frosty air as she looked across at the ocean, which was relatively calm today. The rugged coastline was crystal clear in the winter sunshine and Kate could see down the coast as far as Trevose Head, and northwards up towards Devon and Lundy Island.

'So shall I say we'll go?'

'Why not?' Kate was fascinated by what she'd recently discovered about the Hedgefields. She found there was plenty of local gossip to be had once she'd expressed an interest. One of her regular patients, Ida Tilley, from Pendorian Manor, had gone into raptures about the Hedgefields' big mansion up at Tremorron, which had aroused Kate's curiosity. She hesitated for only a moment. 'It won't be a formal dress-up affair, will it?'

Woody laughed. 'You should be OK in your gownless evening strap and your tiara,' he scoffed, 'plus the Palmer family jewels, of course.'

'Seriously, Woody! Are they very grand?'

'Of course they're not *grand*! They're quite down-to-earth, albeit with lots of dough. But, if you're worried, I'll check that out when I call him back.' He chewed his lip. 'You *must* have made a good impression!'

'Don't be ridiculous!' Kate retorted. 'I hardly said two words to him and I slept most of the way back, if you remember.'

'Then I guess it's because of my informing him of your Superwoman qualities,' Woody said.

Kate looked through her wardrobe and sighed. Although she and Woody had eaten out on innumerable occasions, this was the first time they'd been invited to someone's *house* together. What should she wear? What would the wife be like? And would she have to reciprocate and ask them back? Would they entertain the Hedgefields in Woody's house or hers? Kate was beginning to wish they weren't going. And, of course, Woody would think she was nuts if she told him of her concerns, because men were not known to worry themselves about such trivia.

Woody accepted the invitation and told Kate that it was all very informal and they'd probably be eating in the kitchen.

'Oh, that's good,' Kate said, feeling relieved. 'And will it be just the two of them?'

'I assume so.'

'What's the wife like?'

'I've never met her. I only know she's called Eve and comes from a local farming family, so she should be pretty down to earth,' Woody replied.

'What about children?'

'I know they have two daughters, but one's at university and the other is at some private school up country. Sure you don't want to find out their names, ages, bust sizes, shoe sizes before we go?' He ducked as she aimed a copy of the *Western Morning News* at him. 'I shall wear my one and only cashmere sweater,' he went on, 'with several layers beneath because those big houses are known to freeze in winter. Must be their blue blood that keeps the aristos at a cool temperature.'

'I wouldn't class *them* as aristocrats,' Kate said, 'they're self-made.'

'Well, they must be doing *something* right. We'd regard them as gentry in the States.'

'In the UK,' Kate explained patiently, 'it's *breeding* that makes you gentry. Years of breeding and inbreeding, and usually with a centuries-old stately pile that they can't afford to run.'

'This is such a crazy country,' Woody said, 'and one of the reasons why I like it. Next thing you'll be insisting I use a knife with my fork. What *is* it with you Brits?'

Kate had decided to follow Woody's lead and settled on her standard 'going out' winter outfit of her – one and only – cashmere sweater which, mercifully, was black and loose enough to cover her California tummy. Still, she'd need to remember to hold it in. She teamed the sweater with her new black-and-white checked skirt and wore her long black patent leather boots which had cost her almost a month's salary in John Lewis a couple of years back.

At fifty-nine she still had most of her natural auburn hair colour, thanks to the gene she must have inherited from her mother, who went to her grave at seventy-five years of age without a single white hair on her head. Angie, on the other hand, had inherited their father's genes: early greying hair (Angie had chosen blonde instead) and a penchant for alcohol. This particular weakness had destroyed their parents' marriage, and could have done the same for Angie's, had her late husband not been such a saint. Kate had also inherited her mother's green eyes, now made up 'smokily', as was the fashion. As she studied herself in the full-length mirror Kate was reasonably pleased with her reflection – so long as she remembered to hold in that tummy.

As Kate got into the passenger seat of Woody's car, her mind was still mulling over all the rumours and gossip she'd heard on the subject of Locker Man.

CHAPTER SIX

Kate was impressed with her first sight of Tremorron. It more than lived up to Ida Tilley's description and was situated a couple of miles west of Higher Tinworthy, along the narrow coast road, where she'd had no occasion to go before. In the darkness, it was difficult to discern anything apart from the Cornish hedge on the left side and the moonlit Atlantic stretching out on the right, until they arrived at the gateway that heralded Tremorron House. From there followed a bumpy ride to the house on a meandering stony path with grass growing in the middle.

'I don't suppose you notice all the bumps if you're driving a top-of-the-range Range Rover,' Woody remarked as they rounded the final corner and saw the house ahead. It was very dark but the house was floodlit. Kate could see it was an enormous Victorian pile, complete with a couple of turrets. She wondered if the place was lit up every evening, or if it was only done to welcome guests.

Woody steered his car into a space alongside a collection of off-road vehicles.

'Oh, wow!' Kate exclaimed, as she got out of the car. 'This house looks *enormous*!'

'It is enormous!' Woody said, gazing up in awe as he locked the car door.

The doorbell resounded throatily, somewhere deep in the bowels of the house, and Kate half expected a maid, in cap and apron, to open the door. Instead the door was opened by Aaron, casually attired in a denim shirt and beige corduroy trousers.

'Good to see you! Let me take your coats; I promise you it's warm in the kitchen,' he said. His breath was visible in the icy stone-floored hallway. 'Come on through.'

He led the way across the huge hall towards a door at the back which, in turn, led to a long corridor where, Kate noted thankfully, the temperature increased a little. As they finally arrived in the kitchen, it felt almost warm.

They entered a huge, state-of-the-art kitchen where, stirring something on the Aga with a wooden spoon in one hand and a large glass of red in the other, was an attractive dark-haired lady who Aaron introduced: 'This is Eve, my other half!'

His other half looked to be in her late forties, tall, slim and her dark hair liberally sprinkled with grey. She wore a butcher's apron over a white silk blouse and jeans. There were introductions all round, Eve apologising for being 'one glass ahead', explaining that it was a shame to leave it in the bottle after she'd added most of it to the casserole. She had a mischievous grin and Kate liked her immediately. 'Let Aaron pour you some decent stuff,' she added.

Aaron indicated a vast array of bottles positioned on the long granite work-surface. 'I've got a small selection out so you can take your pick.'

'Wine would be lovely,' Kate said, 'red, please.'

'I'll just have a shandy,' Woody said. 'I'm driving.'

'You could stay the night,' Aaron said, pointing upwards. 'There are seven bedrooms up there!'

'Well…' said Woody doubtfully, glancing at Kate. 'I think we should perhaps go back…'

'It's a very kind offer,' Kate said, 'but I'd worry about my dog. I really need to go back.' She didn't add that she had an unreliable sister who was probably three sheets to the wind by now.

'Oh well, never mind, perhaps another time,' said Aaron.

Another time! Perhaps, Kate thought, he should wait to see how *this* evening goes first.

'Anyway,' Aaron continued cheerfully, 'it's not as if you're likely to be stopped and breathalysed on the way home, is it? I mean, you should have them all well trained, Woody.'

'I'm not in the Force any more, you know,' Woody said with a smile as he accepted a shandy, 'and I rather think my successor might be less lenient.'

At the far end of the long kitchen were two large tan-coloured leather sofas, set in front of a wall of windows leading out onto a floodlit terrace which must be wonderful in summer, Kate thought. She bet it had sea views too.

Kate and Woody sat down on one while Aaron drew up a glass-topped coffee table in front. Kate couldn't see the label on the wine bottle but she knew, with that first sip, that this was a very superior wine. These two plainly did not need to go trolling around looking for bargains in the supermarket.

'I understand you have two daughters,' Kate said, as Aaron and Eve sat down opposite.

'Yes,' Eve confirmed, 'Amber's twenty and has just gone back to uni, and Jade is seventeen and at boarding school.'

'Our two little jewels,' said Aaron.

'Not so little any more,' Eve added. 'What about you both?'

'Well, I have two girls too,' Woody said, 'grown women now, one with a couple of boys. They've turned out well but we had some dramas with them when they were teenagers.'

Eve sighed. 'I know exactly what you mean. What about you, Kate?'

'Maybe boys are easier – sometimes, anyway. I've got two boys, one married up in Edinburgh and just presented me with my first grandchild last August, and the other in Australia, living with his girlfriend.'

'That's a long way away,' Eve said.

'It is. I've only been out there once, and I'm supposed to be saving up for another visit, but it's a slow process,' Kate said. 'Saving, I mean.'

'Well, you certainly can't go all *that* way in an economy seat, can you?' Aaron pulled a face. 'You'd be a *wreck* at the end of it!'

'I'm afraid I shall have to be a wreck then,' Kate said, feeling irritated by the comment.

Eve changed the subject abruptly by asking Kate why she'd chosen to live in Cornwall, and Lower Tinworthy in particular.

'We read about you in the paper,' she said, 'when you got mixed up in those awful murders.'

Kate's involvement in solving the two murders in the previous year was explained in detail, attracting gasps of horror from both Eve and Aaron, and continued even after they'd sat down at the beautifully laid table and tackled their scallop starter.

'You were very brave,' Eve said admiringly.

'I'm not really brave at all,' Kate said, 'but I just sort of *found* myself in difficult situations.'

'You can say that again,' muttered Woody.

'Fortunately, Sir Galahad here was on hand to rescue me on both occasions,' Kate said, patting Woody's arm. 'But, to change the subject, do you *really* have seven bedrooms?'

'We had ten at one time,' Aaron said, 'but madam here insisted on having en suites, so we lost a few.'

'We didn't *need* ten bedrooms,' Eve said sharply. 'In fact, we don't need seven.'

'Well, it just happens to be a big house,' said Aaron. 'My father and grandfather had visitors all the time, so they were frequently occupied, I believe.'

'And we *don't* have visitors at *all*,' Eve said, 'so we could do with a smaller place.' She turned to Kate and Woody. 'I keep telling him that.'

Aaron sighed. 'We are *not* leaving this house,' he said, as he topped up Kate's glass. 'It was good enough for my father and grandfather and it's good enough for me.'

'It costs a fortune to heat,' Eve went on, 'and—'

'We have enough funds,' Aaron snapped.

Kate was beginning to feel a little uncomfortable with the conversation and her opinion of Aaron was beginning to alter – he didn't seem to be quite as affable as he had appeared up to now.

They were just finishing Eve's delicious casserole when Aaron leaned across the table to Kate and said, 'I understand your sister has bought the old boat house down by the beach – The Locker Tea Rooms, or whatever it's called these days? And rumour has it that a body's been found in there?'

'Yes, she has,' Kate replied, surprised that he knew Angie had bought it. 'She's got ideas for turning it into a beach bar type of place. She didn't reckon on the body!'

Aaron didn't speak for a moment. Then he said quietly, 'I didn't know it was for sale.'

'No,' Kate replied, 'I don't think it went on the open market. I think Angie got talking to Polly Lock in the pub.'

'Interesting.' Aaron sat back and dabbed his mouth with the white linen napkin. 'Wish I'd known she was planning to sell. We used to lease it from the council and then, later, from Larry Lock, you know, to put all our boating stuff in there. We let the fishermen store their gear in there too sometimes.'

'We're not sure how she'll make out,' Woody said, 'with The Greedy Gull just up the road. Don't suppose Des will welcome any competition.'

'Particularly as she's been one of his best customers,' Kate added drily.

'Well,' Aaron continued, 'if she ever decides to sell it, I'd be most interested.'

'What on earth would you want that old place for?' Eve asked, frowning.

'Purely sentimental reasons,' Aaron replied. 'But what about this *body*? I mean, hasn't that put your sister off the whole idea?' He turned to Woody. 'Do they have any idea *who* it might be?'

Woody shook his head. 'Not a clue. Don't forget I'm retired now, Aaron, and Bill Robson isn't exactly a close friend.'

'Well, if you ask me, I'd say they should be concentrating on the Locks – Larry and Polly. They had it for years,' Aaron said.

'No doubt they'll question everyone concerned,' Woody said. He then rapidly changed the subject. 'Kate and I have just about got over the jet lag. But we're still waking up in the middle of the night.' They chatted amicably throughout the rest of the meal with no further friction between their hosts. Kate noted that everything was very understated and expensive: Eve's silk blouse, the wine glasses, the tableware, the crockery and cutlery. Nothing ostentatious; just top quality.

It was after eleven when they left, dashing out into the cold January night shouting their thanks and saying, 'We *must* do this again!' Tomorrow, Kate thought, when I'm sober, I might regret saying that.

'Interesting pair,' she said to Woody as they drove off. 'I particularly liked Eve.'

'Yes,' Woody said, 'I like her too. Aaron's OK, just a little brash.'

Kate couldn't fault Aaron's generosity and hospitality, but there was something rather unsettling about the man although she couldn't quite work out what it was…

CHAPTER SEVEN

A couple of days later, as Kate was preparing to go to work, once again she found four members of the press on her doorstep. After last year's shenanigans she wasn't altogether surprised.

'This has nothing to do with me,' she explained patiently.

'But the body was found in a building owned by your *sister*,' one of them said. 'It's quite a coincidence, isn't it?'

'Coincidence or not,' Kate said, 'it has absolutely nothing to do with me – or Angie. But it's my sister you should be talking to.'

'It was *her* that got in touch with *us*,' another one said, 'and we've already had a word with her and her partner.'

'In that case you'll know all there is to know,' Kate said, closing the door. What on earth was Angie playing at, inviting the press to the tea rooms? They'd be sniffing around soon enough without any invitation.

At the medical centre gossip was rife, of course. Everyone had a theory, most of them concerning Polly Lock, and a few still very suspicious about Angie and Fergal. It was Ida Tilley who mentioned Larry Lock.

Ida had trouble with her knees, which was not altogether surprising considering she'd spent half of her life scrubbing floors before the Barker-Jones family had elevated her to the lofty position of housekeeper.

'I'm needin' new knees,' she informed Kate for the umpteenth time. Then, suddenly losing interest in her offending joints, she asked, 'What about this body then in Polly Lock's tea rooms?' She widened her pale blue eyes, and shoved a stray white hair, which had escaped from her bun, to behind her ear.

'Hmm,' Kate murmured as she wrote out Ida's prescription.

'Yer sister's gone and bought Polly's tea rooms, hasn't she?' Ida asked.

Kate nodded.

'Well,' Ida continued, warming to her subject, 'there's been a fair bit of fun 'n' games goin' on *there* in the past! A fair bit of fun 'n' games!'

Kate wondered what was coming. 'Really?'

'She liked the men, did Polly Lock. Still does. Liked the men.' Ida nodded and set her mouth in a tight line. 'All them gentlemen callers! Gentlemen callers galore! And they weren't there for the tea and buns, I can tell you!'

'So, a merry widow, perhaps?' Kate suggested.

Ida leaned forward in her chair. 'Dozens of them, *before* she was a widow! *Before* she was a widow, I'm telling you!'

'So, where was the husband while all this was going on?' Kate asked.

'He was out at sea half the time. Out at sea, catchin' fish, he was.' Ida shook her head sadly. 'He was hardly out of the door when her gentlemen callers would arrive. Hardly out of the *door*!'

'He didn't know?'

'Well, he must've done, dear, cos everyone *else* knew. Everyone knew, so they did. But he only caught a couple of them red-handed, I believe, and there were some awful fights. Awful fights there were!' Ida's eyes lit up with the memory of it. 'He nearly killed a couple of them!' She lowered her voice. 'I'd put money on it, dear, that he killed one of her fancy men. And buried the poor bugger in the cellar! In the *cellar*!'

'Oh, surely not?' Kate was nevertheless fascinated. She'd heard many times that Polly was 'a bit of a girl', but she hadn't realised that Polly's 'fancy men' came calling while Larry was still alive. Somehow or the other she must try to have a bit of a chat with Polly, who had now moved in with the undertaker in Middle Tinworthy. Fortunately, it wasn't somewhere Kate had much reason to visit.

'You mark my words,' said Ida as she picked up her prescription. 'You mark my words!'

That evening Woody came into the kitchen at Lavender Cottage, where Kate was peeling potatoes and said, 'Are you ready for a little surprise?'

'A *nice* little surprise?' Kate asked hopefully.

'A very *strange* little surprise,' Woody replied.

'Don't keep me in suspense.'

Woody cleared his throat. 'Locker Man was wearing a jacket, still in remarkably good condition.'

'So?' Kate asked.

'His pockets had been emptied, *except* for the inside breast pocket. The killer had obviously missed that.'

Kate was now jumping up and down. 'For God's sake, *tell* me! What was in there?'

'In there,' said Woody, 'was a bank card.'

'Wow! Now we know his identity! *Who* is it?'

'It's not as easy as that,' said Woody, who was plainly enjoying the moment, 'because it doesn't quite tally.'

'What do you mean?'

'The name on the card is Aaron Hedgefield!'

CHAPTER EIGHT

'What?' Kate was astounded. 'That doesn't make sense!'

'Correct,' Woody agreed, 'it doesn't. Bill's up there questioning him as we speak.'

'Someone *must* have stolen his card,' Kate said firmly.

'That would seem to be the most likely explanation, unless Aaron *gave* it to the other man for some reason.'

'Why on earth would he do that?'

'Goodness only knows. And then the guy gets himself bashed on the head. It certainly doesn't make sense,' Woody said.

'Unless there's some kind of *connection* between Locker Man stealing the card and then getting bashed on the head,' she said. 'It was definitely the head injury that killed him?'

'Yes, apparently there's no evidence of it being anything else.'

'And have we any idea how long ago all this was?' Kate asked.

'Only that the expiry date on the credit card was November 2000, so that confirms that we're looking at around twenty years ago.'

Kate experienced again that little shiver of anticipation that indicated she had yet another mystery to solve. This would be a difficult one – twenty years ago! But surely Aaron Hedgefield must have *missed* his bank card? Then he must have got in touch with the bank which, presumably, would have kept some sort of record? But would they keep any files for twenty years? Kate needed to get moving on this one if she wanted to help Angie, because Angie couldn't get her little bar in order or clear the rumours swirling around her name until the police – and all their tape – moved out.

'I nearly told Bill not to bother with interviews and things,' Woody said drily, 'because I know Kate Palmer will solve this in no time at all.'

'Don't be sarcastic,' said Kate. Nevertheless, she made a mental note to look into who had been using the old building before Polly transformed it.

This, of course, was where her contact with all the ancients in the area would come in useful.

'Well, at least it should let poor Polly Lock off the hook,' Kate said.

Polly, now living with the undertaker, was reportedly devoting herself to good deeds, bookwork and flower arrangements at the funeral parlour but, apparently, had drawn the line at getting involved with bodies. Unlike Kate.

'We'll know more after Bill's interview with Aaron Hedgefield,' Woody said. 'That's if he decides to tell me. I think he's of the opinion that I really *have* retired now, and he's right, of course.'

'I sincerely hope he does let you know, because I can't wait to hear what happens next,' Kate said, with a glint in her eye.

What happened next was that the following Monday, Kate's last patient of the day was none other than Eve Hedgefield.

'I'm here under false pretences,' she admitted as she stepped into the treatment room. 'I didn't have your phone number and I desperately wanted to talk to you.'

'*Me?*' Kate asked in astonishment.

'I know this is going to sound silly, but I felt you were a kindred spirit. And I didn't want Aaron to know I was contacting you.' Eve appeared exhausted after her little outburst.

Kate gulped. 'How can I help?'

'I wondered if we could have a drink somewhere? I'm just so confused and I need to talk to someone not connected with the family.' She looked close to tears.

Kate thought for a minute, wanting to help and also intrigued by what Eve had to say. 'You are my last appointment, so we could have a drink in, say' – she glanced at her watch – 'about fifteen minutes' time? Where do you want to go, or do you want to come back to my place?'

'That would be best,' Eve said, 'if you don't mind. I'm so grateful.'

When Kate got back to Lavender Cottage, with Eve following behind in her Golf, she prayed Angie would be out. Fortunately, she was.

Kate hastily removed the gin bottle and a couple of empty tonic cans from the work surface and looked round for any other signs of Angie's lunch.

'Would you like coffee or something stronger?' she asked Eve.

'Coffee's fine,' Eve replied. She looked around. 'What a nice kitchen!'

'It's hardly in the same league as yours,' Kate said honestly as she switched on the coffee maker.

'It's nicer, it's friendlier.' Eve sat down at the kitchen table. 'Ours is so big, and so showy.' She looked wistful. 'Aaron always has to have everything big and showy.'

'Oh.' Kate was unsure how to react to this. 'I thought your place was very beautiful, very glamorous.'

'But not cosy.'

'It's a big house, Eve, so you'd probably have a job to make it cosy.'

'It's freezing, even in summer. Right now it's unbearable.' There was no stopping Eve now; she was in full flow. 'And who needs seven bedrooms? I think it's only a couple less than the damned Atlantic Hotel. You've no idea how much I envy you!' Eve rolled her eyes.

'So why don't you move to something smaller? Or get a beautiful modern house built somewhere in the grounds?' Kate knew in advance what the answer would be. Not for the first time she wondered about the Hedgefields' relationship. They seemed to be a mismatch in so many ways.

'Aaron won't even consider it,' Eve replied. 'He'd rather freeze than give up being lord of the manor. Anyway, I really appreciate you giving me your time after a working day, and I didn't come here to talk about property. You know the police have interviewed Aaron?'

'I had heard something about it,' Kate said carefully, 'but I didn't think it was public knowledge yet.'

'Did you know that a credit card found in the skeleton's pocket belonged to Aaron?'

Kate was unsure how much she was supposed to know. 'Well, that does seem very strange,' she said guardedly.

'He reported the missing card to the bank at the time,' Eve went on, 'but it was never found, until now. Someone must have stolen it, but who, and how? It's all tied up with Aaron's dad, of course.'

'Aaron's dad?'

'Nice old boy. Henry. Apparently, some man had been pestering him for money or something. The family thought it must have been some sort of blackmail, and that's what caused him to take his own life, because you couldn't imagine anyone less likely to be suicidal.'

'So, didn't Henry ever discuss it with Aaron?' Kate asked as she set the mugs of coffee on the table, along with milk and sugar.

'No, he didn't – all we knew was that there was some man lurking around who claimed to be a relative and wanted money. Aaron always assumed his father had paid the man off and he just went away,' Eve said, stirring her coffee. 'But it wasn't long after that when Henry hanged himself in the orchard. It was *awful.* It was Aaron who found him, and it's had a profound effect on him. He still has nightmares.'

'How dreadful!' Kate said sincerely, sitting down opposite and sipping her coffee. 'No wonder he has nightmares; you'd never forget something like that.'

Eve nodded. 'It changed him, you know. I'd been going out with Aaron for some years before we got married, but he had a breakdown after his father's death and had to go away to London to have some private specialist treatment. He was gone for six months. He was much better when he came back but never the same extrovert fun-loving Aaron I used to know.'

'What about Aaron's mother?' Kate asked.

Eve sighed. 'Oh, poor Adeline! She was born in Kenya, and the family came back to England when she was in her teens, and I don't think she's ever been really happy here. She was always very highly strung, you know. But she's lost it completely now; been up in The Cedars for years.'

Kate hadn't yet had reason to visit The Cedars. The nursing home, which specialised in mental illness, was on the outer fringes of Higher Tinworthy, and had its own team of nurses and carers, so there had been no reason yet for her to call.

'What an unfortunate family!' Kate said.

'Believe me, money does not ensure happiness,' Eve said sadly. 'But I wanted you to know something about the history of the family because you're new round here. And I know that Aaron intends to invite you both up again.'

'He *does*?' Kate was astonished. 'We've only just *been*!' She stared at Eve for a moment. 'I was planning on asking you here…'

'Oh, don't worry about *that*!' Eve said. 'Anyway, Aaron likes to eat at home.' She leaned forward. 'And we shouldn't be seen to be visiting you, not at the moment. Everyone in the village would know, so it's much less conspicuous for you to come to us.'

'That's very kind of you, but…'

'Aaron isn't particularly kind. He'll have his reasons, you mark my words. I just wanted to fill you in with some background stuff before you come. Aaron will want something – he always does.' With that, Eve drained her coffee and stood up. 'I must go. Thanks for the coffee – and for listening.'

As Eve drove off down the lane Kate tried to work out what the visit had been all about. What had Eve really wanted? Had she really been trying to warn her about something?

CHAPTER NINE

'I was speaking to Bill Robson today and I believe they've got the result of the DNA which would confirm the identity of the victim,' Woody announced the following evening. 'You aren't going to like this but – because now I'm of no further use to him – I'm to be treated as a civilian, and he isn't going to tell me.'

Kate, still in her uniform, had kicked her shoes off and was filling the kettle after another long day on her feet. 'I don't believe it!' She turned around, horrified. 'After all the help you've given him! I told you he was horrible!'

'He's within his rights, Kate, like it or not.' Woody laid a comforting arm round her shoulders.

'I feel the need for a glass of wine,' Kate said, setting down the kettle.

'You and me both,' said Woody. 'Is there still half a bottle of that nice Shiraz in the cupboard?'

'Yes, there is.' Kate found the bottle and poured out two glasses. 'I was quite convinced this body was somehow or other connected to Polly Lock, after Ida Tilley told me all about her so-called gentlemen callers, and how jealous Larry was. Now I'm beginning to wonder… This is becoming more and more confusing. By the way, I had coffee with Eve Hedgefield yesterday. She thought that Aaron's father might have been blackmailed by someone and that's what caused him to take his own life,' Kate said.

'How come you had coffee with Eve Hedgefield?' Woody asked.

'She arrived at the surgery – nothing wrong with her – just keen to see me to chat about something, so I had to ask her back for coffee. She gave me a rundown on the family, and said that Aaron was dead set on asking us up for dinner again *very soon*.'

'That sounds to me like he's after something,' Woody said grimly.

'That's just what Eve said. And do you know what?'

'No,' Woody said, 'but I have a feeling you're going to tell me.'

'I don't think that marriage is a particularly happy one. I get the impression that they disagree on an awful lot, including where they want to live. And isn't it unusual for her to come around here and warn me that Aaron probably wants something? Don't you think that's strange?'

'Just a bit,' Woody agreed.

The following day, as Kate wandered back along the beach after her daily walk with Barney, she noticed Angie talking to a woman outside The Locker Tea Rooms. As she neared she realised the woman was Polly Lock. Instead of heading towards the bridge Kate made a quick right turn along the cobbled street towards where the two women were standing.

Kate reckoned Polly was about her own age, no taller than five feet, two inches, sturdily built with a very large bust and immaculate blonde hair. In the short time she'd lived in Lower Tinworthy, Kate had heard Polly referred to as 'Polly Parton', and her twin assets referred to as 'a nice pair of Pollys'. One way or another, Polly was a prominent Tinworthy character. Kate had met her on a couple of occasions when she'd visited the surgery.

She turned around as Kate approached. 'Hi,' she said, 'I just came down to see what was happenin'.'

Very little was happening as there were no police around, and the cellar area was still taped off.

'I just feel so sorry for Angie, stuck with all this,' Polly went on, pointing at the tape. 'Wish I'd investigated the bloody cellar before I sold it but, truth be known, I never bothered with it. Forgot it was there.'

'I can't even offer poor Polly a coffee,' Angie said, 'because Fergal's knocking seven bells out of the so-called wet room, and he's turned the electricity off.'

Kate realised that this was the opportunity she'd been waiting for.

'I was just heading home to put on the kettle,' she said to Polly. 'Why don't you come up with me and have a cup of tea?'

'I might just do that now,' said Polly, pulling her coat collar up against the bitter wind.

'I can't join you,' said Angie, 'because Fergal keeps yelling for this and that.'

Thank goodness for that, thought Kate, who was hoping for a one-to-one with Polly without the distraction of her sister.

As they wandered up the lane towards the cottage, Kate said, 'I understand you're now working alongside Fred the undertaker. How's it all going?'

'Aw, it's fine. Steady business. Don't matter what state the economy's in, you can't stop people dyin',' she said cheerfully. 'Fred's promised to take me on one of them African safaris later in the year. I've always fancied ridin' around in one of them stripey-painted Jeep things and seein' all them wild animals.'

'That sounds lovely,' Kate said. 'So, you're not missing the tea rooms?'

Polly snorted. 'Not a bit! You know, Larry, my late husband, bought that place yonks ago and did nothin' with it except store junk, and let everyone else store their junk in it too. He leased it out to all sorts of folk, and we just lived in three or four of the rooms.'

They'd reached the cottage and, as Kate ushered her into the kitchen, Polly added, 'When Larry died I knew exactly what I wanted to do with the place. It was an expensive business, though. You don't want to go buyin' them listed places. Pain in the neck, cos you have to get permission to do everythin'. And you can't do this, and you can't do that. This place ain't listed, is it?'

'No,' Kate replied, 'it's not. But I know Angie has had some problems.'

'Just as well yours ain't then,' said Polly, plonking herself on a kitchen chair.

'Tea or coffee?'

'Tea, please,' said Polly, looking around. 'You got it nice in here.'

'So, who else might have used the place before you made it into the tea rooms?' Kate asked, as she placed a mug of tea and some cake in front of her guest. 'Who did your husband lease it out to?'

'Oh my goodness, I couldn't rightly say. Lots of folk. Couldn't tell you how many but I gave the police a long list of everyone I could think of. They were mainly fishermen and builders, most of them dead and gone. And the Hedgefields leased part of it for a long time.'

'I wonder if they all used the cellar?' Kate remarked casually.

Polly shrugged. 'To tell the truth, I didn't pay no attention. But I'll tell you this – my Larry never buried no one down there!'

Kate wondered if the double negative was intentional, but then decided it probably wasn't. 'And you never used it?'

'I *told* you I didn't! Lots of local gentlemen would pop in for a cup of tea, you know, and the police keep askin' me what happened to them all. As if *I* should know! Most of them went upcountry somewhere, or died off' – she sniffed – 'but *not* in the bloody cellar! There was one though…'

'Who was that?'

'Someone called Patrick Somethin'. I can't for the life of me remember his second name. He was a travellin' salesman, and he was very lovely.' Here Polly's eyes misted up. 'He came in for tea every day.' She looked steadily at Kate over the rim of her mug. 'He fancied me, you know? And I fancied him, too, but Larry got wind of it and there was a terrible to-do. Now I come to think of it, he disappeared after that.'

Kate swallowed. 'So, have you any idea what happened to him?'

'Well, no, I haven't. Larry said he was goin' to France, so maybe that's where he went.' She had a sad, faraway look in her eyes. 'On the other hand, that would have been twenty-odd years ago. And maybe Larry just *said* that...'

'But you did say that Larry wouldn't have buried anyone down there,' Kate reminded her.

'Well, maybe if he was *very* angry. He had a terrible temper, did Larry. And he was bloody angry that day.' She turned to Kate. 'I don't rightly know what to think...'

Patrick Somebody. Not much to go on, Kate thought. But it did echo what Sadie had said in the surgery.

'Must be off,' said Polly, standing up and placing her mug tidily in the sink. 'Got to get back and do some flower arrangin'.' She grinned. 'We got some folks in viewin' this evenin' so it's nice for them to have somethin' pretty to look at.'

'Oh, quite,' agreed Kate as she helped Polly on with her coat. 'It's been nice chatting to you. Do pop in any time you're passing. And, if you can recall the name of your travelling salesman, please let me know.'

'I will!' said Polly cheerfully as, with a wave, she headed down the lane.

Kate wondered whether to tell Woody about this conversation. The police had already interviewed Polly and, hopefully, she might have told them about this Patrick person. However, there was really no accurate way to trace every single person who'd gone in and out of the building over the years.

Kate didn't think Polly had been lying. She didn't think Polly was guilty either, and her gut feelings were usually correct. But what about Larry?

*

Kate started to make a list. She liked making lists, and adding possible suspects to it as she came across them. At the moment she could only write two names on this list: Larry Lock and Polly Lock. Would anyone in Tinworthy remember a travelling salesman called Patrick Something? And, if they did, would they know where he had come from?

This one was going to be a challenge. Only the police knew who the murder victim was and her only real suspect at the moment – Larry – had died years ago. Should she add any of the Hedgefields? After all, the body had Aaron's card in his pocket, and what would a travelling salesman be doing with Aaron's card? Kate sighed. Even Miss Marple would have a headache with this one…

CHAPTER TEN

The invitation to Tremorron came the following day for that very evening.

'This isn't right,' Woody said. 'He's *definitely* after something. I've said we'll go, though, so I suppose we should get ready.'

'Eve did warn me,' Kate reminded him.

'He's involved in this Locker business, possibly a suspect; we should steer clear.'

'Why is he a possible suspect?' Kate asked.

'Because the dead man had Aaron's credit card in his pocket and because the Hedgefields used to lease the tea rooms.'

'Well, that's purely circumstantial, surely,' Kate said, 'and, besides, you're not police any more.'

'And you're getting into Miss Marple mode again,' Woody said drily, 'in which case you shouldn't really be getting involved with Eve Hedgefield either.'

'Why not? She's a nice woman. I get the distinct impression that all is not well in that marriage. She needs a shoulder to cry on that she can trust.'

'So, are you into marriage counselling now?' Woody asked, suppressing a grin.

'I get the impression you're having a dig at me, *Abe*!'

Kate had only recently found out that Woody's real name was Abraham Lincoln Forrest, a fact which embarrassed him greatly. His English father had named all his children with historical American names, so proud was he of his new citizenship and the opportunities that had come with it. Kate took gleeful delight in addressing him as Abe at appropriate moments.

'Having a dig at you? Never, my love! In fact, I think you'd be very good at marriage counselling.'

'Don't forget I'm a divorcee, so perhaps I should give counselling a miss,' Kate said.

'I should think that would qualify you,' Woody said, 'but, having said that, perhaps you'd be more of an asset to the police force because I've never known any policewoman as nosy and dedicated to criminology as you are.'

'Good heavens, Woody! Is that a *compliment* I hear?'

He squeezed her hand. 'Just don't let it go to your head.'

'As if!'

At that moment Angie and Fergal walked into the kitchen. Angie appeared particularly despondent. She'd not bothered with make-up and her hair was scraped back and secured with an elastic band. Fergal didn't look much better: unshaven and generally scruffy.

'The fecking police were there again today,' Fergal groaned. 'Are they ever going to take that fecking tape away?'

Angie was peering into the cupboard. 'Where's that bottle of Gordon's gone?'

'Well, I haven't touched it,' Kate snapped. 'It'll be where you left it.'

How many times, she wondered, have we had this conversation?

'*Somebody's* had it!' Angie said accusingly.

'You, I expect.' Kate looked at her watch.

'We've had a very exhausting day,' Fergal said, 'haven't we, Angela?' He collapsed onto a kitchen chair. 'Plumbing's not my thing. I had to get on to YouTube for demonstrations. It was so complicated.'

'And he's very dirty,' Angie added.

'Sure, it's a mucky business. So, I wondered if I could use your shower? *Please?*' Fergal asked.

Kate sighed. 'Go on, then. I don't suppose you thought to bring a towel, soap, or anything?'

'He can use mine,' Angie said, emerging triumphantly from the cupboard with the gin bottle in her hand. 'But we'll have a wee drink first, eh, Fergal?'

'Sure, we might as well,' Fergal agreed. 'Would you have any crisps or anything, Kate? Or nuts? I'm very partial to a cashew.'

'No, I do not. I'm trying to lose the weight I gained on holiday,' Kate replied.

In the meantime, Angie was pouring out generous measures into two glasses. 'Would you like one?' she asked Kate and Woody.

'No, not for me, thank you,' Woody said.

'We're going out to dinner shortly,' Kate said, 'and I'm going to need a reasonably clear head.'

'Anywhere nice?' Angie asked as she took a mammoth swig of her drink.

'To the Hedgefields', at Tremorron,' Kate replied, and then immediately wished she'd made up the name of some restaurant.

Angie stared at Kate and then Woody over the rim of her glass. 'But you've only just *been*!'

'I know, I know, but we're obviously so lovely we've been asked back again.' Keen to change the subject, Kate added, 'I'm going to need the shower in an hour's time, so get a move on.'

'Yes, it's time we were getting ready so I'm going to pop home and have a shower too,' Woody said. He gave Kate a kiss on the cheek. 'I'll pick you up about seven.'

'Why have they asked you back again so soon? You seem to be getting very cosy all of a sudden, what's the reason?' Angie asked, taking another swig of her gin.

'Could it not just be our delightful personalities?' Kate said. *Why had she ever told them?*

'No, it couldn't. It's something to do with that body in our cellar, isn't it? Fergal passed their place on the way to Camelford today and said he saw a police car turning into their driveway.'

'So they were,' Fergal confirmed.

'Well, Woody isn't in the police any more,' Kate said, 'so I don't know how we could become involved with any of that.'

'You do like to play the innocent at times,' said Angie as she downed the rest of her drink. 'Now, you go and have that shower, Fergal.' She looked at the Gordon's bottle. 'I might just have another wee one while I'm waiting.'

'Incidentally,' Kate said, 'what's this about you inviting the press to The Locker? *Nobody* invites the press, they just tolerate them.'

'For God's sake, Kate, don't be such a wuss! It's great advertising! Most people are morbidly curious, and the sooner the tea rooms get nationwide publicity, the more visitors we'll get. Locker Man may not have been a smuggler, but he can still get us loads of customers. They'll be descending on Tinworthy in their thousands come Easter!'

Kate sighed. 'Apart from anything else, Angie, that is not at all respectful to the poor man, whoever he was.'

'But he died *years* ago,' Angie argued. 'So it's not doing him any harm and he owes us a favour for having to put up with the police and all their tape. The press would have been arriving in droves anyway.' She glanced at her watch, drained her gin, and yelled, 'Fergal, are you out that shower yet?'

'I've only just got in!' he yelled back.

Kate sighed as Angie headed towards the stairs. She never knew what her sister was going to do next. Tonight, for example, was Angie sleeping here in Lavender Cottage, or in the tiny half-converted flat with Fergal? She was a real whirlwind, that was for sure.

After nearly sixty years on this earth, she should be used to her by now.

CHAPTER ELEVEN

Kate felt uneasy about going up to Tremorron House again only a few days since their previous visit. In fact, she found it downright embarrassing. She had planned to reciprocate eventually and ask Eve and Aaron down to Lavender Cottage, but not for another month at least. Aaron had told Woody on the phone that he needed some advice, and it wouldn't do at all for his large Mercedes, with its personalised number plate, to be seen in the village. Furthermore, both he and Eve enjoyed their company, he said.

'Whatever he's after,' Woody said as they drove up the bumpy driveway, 'he won't rest until he gets it. Probably wants to sound me out about Bill Robson and police procedures. Thank God I'm not in the Force any more.'

'I don't suppose he'd have asked you if you were,' Kate remarked.

'No, probably not. If he had, I wouldn't have gone. He's aware, of course, that I know about the credit card. It's got to be something to do with that.'

'Maybe he just wants to sound you out on police procedures,' Kate said.

Two minutes later Kate and Woody were again welcomed into the icy hall of Tremorron House, and ushered into the marginally warmer state-of-the-art kitchen.

'No cooking tonight,' Eve said. 'We've sent out for tapas, which should be delivered in about half an hour. I hope you're OK with tapas? We've ordered half the menu so there should be *something* you like.'

'Sounds great,' Kate said.

'Yeah, great,' Woody echoed as they planted themselves into one of the huge leather sofas.

'Eve wouldn't let me make cocktails,' moaned Aaron with a pout. 'Says I make them far too strong and one of you has to drive.' He hesitated. 'That's assuming you're going to turn down our offer again of a bed for the night?'

'Thanks, but there's the dog…' Kate said.

'Oh, yes, the *dog*.' Aaron was uncorking a bottle of wine. 'We used to have dogs, didn't we, Eve? Labradors. Lovely dogs, but very greedy. And such a tie! It was OK when Freddy was here because he lived in.'

'Who was Freddy?' Kate asked.

'He looked after my dad for years,' Aaron replied. 'I guess you'd call him a genuine old retainer. He was older than God, and he'd probably still be with us if he hadn't driven his ancient car into a tree on the Launceston road. I think he must have been having the odd snifter from the brandy decanter!'

'He had an old Morris Minor,' Eve said quietly, 'and the brakes failed.'

'Very sad,' said Aaron. He didn't sound in the least bit sad. 'Anyway, we don't have dogs now so we can come and go as we like. In fact, we're flying out to Miami shortly to join a cruise through the Panama Canal and up the coast to Mexico.'

'Lovely,' said Kate, who had no great wish to cruise.

'*If* you like cruises,' said Eve.

'*Everybody* likes cruises!' Aaron was waving the bottle around. 'Are you having some of this again, Kate? I remember how much you enjoyed it before.'

'Yes, please,' said Kate.

'*I* don't like cruises,' said Eve. 'I can remember a time when you didn't like them much either.'

'Don't start that again!' snapped Aaron. 'Most of the people round here would give their eye teeth to go on a cruise like that!'

There was an uncomfortable silence for a moment before the doorbell rang and the tapas arrived. Both Eve and Aaron then became engrossed in placing the containers on a hotplate and finding cutlery, after which everyone began to help themselves.

'You could feed the five thousand with this lot,' Aaron said as he heaped his plate, 'but I don't like the idea of my guests going hungry.'

'Little chance of that!' Kate said as she sat down with a plateful of seafood. For a few minutes the only sound was that of the scraping of knives and forks on plates and murmurs of appreciation.

Then Aaron put aside his plate, leaned forward and said to Woody, 'I have to confess that I had an ulterior motive for wanting you to come up here tonight, Woody. I've got rather a perplexing problem and I hoped you could shine some light on the mystery for me.'

'OK,' replied Woody. 'What is it?'

'Well, I've no idea what the police are up to – or who this body in The Locker Tea Rooms is supposed to be' – he paused and took a deep breath – 'but they've matched his DNA with *mine*!'

Woody let his fork drop. '*What?*'

Kate's prawn went down the wrong way and she had to take a hasty gulp of water.

'That guy, his DNA was an exact match to mine! How the hell can that be? It must be something to do with the credit card which would have my DNA on it, wouldn't it? That Robson bloke has been quizzing me for days, but what can I say? I have *no idea* why it matches.' He paused for a moment.

'So your DNA was in the records, then?' Woody said.

'Yes it was, and no doubt you're wondering why. The truth is I got up to some wild stuff when I was a kid.' He hung his head, looking ashamed. 'I lost my licence for drink-driving after I injured someone, and even had an ABH charge against me.'

'What's ABH?' Kate asked.

'Actual Bodily Harm,' Woody explained. 'Not quite so serious as Grievous Bodily Harm, but not something you'd want on your record either.'

Eve reached across and grasped Aaron's hand. 'I'm afraid it's true. Aaron was a real handful when we first got together. He was into drugs, he got into fights, which is when he got the ABH charge. It was all a long time ago, but it meant they have his DNA on record. And that man, whoever he was, has exactly the same DNA as Aaron. It's got to be a mistake.'

'I don't think they'd make a mistake like that,' Woody said. 'They're pretty careful about checking these things.'

Kate sipped her drink, trying to work out how the DNA could possibly match, and why he was telling them.

'Is there anything I can do? Get it checked again, or something?' Aaron asked.

'Well, I guess Robson will sort it out,' Woody said doubtfully.

'I'd like *you* to work it out,' Aaron said, looking directly at Woody.

'But I'm no longer in the police,' Woody began, 'and—'

'Yes, but you understand police methods, what they may be thinking, how often they get this DNA business *wrong*. I need your help to clear my name, Woody, and my father's. If this man died twenty years ago it seems entirely possible to me that this was the man who came here threatening my father and I need to know who the man was, and why his DNA is the same as mine.'

'Aaron, I don't have psychic powers, I only wish I had!' Woody took a gulp of his beer. 'I have to tell you that Robson now tells me *nothing*. I was useful to him for a while, because he didn't know the area or who was who, but now he no longer confides in me, so

I'll know no more than you do. But I'm sure Bill Robson will do an excellent job and get everything cleared up.'

'I'm afraid I don't share your optimism,' Aaron said, 'so I'd like you to look into this for me and shed some light on the situation. Because I'm damned if I can.'

'I know no more than you do,' Woody repeated calmly.

Aaron leaned further forward, undeterred. 'You have contacts. I need you to find out who this man is, *was*, and why the police are connecting him to me.'

'But—'

'I'll pay,' Aaron interrupted, and Kate observed his dark blue eyes which were now cold and steely. She shivered. You wouldn't want to cross this man, she decided.

'I don't want paying,' Woody said, taking a hasty gulp of his drink. 'I'll do what I can, but you must realise I no longer have access to anything or anyone in the police station. Kate's the one who's got the gift for ferreting out information she shouldn't have access to.'

Aaron looked at Kate, seemingly to find her suddenly more interesting. 'I would welcome any help you could give, Kate. I have to maintain this family's reputation, you know. We're well respected round here, and I employ a great many local people, like my father before me.'

'Well,' said Kate, 'it would seem to me that if this man's DNA is an exact match, then the only explanation is that you have an identical twin.'

Aaron gasped. 'That's ridiculous! Surely I would *know* if I had a twin!'

'Has no one ever mentioned that to you?' Kate asked, looking him in the eye.

'Well, no, who would mention it to me?' Aaron appeared to be completely shell-shocked.

'The only person who would know would be your mother. Couldn't you ask her?'

'My mother is in The Cedars, has been for years. Her mind is completely gone. She doesn't even have any memory of the fact that I'm her son. Whenever I go there she thinks I'm the doctor.'

'Would you be prepared for me to go there and visit her?' Kate asked, aware, from the corner of her eye, that Woody was giving her menacing looks.

'If you think it would be any good…' Aaron sounded doubtful.

'Well, we have to start somewhere,' Kate said firmly.

'What I'd really like to know is how that man got hold of your credit card,' Eve said, 'but of course you're always leaving your cards lying around, and, if he was planning to blackmail your father, perhaps he saw your card abandoned and took it spontaneously. A man like that wouldn't be above an opportunist crime. But that means, of course, that he would have to have been in the house. So your father must have had a good reason for letting him come in. What better reason than it was someone who made out he was a son Henry knew nothing about?'

'How could he have a son he knew nothing about?' Aaron asked.

Kate raised her eyebrows as she glanced at Woody. Surely old Henry was perfectly capable of having an affair? Particularly if his wife was sectioned much of the time.

'That's ridiculous, of course, and, whoever he was, he was obviously up to no good,' said Eve.

Aaron turned to look at Woody. 'I have no doubt someone was trying to blackmail my father, or extract money from him in some way. I fear that my father may have lost his temper – who wouldn't? – and perhaps they came to blows. Perhaps my father accidentally killed him? It would explain why the body was found in the old boat house and why Dad was so stressed afterwards that he took his own life.'

'I'll find out what I can, Aaron,' Woody said, 'but I'm not at all optimistic that I can come up with the answers you're looking for.'

'You have a good reputation round here,' Aaron continued, 'and I know I can trust you.' He glanced across at Kate. 'I hope that what's been said this evening will go no further than these four walls.'

'Of course not,' she said. She quite liked the idea of Woody being involved in this, because then he wouldn't be able to tell *her* not to get involved, like he always did – particularly after his remark to Aaron about her aptitude. She didn't much like Aaron's somewhat chauvinistic attitude but she couldn't deny that the whole situation intrigued her.

'Anyone for dessert?' Eve asked, as she produced what appeared to be a lemon soufflé. 'Here's one I made earlier.'

'Well, that was quite an evening!' Kate remarked as they drove home along the coast road in total darkness.

Woody swerved the car. 'Sorry! Did you see that badger? I nearly hit him.'

It was the thing Kate hated most about night-driving on country roads – dodging animals mesmerised by the car headlights. And, in the daylight, seeing the resulting carnage along the roadside: badgers, foxes, hedgehogs.

'Well done for avoiding him,' Kate said. 'What do you think about Aaron's revelation? It all sounds so incredible. There's something very strange going on there.'

'Yes,' Woody confirmed, 'there certainly is something strange going on there. I can't believe this DNA business.'

'Aaron must have a twin,' Kate said, 'or else he's so fond of himself he's had himself cloned!'

'Surely Aaron would know if he had a twin?' Woody said.

'Probably there's a mistake with the DNA. Perhaps it's not always accurate?'

'Kate, DNA is *always* accurate. It would be an exact match.'

'Well, in that case Aaron definitely *had* an identical twin.' She made a mental note to check that out.

After a few moments, Kate said, 'They're a strange couple. Eve doesn't like the house and she doesn't like cruises.'

'I don't think she likes *him* that much either,' Woody added.

'I wonder why she stays then?'

'Why do you think? Because he's loaded, that's why,' he replied.

'I don't think she's that type,' Kate said, 'and I wouldn't mind betting that, once the younger daughter is off their hands, she'll be off.'

'Hmm,' Woody said. 'I'm quite aware Aaron's trying to hide something, but I'm damned if I know what it is. Who was this guy who appeared out of nowhere, stole the credit card and caused old Henry to hang himself? Could he and Locker Man be the same person? Did the old boy really finish him off?'

'If this mysterious blackmailer existed at all.'

'Well, Locker Man existed once,' Woody said, turning onto the main road.

'Perhaps you're right; perhaps they were one and the same person,' Kate said. 'The timing fits.'

'Have you any better ideas?'

'No, but I'd like to know who that man was, not only to help Aaron out but because once we know that then Angie can get on with her bar.'

'Angie's bar is the least of our concerns at the moment,' Woody said. Kate looked into the black of night and chose to ignore Woody's words. Despite the complicated nature of the crime, she could feel the familiar buzz that she'd experienced when on the case for her last two amateur investigations. Her mind was whirring with possibilities and she was determined to find out the truth.

CHAPTER TWELVE

Kate didn't sleep well. The conversation they'd had at Tremorron kept going round and round in her head and nothing was making a great deal of sense. As she drove to work, she was still mulling over the indisputable fact that Aaron *must* have a twin.

'You look knackered,' Denise said. 'Had a heavy night?'

'Something like that,' Kate replied, 'so treat me gently. Who's first on my list?'

'Oh now, let me see. Ah yes, you've got Mark Edderley, and he's a bit late. Nice bloke, though. Cut his leg in some sailing accident or something. I think Sue sewed him up and now he'll want the stitches taking out. Yes, here he is!'

A stocky man in his forties, with unruly sandy-coloured hair and an infectious grin, was heading towards the desk.

'Hi, Denise!'

'Hi, Mark! This is Kate, who'll be removing your embroidery today.'

'Hello,' said Kate. 'Come with me.' She led him into her room where Mark sat down and rolled up the leg of his jeans.

As she prepared to remove the stitches, Kate asked, 'How did you manage to do that?'

He grimaced. 'It wasn't really a sailing accident; it just sounds better to say that. It was more of an *after*-sailing accident in the pub, where I managed to slip and cut my leg on my broken beer glass. Don't ask!'

'Oh dear,' said Kate, 'did you overdo the celebrating?'

'We were christening a friend's new boat,' Mark replied. 'We sailed it round from Dartmouth to the Tamar. Are you a boat person, nurse?'

'Kate's the name. No, I'm not much of a boat person. Sharp end, blunt end, on the water – right?'

He laughed. 'That's about it! Anyway, Aaron was buying the rounds of drinks as usual—'

'Aaron?' Kate interrupted.

'Yeah, Aaron Hedgefield. Know him?'

Kate knew she had to be careful. 'Well, yes, he kindly gave me and my friend a lift back from Heathrow in his luxurious car. I slept nearly all the way home.'

'That sounds like Aaron, generous to a fault,' Mark said as he watched Kate removing the stitches. 'We go back a long way, Aaron and I. Knew each other as kids, although he went to a posh boarding school and I went to the Tinworthy School here.'

'You must know him well then.' Kate wanted to keep this conversation going to find out as much as she could about Aaron Hedgefield from a new perspective.

Mark sighed. 'You know what? At one time I'd have said yes, but he's changed a lot over the years. He was a real extrovert, funny, generous, friendly. But he's changed. I mean, he's still generous enough but his spark has gone ever since his dad hanged himself. I guess you might have heard about that?'

Kate nodded.

'Say, you're with Woody Forrest now, aren't you?'

'We're friends,' Kate said.

'Woody's OK,' Mark said. Then, as he stood up, he said, 'Oh so you're the nurse who got mixed up in the murders last year, aren't you?'

'Word certainly gets round,' Kate said, smiling.

'Well, you'd better get to work on this Locker Man everyone's talking about! Never a dull moment, eh? I hear his suit lasted well. Wonder if the old school tie did?'

He didn't appear to be aware of the credit card. 'Never a dull moment,' Kate agreed as she opened the door to show him out.

After the dramas of the previous year, followed by the Californian trip, Kate would have welcomed a few dull moments.

When Kate got back from the surgery she got out her list again. She needed to add Henry Hedgefield, Aaron Hedgefield and possibly even Adeline Hedgefield. There was no sign of Angie. Doubtless she had been at The Locker Tea Rooms all day.

Kate worried about Angie. Although she was two years older than Kate, Angie had always been a worry to somebody. To their mother, who said that Angie had their father's genetic make-up, alcoholic, shiftless, and always seeking something just out of reach. Angie's late husband had given her a free rein to explore the world of acting, where Angie dreamed of Hollywood and Oscars. She might have excelled if she'd just laid off the gin for a while. But, after missed or mumbled auditions, and the resulting rejections, this had only served to increase her alcoholic dependence. Both of Kate's sons, while approving in principle of the move to Cornwall, had asked their mother if she was wise to head down there 'with Aunt Angie in tow. You *know* what she's like,' they said.

Kate did indeed know what she was like. Since coming to Cornwall Angie had had a brief but enthusiastic flirtation with abstract art *and* the local gallery owner and now, having inherited some money from her late mother-in-law, was hell-bent on running a bar with the charming, if feckless, Fergal.

Thus, Kate's dreams of Angie partaking of long walks with the dog, perhaps joining the WI, or taking part in some form of worthy rural pursuit, had come to nothing. Nevertheless, she was still hopeful that her scatty sister might just find something that satisfied her. Other than gin. And that didn't look too likely at the moment.

Fergal was a charmer, good-looking, charismatic and full of Irish blarney. He'd had a wife at one time, but she'd taken herself off to the USA with another man and all the money out of the joint account. A penniless Fergal had found his way, via London, to Plymouth where he did a variety of odd jobs, including working in bars and a stint working as a pub chef, and lived in a rented caravan. He'd retained one job because it came with a car: selling postcards, maps and tourist trivia to shops all over Cornwall and Devon, which is how he met Angie. Now he was about to co-host The Locker Tea Rooms, or whatever they decided to call it. And, when the upstairs space was suitably converted, he planned to move in there and base himself full-time in Lower Tinworthy.

The tourists would love him, of course, but Kate was none too sure how he and Angie would get through the winter. Could their relationship survive? With no money coming in, and a half-converted flat, would they get fed up with each other and the whole project? Did Angie love Fergal enough? Des Pardoe, at The Greedy Gull, would most definitely *not* love him – assuming, of course, that the tea rooms proved to be any sort of competition to The Gull, which Kate doubted. Not for the first time Kate wondered about Fergal. Could he possibly be involved in this Locker Man business, and did he know more than he was saying? Could the body be the reason for Fergal's appearance in Cornwall?

She was distracted from her worrying by the telephone.

'Hi!' Woody's voice said. 'How's your day been?'

'I met Mark Edderley at the surgery today,' Kate remarked. 'He crews on Aaron Hedgefield's boat apparently.'

'Yeah, I've met him. Nice chap. What was wrong with him?'

'Oh, just needed some stitches removing. Apparently they were celebrating having brought Aaron's boat round from Dartmouth to the Tamar, and Mark fell over and cut his leg on a broken glass. I guess you'd call it *apres*-sail. I gather he and Aaron were celebrating in a pub somewhere. It was a nasty cut. He wondered if the old school tie had survived as well as the suit Locker Man was wearing.'

She could hear Woody taking a deep breath. '*What* did you say?'

Kate repeated what she'd said.

'We've only *just* found out that the corpse was wearing what looked like one of Aaron's old school ties. How could Mark possibly know that?' Woody asked.

'Oh, he must have heard it somewhere, I suppose,' Kate said.

'There is *nowhere* he could have heard it. It's only just been identified. I suppose there's the odd chance that Aaron may have told him, but I would doubt it.'

'Which means?'

'Which means our friend Mark knows something he shouldn't.' Woody was silent for a moment. 'Bill Robson has to know about this because Mark most definitely needs to be questioned. Anyway, getting back to Aaron, now his boat's back on the Tamar, he's promised me a sail just as soon as the weather improves.'

Kate cleared her throat. 'Do you think it wise for us to be seen to be so chummy with him?'

There was silence for a minute before Woody asked, 'Why not? I know I said to you that we had to be careful but Aaron's not been arrested or anything yet, and there's no firm evidence other than this DNA business, so we have to presume he's still in the clear, for the moment anyway. I promise you I won't go sailing with him if there's any doubt as to his innocence.'

Kate knew Woody was desperate to do some sailing, but still. 'Well, surely the police are still interested in him?'

'Of course they are! That guy, whoever he was, stole Aaron's credit card! There's a chance Aaron got a glimpse of him, and he's the only person who could give the police some idea of who he might have been.'

'So you agree with me that there's something fishy about all this business?' Kate asked.

'Well, that's obvious, but I'm not with the police any more so there's only so much I can find out, no matter what Aaron Hedgefield thinks I'm able to do.'

'What he wants,' Kate went on, 'is for you to find out what Bill Robson might be thinking. Now, why would he want to know *that*?'

'I have no idea what Bill Robson is thinking and, for sure, he's not going to be telling me anyway. Now, can we let the matter rest?'

'OK, but it's just that, although I like Aaron very much, I suspect he's using you.'

'Kate, he's asked for my help. I told him, as you know, that there was very little I could do. Now, I was going to suggest we went out for a nice meal somewhere at the weekend, but not if you're going to go on about Aaron Hedgefield all evening.'

'Of course I won't,' Kate said. 'Can we go up to The Edge?'

'I don't see why not.'

The Edge of the Moor was a half-hour drive from Lower Tinworthy, up on Bodmin Moor. It was a long, low, ancient stone building, not unlike Jamaica Inn, and it would forever hold a special place in Kate's heart. It was where Woody had taken her on their very first date. Close to a year ago, Kate thought, and what a year it had been!

Kate fully understood that it was owing to the very close shaves she'd experienced during the previous twelve months that meant Woody was, first and foremost, concerned for her safety. Hence his favourite, oft-repeated mantra, 'Do *not* get involved!' But, of course, she always *did* get involved. Kate had always been interested in people which was one of the main reasons that she'd become a nurse. Due to her work at the medical centre, she was not only able to get to know people by chatting to everyone who came in – and who frequently told her all manner of interesting titbits – she also had access to their medical histories, not that she would ever share such privileged information with anyone else – except Woody, perhaps – but it did mean she could gain a fuller picture of people. Kate knew that the police fired relevant questions and were only interested in facts, but people didn't *chat* to the police because they were intimidated by them. They were buttoned-up and monosyllabic as a rule. But they chatted to *her*.

It was these advantages that she had over the police that might help her get the upper hand in solving the puzzle of Locker Man. Although Kate had to admit that right now it was as much of a mystery to her as it was to everyone else. She'd get out her list when she got home and add Mark Edderley to it.

'Have you given any more thought as to how you plan to find out about Locker Man?' Kate asked as they entered the restaurant.

'I thought we weren't going to talk about this?' Woody replied, with irritation in his voice.

'Well, I only wondered if I could be of any help.'

'Now that you mention it, you probably could be of some help. If I'm going to find out if Aaron had a twin, the obvious person to talk to is his mother, and that's much more your department than mine.'

'Eve said she's been in The Cedars for years,' Kate remarked.

'So perhaps it's time you paid her a visit,' Woody suggested.

'I'll find an excuse,' Kate said with relish.

'Now, let's forget Locker Man and think about our dinner. I'm going to have a great big juicy steak,' Woody proclaimed as they sat down at the polished oak table, set for two, close to the inglenook. 'And a decent bottle of wine, or two. We'll get a cab home.'

'We will? But—'

'But nothing. You can drive me up here tomorrow, and I can fetch my car then.'

'Oh, all right. Is this a special occasion then?' Kate asked.

'Yeah, we're having a civilised evening with no further mention of Aaron Hedgefield, Locker Man, Bill Robson, et al.'

'So what'll we talk about then?'

Woody summoned the waiter. 'The weather, perhaps? I mean it's bloody cold. Then again, it *is* January.'

'And it isn't California,' Kate added.

'Talking of which, my mom thought you were great,' Woody remarked. 'She said—' He stopped as the waiter approached and noted the wine they wanted.

'What did she say?' Kate prompted as the waiter moved away.

'Oh, just that I should look after you and not let anyone else snap you up.'

Kate snorted. 'Who on earth would want to snap *me* up?'

'Well, there are all these old boys forever hobbling into the surgery, looking for a chat and a bit of company. I should think you'd be spoilt for choice. And you could always prescribe them some Viagra.'

'If we weren't in here I'd chuck something at you!'

'Just as well we are then.' Woody leaned back and studied her. 'Seriously, Kate, would you want to get married again?'

What? Married! Was the man *proposing*?

'It's not on my list of priorities,' Kate said, as the waiter reappeared with the wine and filled their glasses.

'It's not on mine either,' Woody said as the waiter disappeared.

Kate wondered if the little shiver coursing through her veins was due to relief or disappointment. She wasn't sure. Much as she enjoyed being single, she would not want Woody to be looking elsewhere. No doubt about it, he was a damned attractive man, with his close-cut, greying-black hair, and his deep brown eyes. Even Angie had thought so once, although she wouldn't now admit it for the world, since Kate had 'snatched' him, as she put it.

'So why bring the subject up?' Kate asked hesitantly.

He sipped his wine. 'I just wanted to make sure that you were happy with our current arrangements: you on one side of the valley, me on the other.'

'There are thousands of married couples who would *love* that,' Kate said, smiling.

'You're right. Anyhow, as long as you're happy with things the way they are?' He looked at her quizzically.

'I'm very happy with things the way they are,' Kate replied, smiling.

'Me too,' he said, reaching for her hand.

CHAPTER THIRTEEN

On Monday morning Ida Tilley was back in the surgery. 'It's me knees again,' she informed Kate as she hobbled into the treatment room. 'I'll be needin' new ones cos I've been down on them all week scrubbin' floors,' she sighed, 'just in case Mr Seymour might pop down with a few friends.' Mr Seymour didn't do a lot of popping down and so, for most of the year, Ida rattled around in Pendorian Manor all by herself.

Kate had heard this countless times before, and all the X-rays indicated that Ida was not yet ready for knee replacements. Now, as Kate poked and prodded Ida's podgy kneecaps, she said, 'A few exercises might help, you know. They've just stiffened up. Do you do a *lot* of kneeling, Ida?'

'Well, not no more I doesn't. Don't do the floors often. Not no more. Only kneel when I says my prayers at bedtime to thank the Lord for my good fortune to live in that house.'

'It's a lot of house to look after. Have you ever thought of retiring?' Kate asked. 'Finding something small and cosy?'

Ida glared at her. 'Why would I be wantin' that? I couldn't afford no house. Mind you, I had my chance, so I did. I had my chance. If I'd married Freddy Parr, cos he'd got himself a real nice little house up at Tremorron. Nice little house it was. Still, if I'd married him I'd be a widow now. A widow.'

'At least you'd have a nice little house.'

'He was a fine man. Worked for them Hedgefields up at Tremorron. Worked there fifty years he did. Fifty years. But it was never the same after old Henry pegged it. A gentleman, he was, old Henry. Like

Mr Seymour. Freddy was a gentleman too – not that he was high-born like, cos he wasn't. His dad was only a labourer but Freddy wanted somethin' better for himself. Somethin' better. He was in charge of everythin' up there, you know, cos in them days there was maids and valets and everythin'. Old Adeline didn't much care for gettin' her hands dirty, so she didn't. She was a bit of a… didn't go out much.'

'A recluse?'

'That's it. A recluse, that's what she was. She's in The Cedars now, you know.' Ida shook her head sadly. 'Don't know no one.'

Kate was fascinated. 'So your Freddy died?'

'Drove straight into a tree, he did. A bleedin' tree! You want to know why? Cos his brakes failed, that's why.' She leaned forward. 'You want to know somethin' else? Somebody'd been fiddlin' with them brakes, wanted poor Freddy gone. He looked after that little car and he'd have known if the brakes were dodgy. He was a lovely man, never upset no one.'

'Surely the police would have spotted that, Ida?'

'Maybe they did, maybe they didn't. The garage what checked Freddy's car was run by Micky Fisher. Bent as a corkscrew, he was. Bent as a bloody corkscrew.' Here Ida tapped her nose. 'He wasn't ready to die, he was a good driver. Poor Freddy.'

'So, what are you saying, Ida?'

'I ain't sayin' nothin'. Now, what about me knees?'

*

Why, Kate wondered as she drove home, would anyone want to tamper with the brakes of a harmless old man's car? He'd worked for the Hedgefields, but was that relevant? Probably not, but she couldn't help wondering.

'Did you know that the old boy who used to work for the Hedgefields, Freddy, was killed when he drove into a tree?' Kate asked Woody later.

'Well, Aaron told us that,' Woody replied.

'Yes, but he didn't tell us that there was a rumour his brakes had been tampered with,' Kate said.

Woody looked at her thoughtfully. 'There are always rumours in a place like this, Kate. Who came up with this nugget of information?'

'Ida Tilley, from Pendorian Manor,' Kate replied. 'Freddy wanted to marry her once.'

'*Ida Tilley!*' Woody snorted. 'You can't believe people like her.'

'She said that the guy who owned the garage at that time was a bit of a crook. Micky Fisher, I think she said his name was.'

'Ah, Micky Fisher.' Woody thought for a moment. 'Micky Fisher went out of business around the time I came down here. You're right; he didn't have a very good reputation. People said he'd give any old banger an MOT certificate without even examining it if you paid him enough. But I never met the guy.'

'Surely the DI at the time would have looked into it all anyway?' Kate said. 'Who did you take over from?'

'Old Doug Dewberry,' Woody said. 'He was a real character.'

'On the straight and narrow?' Kate asked.

'Hmm,' Woody said after a moment, 'I wouldn't put money on it.'

'There you are then.'

Kate didn't care much for general gossip but there were times when extracting a few titbits of specific information could be quite useful, to say the least. Just such an opportunity occurred the following day. Kate's third patient of the morning just happened to be Ron Lawson, who was one of the co-owners of Tinworthy Motors. The coincidence gave Ida's suspicions extra significance in Kate's mind.

'I think I've broken me finger,' he said, as he held out a grease-stained, black-nailed hand for Kate's inspection. 'I got it caught in the bonnet of a Renault, and it ain't half sore.'

Kate examined it as gently as she could, but he still yelped with pain with each move.

'I think you have broken it,' she confirmed, 'but all I can do is strap it to the middle one to splint it and it'll mend on its own in time. Toes and fingers just have to mend by themselves. Are you able to rest it?'

Her patient guffawed. 'We can't do no restin'! Got a backlog of work, we have! Got to keep our heads above water – know what I mean?'

After Kate had strapped his fingers together and he got ready to leave, she said, 'How about I give you a prescription for some pain-killers?'

'Yeah, that'd be good.' He yawned.

'Have you had the garage long?' she asked casually.

'Goin' on six years, I think. Why you be askin'?'

'No special reason. I wondered if you'd ever worked for Micky Fisher? I believe he owned it at one time.'

'No, thank God, I never worked for him. He got us all a bad name, and it's taken me and Len them six years to sort it all out and build up our own reputation.'

Kate handed him the prescription. 'Really?'

Ron leaned forward and tapped his nose, which seemed to be a Cornish prelude to Something Important being announced. 'He was a bit of a crook, was Micky. Overcharged, didn't do a very reliable job – but he had his cronies to bail him out.'

'Gosh!' said Kate. 'It's a wonder his business survived at all!'

'Like I said, he had his cronies. Most of them are gone now, except folks like Gavin Perry what owns The Cedars nursin' home and charges a bleedin' fortune. And Aaron Hedgefield, of course.'

'How interesting!' said Kate. Then, thinking quickly, 'I thought Aaron Hedgefield was a bona fide businessman?'

Ron snorted. 'He got Micky out of trouble a few times; reckon Micky owed him. That's all history now cos we're running a straight business, all above board. You bring that Fiat of yours to us when it needs servicin' and that, and we'll give you a bloody good rate.'

'Oh, I will,' Kate said as she closed the door behind him.

Kate sometimes forgot that everybody knew everybody else in an area like Tinworthy, or at least knew all about them. Having come from the city this was a novelty and a revelation, but it was also an advantage when you were told so many interesting titbits. Titbits were invaluable in trying to solve crime. And this plot was thickening by the minute. Kate was determined to get to the bottom of it.

CHAPTER FOURTEEN

On the Thursday, as Kate had no special plans, she decided it was high time to pay a visit to The Cedars and acquaint herself with Aaron's mother, as she had promised to do. She was increasingly keen to see if she could find out anything at all about this phantom twin. Adeline had been in there for years and Kate had never visited before – so might the staff think that was rather strange? After much thought she decided the only thing was to go and say she was a friend of the family, which was near enough the truth.

As Kate had never seen inside The Cedars before, she was unsure what to expect: residents sitting round the walls staring at an enormous deafening television, some asleep, some half-asleep? Her impression of residential and nursing homes had, up to now, not always been very positive. Therefore, she was pleasantly surprised to find The Cedars had a welcoming vestibule with yellow walls, lots of bright pictures and a collection of prolific plants. No blaring TV, no one shuffling around. Yet, anyway.

'I've come to see Adeline Hedgefield,' she told the plump little nurse who appeared as she entered. 'I'm a friend of the family, so thought I'd pop in.'

The nurse indicated a visitors' book on the table and asked Kate to sign it.

'Nice for Adeline to have a visitor,' the nurse said. 'I can't remember the last time anyone came to see her.' She watched Kate signing the book. 'Not that she'd have any idea anyway. She's on medication now so she's quite calm and happy in her own little world.'

Kate felt sorry for anyone who didn't have visitors, and felt a little guilty that she was going there only to try to make sense of this twin business. What if Aaron *did* have a twin? How would she break the news to him? She'd wait to see what she could discover from Adeline's damaged memory before she began to wonder about breaking news like that.

The nurse glanced at Kate's entry in the book. 'I *thought* I recognised you! You're that nurse who nearly came to a nasty end last year!'

Kate grinned as she laid down the pen. 'That's me!'

'Well, nice to meet you! I'm Fran. Follow me; Adeline's in her room – doesn't do a lot of socialising. She's in the Primrose Wing.'

Kate followed Fran along a corridor, dodging a couple of wheelchairs on the way, until she stopped at Room 15, and opened the door. Kate was ushered into a large bright room, furnished with a divan, two comfy-looking armchairs, and a couple of tables. The furnishings were all covered in an attractive leafy print. Standing gazing out of the window at a field full of sheep was a tall, elderly lady, dressed in slacks and a jumper, her white hair tied back in an untidy chignon. When she turned around Kate saw that the front of her navy-blue jumper was adorned with brooches of all shapes and sizes from neck to hem.

'Adeline likes brooches,' Fran said somewhat unnecessarily. Kate reckoned there must have been at least twenty of the things dangling from Adeline's chest. 'Whatever she decides to wear we have to pin the damned things on it every day,' Fran added in a hushed voice. Then, 'Adeline, you have a visitor!'

Adeline stared at Kate, who moved forward and held out her hand. 'Hi! I'm Kate and a friend of Aaron and Eve's. I was just passing by and thought I'd pop in.' As she spoke Kate realised this was a daft thing to say, since no one could be 'just passing by' The Cedars, which was situated all by itself at the end of a long lane.

Adeline didn't seem too bothered by this. She stared at Kate, ignoring her outstretched hand, and asked, '*Whose* friend?'

Kate noted she had a rather aquiline nose and very dark, fathomless eyes.

'Aaron and his wife, Eve. Your son and daughter-in-law?' Kate lowered her arm and then delved into her bag. 'Look, I've brought you some chocolates.' She placed the Cadbury box carefully on a low table. 'I hope you like them?'

'Have you not brought me a brooch?' Adeline asked. Then, turning to Fran, asked, 'Has this woman not brought me a brooch?'

Fran squeezed Kate's arm and shrugged. 'I don't think Kate knows how much you like brooches.' Then, in an undertone to Kate, 'I'll leave you to it. Just make your way back when you're ready to go and sign out.' With that she disappeared.

'Well,' Kate said brightly, 'if I'd known how much you like brooches I'd certainly have brought you one.'

Adeline frowned. '*Who* did you say you were?'

'I'm Kate, a friend of your son's.' Kate was mesmerised by a bejewelled lizard climbing up towards Adeline's right shoulder.

'My son? What son?'

'Aaron,' Kate replied. 'Shall we sit down?'

Adeline lowered herself carefully onto one of the chairs, never taking her eyes off Kate. 'I haven't got a son,' she said. 'Do you like my lizard? These are real emeralds, you know. My husband gave it to me.'

'Henry?' prompted Kate.

'Do you know him?' Adeline asked.

'No, I don't,' Kate admitted, wondering if, by using the present tense, the old lady was unaware of his demise. 'But it's a lovely brooch.'

'I like this one too,' said Adeline, leaning forward. She pointed to a 'diamond' butterfly wobbling on her right breast.

'Very nice,' Kate agreed. She hesitated a moment, then asked, 'Has Aaron been in to see you lately?'

'*Who?*'

'Aaron, your son.'

'What son? I don't have a son,' Adeline said, looking round and out of the window again.

Kate wondered how to follow this. As she was about to speak, Adeline added, 'I had a *daughter*. Poor little Emily Jane.'

She was more confused than Kate had anticipated and there seemed little point in probing much further. But she'd give it one more try.

'Did you not have *twin* sons, Adeline?'

Adeline thought for a moment. 'Would that be two?'

'Yes, two boys.'

'I don't think so. Maybe. *Maybe* baby!' She giggled.

'*Try* to remember, Adeline!' Kate rubbed her forehead, hoping to get Adeline back on track.

'Why?' Adeline was leaning forward and staring hard at her again.

'I'm just interested,' Kate said lamely. 'I think you might have had twins, two little boys?'

'Perhaps it was you who had them?' Adeline suggested. 'Did you lose them somewhere? Did you find Emily?'

The conversation was going nowhere.

'Yes, I have two sons,' Kate agreed, 'but they aren't twins and I haven't lost them.'

Adeline yawned, plainly bored. 'Didn't I see you down in Antibes or Cannes?'

'I've not been to Antibes or Cannes,' Kate replied. She stood up. 'Would you like a chocolate?' She indicated the box on the low table.

'Chocolate makes you fat!' Adeline said sternly, patting her flat tummy. 'I never eat chocolate.'

Kate sighed. 'Oh well, just give the box to one of the other residents then.'

'No one else lives here,' Adeline snapped. 'I'm here alone with only the servants. Freddy will show you out.'

She'd been dismissed. 'Nice to have met you, Adeline.'

Adeline didn't trouble to reply, so intent was she on trying to open the box of chocolates.

As Kate closed the door behind her, she wondered if it was even worth considering a further visit to The Cedars. Perhaps she'd find a brooch for Adeline somewhere, which would give her an excuse to come back, and perhaps the old lady would open up some more.

As she signed out, Fran reappeared. 'Oh,' she said, 'if you'd waited another ten minutes you could have had a cup of tea when the trolley comes round.'

'I think I'd best be on my way,' Kate said, 'but I'd like to call to see her again sometime.'

'She'd like that,' Fran said.

I doubt it, Kate thought. But she was intrigued by Adeline and wanted to see her again.

*

As she drove home, Kate mulled over her conversation with Adeline. She'd remembered Henry and she'd remembered Freddy, but had no memory of giving birth to Aaron, far less twins. She did mention a daughter, Emily, which was strange. Could that be true?

There was nothing else for it; she was going to have to delve into Births, Deaths and Marriages, to see what might come up. She could check with the surgery. If Adeline had given birth to a baby girl it would be in her medical records, surely? In the meantime, she'd look into the depths of her jewellery drawer to see if she could unearth any brooches. Kate hadn't worn a brooch in more than thirty years and any she might find would certainly not be diamond- or emerald-encrusted. But it just *might* provide a passport into the depths of Adeline's confused mind.

CHAPTER FIFTEEN

When Kate got home she put on the kettle and dug out her laptop. She considered Ancestry UK, Find My Family and various other sites before remembering that she'd once had a subscription to Generations Together when she was doing some research into her own family background a couple of years ago. Would she still have a note of her password and would it still be valid? She eventually found the password in her old diary and decided it was worth a try. She was amazed to get straight into the website. Of course it now required a further subscription but Kate considered it was worth it.

Where to start? She entered 'Henry Hedgefield' and found five of them, but only one in the south-west. This Henry Hedgefield was born in 1941 in Truro. She also found one Henry Hedgefield in the death records, and he had died in 2001, which tallied. There were also a couple of mentions of him in the electoral rolls which stated he resided in Tinworthy, Cornwall. After two cups of tea, she also found him in the marriage records; he had married Adeline Saunders in 1972 in Launceston, Cornwall. Kate looked for Adeline Saunders in the birth records and found three but couldn't find anyone within the right date range.

Kate then set about searching Aaron Hedgefield. She guessed he was in his mid-forties. Hadn't Eve said something the other night about him being forty-five? She found him in the marriage records but there was no trace of him in the birth records. With Hedgefield being quite an unusual name Kate expected to find him easily. But nothing. Perhaps he had been born overseas. Kate couldn't think why that should be, but it seemed the only likely explanation. She decided to look for the daughter Adeline had been so insistent about, Emily Jane. Once again, Kate found no record of a Hedgefield baby of about the right date, in the right location, in the birth records, but there *was* an Emily Jane Hedgefield in the death register. She had died in the fourth quarter of 1973. If her death was registered, but *not* her birth, it must mean that she had died very young, probably only days old.

So Adeline had *not* been fantasising; she really *had* had a daughter called Emily and the poor little mite had only lived for a matter of days. Poor, poor Adeline! Kate wondered if that had been a catalyst for her present condition. The only way of finding out more details was from Adeline's medical notes; her particulars were presumably in the medical centre files somewhere. Surely, if she had had twins, the details would still be there?

So that she had time to check the medical records, Kate went into work early on Monday morning. She decided not to mention her intentions to Woody, who would almost certainly tell her to leave well alone/none of your business/do *not* get involved – even though this time she was doing it at Woody's suggestion. After all, he was the one who'd agreed to help Aaron, however grudgingly. Kate knew Woody had her best interests at heart, particularly since he'd rescued her twice, not just from danger, but from certain death. But, on both these occasions there was still a killer roaming around. Now, after twenty years, that was highly unlikely. Surely there couldn't be much danger in merely trying to find out if Aaron Hedgefield had had a twin. Kate was convinced that had to be the case; what other possible explanation could there be for the DNA match?

Kate studied the rows of cabinets in the long, narrow office behind Denise's desk. The filing system, or lack of it, appeared haphazard at the best of times, particularly when she was attempting to locate old records. When Denise came in to find a file she asked, 'You OK there? Need any help?'

Kate could hardly ask which cabinet contained the Hedgefield history, since she had no valid excuse for looking them up. Fortunately, Denise did not query her intentions. 'I keep meaning to label all these files with the initials of the surnames they contain, but I never seem to get round to it.' Denise sighed heavily as the bell rang on the reception desk to herald the arrival of another patient.

It took some time to sort out Denise's rather erratic filing system but finally she found the Hedgefield files. Kate knew there would be no information about Henry, because that would have been sent to the central storage department after his death.

Finally, Kate found Adeline's file. Adeline had married Henry in 1971 and came to live in Tremorron House. In 1972 she gave birth to a daughter, Emily, who'd lived for only two days. There was no doubt about it, whatever else was going on in Adeline's troubled mind, she'd never forgotten her little daughter.

Feeling sad, Kate continued reading. After the baby's death Adeline had had a complete nervous breakdown, and a psychiatric nurse had been employed to look after her. There were various notes about her condition and the drugs that had been prescribed. The nurse continued to care for Adeline until the summer of 1974 when Adeline attacked her, and the nurse left, after which Adeline was admitted into the Beauvois Clinic in Geneva, Switzerland, for treatment. There were no notes as to what treatment she received there, but she must have become pregnant again shortly *before* she left the UK, because Aaron was born the following March, presumably in Switzerland. If this was so, then Kate had been right – he *had* been born abroad. There was no mention of twins. Adeline returned to Cornwall in May 1975 with two-month-old Aaron, after which she appeared to have become a complete recluse. Adeline continued to be treated for severe depression. *Adeline*, said the notes, *shows little interest in doing anything or going anywhere, or even showing any interest in her baby son*. Poor Aaron, Kate thought, I hope his father loved him, at least. What an unfortunate family they were! Many women who lost one baby would perhaps shower another with love and attention but losing a baby affected women in different ways and it was feasible that her mental health had deteriorated significantly by this point. Adeline's problems seemed to accelerate and she was sectioned twice in the following years: once when she tried to knife poor Henry and another time, some years later, when she was found stark naked wandering along the Launceston road. The last time she was admitted into The Cedars was in 2012. Kate was horrified – what a strange, disturbed life the poor woman had endured. She felt very sorry for Aaron, too, because it appeared he'd never been accepted by his own mother.

With all those thoughts somersaulting in her head, Kate drove home at the end of her shift, looking forward to sitting down, reading the newspaper and having a nice quiet cup of tea. But when Kate arrived home she could hear much giggling going on upstairs. She stopped in her tracks. Surely Angie and Fergal weren't at it so early in the day? She made her way up the stairs on tiptoe and realised halfway up that the giggles were emanating from the bathroom, the door of which was open, and from which scented steam was pouring out.

Kate stopped on the landing. Both of them were presumably in there, but which of them was actually in the bath? 'Angie?' she called.

'It's OK, Kate, you can come in,' Angie shouted.

Cautiously Kate opened the door and then stopped short. Through the steam she could see two bodies squashed into their normal-sized bath, facing each other with knees bent, and Fergal modestly covering his bits with a pink flannel. The water sloshed backwards and forwards, dangerously close to the top.

'What the hell are you doing?' Kate asked.

'We're having a bath,' Angie replied.

'That water is about to overflow,' Kate said, 'and—'

'Don't go getting your knickers in a twist,' Angie interrupted. 'Poor Fergal's been working hard getting that shower installed in The Locker and he needed a wash.'

'Remember,' said Fergal earnestly, 'we're all supposed to be trying to save water, are we not?'

'Don't tell me that's my flannel?' Kate asked, exasperated, staring at Fergal. 'And why are you in there too, Angie?'

'No, it's my flannel,' Angie said, 'and Fergal fancied a bit of company.'

'She just won't leave me alone, Kate,' Fergal said. 'I can't even get rid of her in the bath.' With that they both dissolved into fits of giggles.

Kate rolled her eyes, then closed the door and prayed the water wouldn't overflow. As there was obviously going to be no peace at home, she decided to give Woody a call to see if he'd like to go out for a drink.

'You've been very quiet lately,' Woody said, regarding Kate with suspicion as he placed a glass of wine in front of her in The Greedy Gull.

'Have I?'

'Yes, you have, and that always worries me. I suspect you've been up to something. It's not like you to keep your nose out of a murder inquiry even if it *is* twenty years too late.'

Kate was actually bursting at the seams to tell him about her findings but was a little nervous as to what his reactions might be. 'Well,' she admitted, 'I have been doing a teeny-weeny bit of research.'

Woody rolled his eyes heavenward. 'Why am I not surprised? What exactly have you come up with this time, Miss Marple?'

'You needn't have a go at me because it was *your* idea that I got involved when you suggested it to Aaron,' Kate said.

Woody sighed. 'Well, I've been doing some investigating myself. I've told Robson about what Mark Edderley said about the tie. He's got to be involved in some way, and I'm keeping an eye on him. OK then, tell me what *you* found out.'

'Well, not a lot really, but I did unearth one or two interesting facts.'

Woody observed her steadily over the rim of his pint of Doom Bar, then lifted an eyebrow.

'Don't do that,' Kate said, 'because you know it makes me come over all funny.'

He placed his glass down on the table and wiped some foam from his lips. 'We'd get arrested in here. Now, what do you mean by interesting facts?'

'Well, Adeline said—'

'*Adeline said*. What do you mean, "Adeline said"? Don't tell me you've been up to The Cedars already?'

'Oh, just a couple of days ago. It was *you* who suggested it!'

'Well, you haven't wasted any time!'

Kate gulped some wine. 'No, because I feel sorry for Aaron, and surely he needs to know if he once had a brother even if he never met him.'

'Fair enough. I hope you didn't go upsetting the poor old dear, because I'm sure Aaron would have something to say about it if you did.'

'Of course I didn't upset her,' Kate said, slightly guiltily. 'Anyway, according to the nurse I chatted to, Aaron doesn't visit very often, if at all. But, Woody, they have a difficult relationship. I wonder if she has ever shown him any real affection.'

'How do you know that?'

'I told you – I did some research. Let me tell you this: there is no record of Adeline having twins. She had a little girl who died, which she does remember, but has no memory of having Aaron. So God only knows where the DNA match comes from.'

'Adeline told you that? And you believe her?'

'I checked some ancestry stuff online and I also checked the medical records at the surgery. Adeline had a little girl who only lived for a couple of days, went into a deep depression, and then had Aaron a couple of years later, in Switzerland.'

'What the hell was she doing in Switzerland?'

'Well, she was admitted into some kind of sanatorium, as it was called, in Geneva because, according to her notes, her mental health had become increasingly fragile. She even attacked the psychiatric nurse who'd been employed to look after her. She must have become pregnant before she left the UK because she had Aaron seven months later over there. And she did *not* have twins on either occasion.'

For once Woody was silent. After a moment he said, 'I wonder if Robson's been doing some research too? If I was still up there that's what I'd be doing. I don't suppose he's checked the medical records.'

'I doubt that he'd be allowed to. But they coincide with what I found online, and believe me, Adeline's memory hasn't altogether deserted her.'

'What was she like?'

'Oh, quite nice, in a confused way. Rather an elegant, aristocratic-looking lady. But what I can't figure out is why she took no interest in Aaron. You'd think that having lost one baby, she might want another. But then again, if she was still grieving for her little girl she may have found having another baby very difficult.'

'I compliment you on your research, Kate, but it still doesn't solve the problem of the DNA.'

'No,' Kate agreed, 'it doesn't. I'd love it if we came up with some information that Robson missed!' Kate had a burning desire to get one up on Bill Robson ever since he'd accused her of meddling in a crime inquiry some months previously. Theirs had been something of a personality clash. He was an abrupt, humourless little man and, as the new detective inspector, was as different from Woody as it was possible to be. 'You said something earlier about doing some investigating yourself?'

'Yes. I've been checking on Mark Edderley.'

'Mark?'

'He's not quite as saintly as you might think. He and Aaron Hedgefield were thick as thieves at the time Aaron was using The Locker for storing sailing stuff and – furthermore – Mark was also into drugs and fights at the same time as Aaron.'

'From the way he spoke I thought…'

'Kate, I know you want to believe the best in people, but Mark is definitely a suspect as far as I'm concerned. How could he possibly know about the old school tie?'

Kate sighed. This was not going to be easy. She considered her list. Apart from Larry and Polly Lock, there was now Henry Hedgefield, Aaron Hedgefield and Mark Edderley, and they were only the people she *knew* about. The tip of the iceberg. Was Adeline capable of killing? She'd attacked her nurse so obviously had a violent streak. Even if she was, it was very unlikely she'd be able to transport the body to The Locker and bury it in the wall. Who else might have frequented the place at that time and how could she possibly trace them all, particularly as some were probably no longer alive?

CHAPTER SIXTEEN

Bobby's Best Buys was situated down by the river, close to the beach and also to The Locker Tea Rooms where Fergal was still battling with the plumbing system in his quest to install a shower. He did seem to be working hard, so maybe Kate's worries about him were unfounded.

Bobby, sixtyish, stout and balding, sold most things. Provided, that is, you weren't needing anything too exotic. 'If I can't spell it, I don't stock it,' Bobby had informed Kate on her first visit. On this occasion, she considered she was reasonably safe since she only wanted butter.

The sky had darkened and it had begun to rain, increasing the gloom in Bobby's badly lit, already gloomy shop, which was deserted. There was no sign of Bobby.

Kate waited a moment and then rang the bell on the counter. It took a few minutes for a dishevelled-looking Bobby to emerge from the back of the shop where, Kate suspected, he'd been having a crafty cigarette.

'Ah, Mrs Palmer,' he said with a sigh. 'I can count on one hand how many folk have come in here today.'

'Well, it is January, Bobby,' Kate reminded him. And the supermarkets are so much better stocked and cheaper, she thought.

'Sometimes wonder if it's worth my time stayin' open,' he went on, running a hand through his few remaining hairs which were standing on end.

'Another few months and the tourists will be back,' Kate soothed as she looked round Bobby's shelves in the forlorn hope of seeing something she might need. 'I'd like some butter, Bobby, and perhaps some of these lovely farm eggs.'

'Yeah,' said Bobby, 'and I got some nice Cheddar just come in.'

As Kate was trying to recall how much cheese they had, the door burst open and in came Ida Tilley, weighed down with heavy shopping bags.

'Well, Ida, and what you forgotten *this* time?' Bobby asked.

'I've not forgotten nothin',' Ida snapped, 'I've just missed the bleedin' bus. That Dave Dooley must've been early, and he's *never* early, is Dave. Always late. But that bugger was early today! How am I supposed to get up to Pendorian with all this shoppin' – tell me that!' She glanced sideways at Kate.

Kate peered out at the rain. 'I'll go get my car,' she said to Ida, pulling the hood of her raincoat over her head, 'and then I'll come back and take you up to Pendorian Manor.' She paid Bobby for the butter and the eggs.

'Oh, I wasn't hintin' or anythin', nurse,' Ida said, 'but I can't say no to a lift, can I, Bobby?'

'No, you can't say no to a lift,' Bobby agreed, winking at her. 'And you wasn't hintin' at all.'

Kate, having left Ida standing in the shop doorway, picked up her shopping and headed out into the gloom, splashing through newly formed puddles as she dashed up the pot-holed lane that led to Lavender Cottage.

Fifteen minutes later she was loading Ida's three large, heavy shopping bags into the back of the Fiat, while Ida got herself into the passenger seat with much huffing and puffing. On the drive to Upper Tinworthy Ida gave Kate a detailed account of her arthritis, her blood pressure and her dodgy knees, and Kate was relieved to draw up in front of Pendorian Manor's impressive front door before Ida could recall any further ailments.

'That's ever so kind,' said Ida, clambering out with a great display of knickers, the elasticated legs of which were perilously close to her knees. They certainly hadn't come from Demelza's Boutique, the only ladies' shop in the Tinworthys, which did a fine line in pussy pelmets and thongs. 'Do you fancy a cup of tea?'

Kate hesitated for a moment. Ida might know a thing or two that could be useful to her research on the Hedgefields, if she could manoeuvre the conversation in that direction. Besides, she'd never been inside Pendorian Manor and she'd wondered what it was like ever since the murder of its mistress, Fenella Barker-Jones, a year ago.

The hall was large, oak-panelled with doors leading off in every direction, and had a majestic central staircase with carved newel posts and red carpeting. Some gilt-framed portraits, which were presumably Seymour's disapproving ancestors, frowned down at her from each side.

'Mr Seymour's relatives,' Ida commented proudly, as she led the way into an enormous kitchen. The centrally placed scrubbed pine table could probably have seated twenty people. Instead, two ginger cats were sprawled on the top, sandwiched between some piles of newspapers, a jar of marmalade and a box of biscuits. Round the walls was a haphazard collection of dressers and cupboards.

'Sit yourself down,' Ida commanded, indicating a shabby armchair next to the old cream-coloured Aga, on which another tabby cat was fast asleep. 'Get off, George!' she yelled at the cat. George slowly opened his eyes, stretched, yawned and jumped unwillingly onto the floor, from where he sat and stared at Kate with undisguised loathing. While Ida was filling the kettle at the large Belfast sink, two Labradors, tails wagging, came from somewhere at the far end of the kitchen to greet their visitor. Kate remembered the dogs from when she occasionally met Seymour Barker-Jones, shortly after his wife was killed, and when she walked Barney up on the cliffs.

As Ida unpacked her groceries and Kate stroked the dogs, she asked, 'Has Mr Barker-Jones been back recently?'

Ida shook her head. 'He don't come down much no more, not since Fenella passed on.' She sighed, sniffed and blew her nose lustily.

'Passed on' was one way of putting it, Kate supposed, as she recalled the awful sight of Fenella, with a knife through her heart, slumped against the kitchen table in the Women's Institute. Her husband, Seymour, was reputed to be a leading light in MI5, a government advisor and, above all, a Very Important Person. So important that, rumour had it, he was almost certainly in line for a knighthood.

Ida had been a housekeeper here for around fifty years, working for Seymour's father before him, and was now rattling around on her own in this huge house. Her main task was to keep the place occupied and aired, to look after the dogs and cats, and to enlist help if necessary when 'Mr Seymour' decided to come home, which was rarely.

'Don't you get lonely at times, Ida?' Kate asked as she watched Ida pouring boiling water into a large brown teapot.

Ida shook her head. 'I'm used to it, I am. And I've got the animals.' She waved a hand around. 'At least he got rid of the mistress's horse cos, before that, I was havin' to make sure that Joe Martin, from down the village, came to feed and exercise the horse every bleedin' day. Milk and sugar?'

'Just milk, please. You must have many happy memories though, Ida?'

'Oh, I does.' Ida handed her a mug of tea. 'There were some lovely times back then, so there were. Lovely days they were.' She stared out of the window moist-eyed.

'The days when Freddy was courting you?' Kate prompted.

'Fancy you remembering that!' Ida exclaimed as she sat down on the armchair opposite.

'Well, I suppose it's because I feel so sorry for the Hedgefields,' Kate said, 'because, in spite of all their money, they seem to be a rather unfortunate family.'

'You can say that again! Poor Freddy feared for his life sometimes with that madwoman around!'

'Really?'

'It was *her*, that Adeline. Nutty as a fruitcake. They've put her away now, thank God.'

'So I believe,' Kate said guardedly, wondering if Ida was referring to Freddy's demise. 'I hear rumour that she lost a baby girl once.'

Ida slurped her tea. 'Didn't think folk remembered that. Anyway, the poor little thing didn't live long.'

'That's so sad. Poor Adeline,' Kate remarked.

Ida sniffed. 'That woman didn't have one maternal bone in her body,' she said, warming to her subject. 'None at all. She was no better when she had the boy. Strange woman. She went doolally after she lost the little girl and Henry was at his wits' end and had to get a nurse in.'

'Did she?' Kate could not admit to having studied the medical records.

'She did, she went doolally. It was a special nurse he got, not like you, but a nurse what deals with them not right in the head.'

'A psychiatric nurse?' Kate prompted.

'That's it,' said Ida. 'Jenny her name was. We got ever so friendly, we did.'

'Who, you and the nurse?'

'Yeah, me and Jenny. See, we used to go to them dances every Saturday night in the village hall.' She leaned forwards, her eyes bright. 'They was great dances. But, do you know, it was ages before I could understand a bleedin' word she said! Ages it was! She talked that funny!'

'Funny?' Kate tried to imagine the addition of a psychiatric nurse with a speech impediment joining the already strange household.

'Yeah, she came from Liverpool, see.'

'Oh, you mean she had a *Liverpool* accent? Popularly known as Scouse? Like The Beatles?'

'Worse than them Beatles, cos they was *singing*. She was *talkin'*, see? I got sort of used to it though.' Ida giggled. 'Jenny used to say she didn't know what I was sayin' either! Said we spoke ever so funny down here!'

'Well, regional accents can be very interesting,' Kate agreed. 'Was she nice?'

'Oh yeah, she was nice. And pretty too. The boys all fancied her, but I didn't mind, see, cos Freddy fancied me. I'll tell you somethin' else: Henry Hedgefield fancied her too!'

'*Did* he now?'

'Yeah, he did, the devil! Adeline was mad with jealousy – on top of everythin' else!' Ida lowered her voice. 'I shouldn't be tellin' you this…'

Kate was agog. 'Your secret's safe with me, Ida.'

'Adeline found them in bed! Together! Henry and Jenny! Together they were, in bed!' She paused for effect. 'More tea?'

'Oh, just half a cup, please, Ida,' Kate replied, holding out her mug and keen to keep this conversation going as long as possible. 'How did Adeline react?'

Ida stopped halfway through pouring the tea. 'She went and got the breadknife, that's what she did! And she went for poor Jenny! She did, she went for poor Jenny. With the *breadknife*!'

'How awful! Did she hurt Jenny?' Kate decided she'd definitely keep Adeline on her list.

'No, cos Jenny moved quicker than Adeline. But she had to go, of course. Back to Liverpool. She got a job up there and never came back. Never came back. Said I should go up there to visit her, but I never did. Never did. All that way! I never felt the need to leave Cornwall really.' She stared at Kate. 'Why would I want to leave Cornwall?'

'Why indeed,' agreed Kate hastily. 'So you never met up again?'

'No, never. We still sent each other Christmas cards and birthday cards like, for over twenty years. Yeah, a good twenty years. Then I never heard nothin' more. So, I'm guessing she's dead, cos I never heard no more after that.'

'Did she never marry?'

'No, she didn't. Not as I know of, anyways. Don't know why cos she was a looker.'

'Can you remember her surname, Ida?' Kate asked.

Ida thought for a moment. 'Can't rightly remember now.'

'I'm just interested in names and people's history,' Kate said. 'Perhaps I can look up her name on the internet and see what I can find out for you.'

'Oh, ain't you clever! That would be good. Biscuit?' Ida passed the biscuit box across.

'No, thanks, Ida. Got to watch the weight.' Kate patted her tummy. 'So you've no idea what her surname was?'

'I know it began with a J, same as her first name. Might have been Jones, or Johnson, somethin' like that. It might just be in my old address book somewhere – I could go upstairs and have a look, if you like?'

'If you manage to find it I might be able to discover whether she ever got married or what happened to her, and I could let you know,' Kate said.

'Could you *really*? That's kind of you, nurse. I'd really like to know what become of her and I don't know nothin' about no internet, see.'

'Why don't you call me Kate.'

'OK then, I will. Give me a moment and I'll have a look to see if I can find that old address book.' With that Ida got up, accompanied by some grunts, and shuffled towards the door.

Kate had no idea if she'd be able to find this Jenny woman or not. She needed as much detail as possible from Ida. While she awaited Ida's return she fussed the dogs, and gave them both a custard cream. All the others were chocolatey and she knew better than to give any form of chocolate to dogs.

After about five minutes Ida returned. 'Jordan!' she shouted triumphantly. 'It was Jenny *Jordan*!'

'Do you have an address for her?' Kate asked. Then, seeing the puzzled expression on Ida's face she added, 'It just makes it easier to narrow it down and it might be useful to have it.'

'Yeah, here it is. Let me see now… ah yes, 24 Pretoria Road, that was in Liverpool somewhere, I suppose.'

'Anything else you remember, Ida, you let me know.' Kate handed Ida one of her cards. 'Now I must be on my way.'

'Well, thank you kindly for the lift,' said Ida as she accompanied Kate to the door. 'And don't forget that I'll be needin' new knees before long.'

CHAPTER SEVENTEEN

Jenny Jordan. So, Henry Hedgefield was having an affair with the nurse who had been employed to care for his wife, who was suffering intolerable grief for the death of their daughter. Poor Adeline! Kate felt increasingly sorry for her with every new piece of information she uncovered. This was rather a long shot, but Kate wondered whether Jenny Jordan's affair with Henry Hedgefield might have resulted in a baby.

She sat down with the laptop and typed in her password and went back onto the genealogy site, Generations Together. She discovered a few Jenny Jordans, but thanks to Ida supplying the address she was able to find Jenny Jordan at that address in the electoral register records for 1980. Then Kate concentrated on finding her birth record. She typed in *Born Liverpool, 1944*, and prayed she'd got the date right. Up on the screen came:

Jennifer Anne Jordan, born 4 April 1944, Sefton, Liverpool.

Then Kate decided to test her theory and she typed Aaron Jordan into the search bar and typed in his year of birth as 1975.

From her wide experience of reading and watching crime stories Kate had discovered that there is generally a defining moment in any case, and Kate thought this could be one of those moments because there on the screen she saw in the Civil Registration Birth Index, 1916-2007 the name Aaron Jordan! And he'd been registered in Liverpool.

Holding her breath, Kate clicked onto the link to view the actual image of the register entry, and there it was: under 'name of child' was Aaron Jordan, maiden name of mother was also Jordan, and he was born in 1975, in the first quarter, so January, February or March.

But that wasn't all. Directly below Aaron's was the name – *Benjamin* – Benjamin's mother's maiden name was also Jordan, and the reference page numbers for the two boys were consecutive, which meant they could only be twins.

If Aaron Jordan was Aaron Hedgefield, then he must have been adopted by the Hedgefields. But what had become of his twin Benjamin?

Her heart pounding and her hands quite sweaty, Kate began searching for references to Benjamin Jordan, wondering if he had died as a baby like the unfortunate Emily. There was no other record for him apart from his birth.

Kate was increasingly certain she might have found Locker Man. She felt a small lump forming in her throat. She would never have believed scanning through a list of names on an internet genealogy site could be such an emotional experience. But knowing that this little baby boy could have come to such a sad and premature end – probably murdered with his body hidden away for over twenty years – very nearly brought her to tears.

Kate re-entered Jenny's name in the search bar to see what she could find. If Jenny had kept Benjamin and married, then perhaps his surname had changed too. But Jenny hadn't married, or at least she had the same name when she had died in 1999, which explained why Ida had received no more Christmas cards from her for the past twenty years. Yet surely Ida had no idea that her friend, Jenny, had given birth forty-five years previously or she would certainly have mentioned it. Ida wouldn't have been able to resist sharing such a tantalising piece of gossip. So why hadn't Jenny ever told her? Surely you would tell your close friend? Then, on further consideration, Kate recalled that it was still a disgrace to have 'babies out of wedlock' in 1975, so perhaps Jenny was ashamed? Or, more likely, she was afraid Ida would know who the father was likely to be. And there was surely no mistaking who the father was! The boys were born seven months after Jenny left the Hedgefield household in September 1974.

To be sure of her facts Kate needed another piece of information; she needed to know whether Aaron Jordan had been adopted, and if he was, that detail would be noted on his original birth certificate. Kate ordered the birth certificates for both Aaron and Benjamin Jordan along with the death certificate for Jenny Jordan, paying for express delivery in the hope they'd arrive the next day. Already a plan was forming in Kate's mind as she logged off. She was going to pay another visit to Adeline, but first she needed to find a brooch.

*

In the depths of her jewellery drawer Kate finally located what she was looking for: a silver butterfly brooch decorated with red and green stones. It was a piece of inexpensive costume jewellery and Kate wasn't altogether sure if Adeline was discerning enough to still appreciate the real thing, or whether she just liked brooches of any kind. Kate found a small gift box, emptied the safety pins she'd been storing in it, lined the box with cotton wool and placed the brooch inside. She remembered Angie handing her a large, much-wrapped parcel one Christmas, when they must have been in their mid-teens. When she'd finally removed the layers and layers of wrapping, Kate found a tiny bottle of eau de cologne from Woolworths.

'Always remember presentation's the name of the game,' Angie had said as Kate had stared in disbelief at the minuscule gift. Kate hoped Adeline would feel the same way as she stored the box safely in her top drawer ready for her next visit to The Cedars.

When Kate went downstairs and put on her coat, Barney danced around her excitedly. 'No, you can't come with me, Barney,' she said. 'I can't take you with me, but I won't be long and I'll take you for a walk when I get back.'

She went into the garden and picked a small posy of snowdrops then set off for the harbour. The Locker Tea Rooms stood empty and full of dust, where Angie and Fergal had begun to remove the plaster from the walls to expose the original stonework. There was no sign of Angie and there were no police personnel there, so she went inside and carefully climbed down the ladder into the cellar, feeling an involuntary shiver as she did so. Angie had mentioned that the police said they'd be all done in a day or so.

The place where the body had been found was still taped off, so Kate carefully placed the flowers on a shelf on the wall just beyond the cordon, then stood and stared at the place where Benjamin Jordan had lain for more than twenty years. She thought of the young man he'd once been – the baby boy whose name she'd discovered in the birth register – and she felt tears pricking her eyes. They were tears of sadness but also tears of anger, and she was suddenly filled with an overwhelming desire to bring him some measure of justice.

Why had he died there? Who had killed him? Could it have been Henry Hedgefield as Aaron had suggested? What reason could Henry Hedgefield possibly have to kill his own son? If Henry was father of both boys why did he only acknowledge one of the twins? Why didn't he want Benjamin? Kate hoped she might be able to find out a little more when she received copies of the twins' birth certificates.

Still feeling profoundly sad, Kate left The Locker Tea Rooms and went back to collect Barney, because what she needed now was a good, long walk on the cliffs to mull over everything. It solved no problems of course but, as always, she felt calmer as she walked back.

*

Shortly after she got home from her walk, Woody appeared on the doorstep.

'Do you fancy getting something to eat at The Gull?' he said.

'It's a bit early,' Kate said. 'It's not five o'clock yet. Why don't we go down to Angie's for tea and a cake? I think the tea room area is pretty well finished by now, and she needs to get some experience.'

'OK, why not? Go get your coat.'

When Kate and Woody walked into the tea rooms Angie, who was behind the bar, looked at them both in amazement. 'What are you two doing here?'

Kate looked at Woody, and back to Angie. 'Well, that's a nice welcome, I must say! Where else would you recommend we go for a cup of tea and a bun?'

'Oh, you're *customers*!' exclaimed Angie. 'We're not officially open yet, but I can do the tea and I've got some teacakes *somewhere*...'.

'That'll do nicely,' said Kate, as she and Woody sat down at a table by the window.

'I don't want to be overheard, not even by Angie, because I want to talk to you about this Aaron Hedgefield business,' Woody said, lowering his voice.

'I'm listening.'

'I tried to get some information out of Bill Robson today as to how the case was progressing, and he told me outright to keep my nose out of it,' Woody said quietly. 'He took great pleasure in telling me I was a civilian now and if he suspected I was interfering in police business he'd have me arrested. He's not such a nice bloke as I thought.'

Kate sniffed. 'I could have told you that,' she said with a warm feeling of satisfaction. 'So basically, he told you not to get involved?'

'He did.'

'And how do you like it?'

'OK, OK! But when I tell *you* not to get involved, I'm only thinking of your safety. Anyway, on this occasion I'd quite like you to get involved.'

'Well, that's a turn-up for the books! You are actually giving me permission?'

They stopped talking while Angie appeared with two cups and saucers, a teapot, hot water jug, milk jug and sugar bowl, all patterned with bluebirds amid leafy trellises. 'Don't you dare make any remarks about this being twee,' she said.

'I wouldn't dream of it,' said Kate, grinning, as she poured the tea. Then, turning to Woody, 'You were saying?'

'Things are different this time. I mean, it's not as if we have a murderer on the loose. All this happened twenty years ago. You might be able to find out a bit of background. Talk to your old ladies again and see if they've got any more information about the Hedgefields and see if you can track down this mysterious twin.'

Kate suppressed a smile. She knew she should tell him what she'd found out about Jenny Jordan and the twins. She held back because she had another idea as to how she could further her research, but she was pretty sure Woody wouldn't agree to it. She would have to come at it from an unexpected angle.

Angie reappeared with two bluebird-and-trellis patterned plates, each bearing a warm teacake with melting butter. 'Enjoy,' she said.

'To change the subject,' Kate said, taking a generous bite, 'is there anything you fancied doing for your birthday? It is next weekend, isn't it?'

'Yeah, the eighth, but I'm not into celebrating birthdays any more.'

'Yes,' Kate said, 'but I wondered about maybe having a weekend away somewhere?'

'At this time of year? Not bloody likely!' Woody said.

That was a blow. Kate was hoping he'd be keen on a trip to Liverpool. She needed an excuse to go there so that she would have the opportunity to do some research on the ground rather than on the laptop. The idea had come to her while she was walking Barney up on the cliff. She wanted to go to the place Jenny Jordan lived and the place the twins were presumably born and find out what she could about what happened to Benjamin.

'I think it would be nice to get away from all this Locker business so we can really enjoy your birthday.'

'If you like…' Woody murmured, but it was obvious he wasn't paying any attention because he added, 'Hey, this pastry is good! You don't suppose Angie made it, do you?' He looked around but Angie had disappeared.

'I very much doubt it,' Kate said. 'She's had a go at a lot of things, but baking isn't one of them.'

CHAPTER EIGHTEEN

The copies of the birth certificates and Jenny's death certificate arrived two days later. When Jenny Jordan had died in May 1999 of breast cancer aged just forty-eight she had still been resident at the same address as Ida had given Kate. Jenny had definitely given birth to twins, there could be no doubt about that. Aaron Jordan and Benjamin Jordan had been born on the same day, 25 March 1975, and they had the same mother, Jennifer Anne Jordan. Apart from the names of the boys, the birth certificates were identical in their appearance – apart from one thing. In the top right-hand corner of Aaron's certificate the word 'Adopted' had been written. Kate knew she now had to try to order the adoption certificate as final proof. It was a complicated online procedure on the government website and she felt relieved when she eventually made the final click. Now she had to wait.

Kate made up her mind to pay another visit to The Cedars straight away.

She found Adeline in her room, sitting at the table, and writing furiously.

'Oh, hello,' Kate said cautiously as she closed the door behind her. 'I see you're busy. Are you writing a letter?'

Adeline glanced up briefly and then continued writing. 'Yes,' she said, 'to my husband.'

Kate didn't have a ready reply to that. 'Oh,' she said, 'good.'

'No, it's not good,' Adeline said, 'because he's gone away.'

'Where's he gone, Adeline?'

'None of your business!' Adeline snapped.

'Perhaps I shouldn't interrupt you then?' Kate asked.

'No, you shouldn't.'

'I've brought you a brooch.'

Adeline laid down her pen, stood up, smiled, and said, 'A *brooch*! Let me see it!'

Looking at the front of Adeline's black sweater as she stood up, Kate wondered if there could possibly be a square inch anywhere on which to pin it. She handed over the little box which contained the brooch nestling in cotton wool. It had cost practically nothing in the first place, but Kate hoped the presentation made it look more expensive.

'Lovely!' exclaimed Adeline. 'Are they garnets?'

'I hope so,' Kate said doubtfully.

'My mother wore garnet earrings,' Adeline said, looking in vain for a square inch of sweater. 'She wears them when she and Father go to the Muthaiga Country Club. One time when they were away we had zebras in the garden!' She gave a high-pitched giggle.

Zebras? Then Kate recalled that Adeline had been born in Kenya, and probably her parents had even been members of the infamous Happy Valley set, about whom Kate had read avidly.

'How lovely!' Kate exclaimed. 'How lovely to have zebras in the garden!'

Adeline stared at her as if she was mad. 'They eat things,' she said, 'but the servants chased them away!'

'Oh, good,' Kate said, not altogether sure if Adeline considered this to be good or not. 'It must have been very different when you came to England?'

'I'm not going to England,' Adeline retorted.

'No, of course not,' Kate said, wondering whether this was a good moment to bring up the subject of Henry and any strange visitors he may have had, assuming Adeline had even been around at the time.

'I believe you entertained lots of visitors at Tremorron,' Kate said tentatively.

'Millions,' Adeline confirmed. 'Do you think there's room for these lovely garnets at the top of my sleeve?'

'I don't see why not,' Kate replied. 'Would you like me to pin it on there for you?'

'No,' said Adeline, 'I shall do it later.'

'Millions, you said; millions of visitors at Tremorron? Well, I don't think Aaron entertains on that scale these days.'

'*Who?*'

'Aaron. Your son? Remember him?'

Adeline thought for a moment. 'Evil,' she said, picking up her pen again.

'Evil? Who's evil?' Kate said.

Adeline sat down and thought for a moment. 'My mother comes sometimes,' she said. 'At night.' She smiled. 'She comes in through the window and floats towards my bed. It's so lovely to see her again.'

'Yes, I'm sure it is.' Kate wondered how to bring the subject back round to Aaron. 'Perhaps she visits Aaron too?'

'*Who?*'

'Aaron, your son.'

Adeline stood up again and glared at Kate. 'I remember *you*! I *told* you I didn't have a son!'

'Just a daughter?' Kate prompted. 'But Adeline, didn't you adopt a little boy? Didn't you adopt Henry's son?'

Adeline began to cry. Kate felt dreadful; *why* had she said that? She stood up and went to hug Adeline.

'Don't *touch* me!' Adeline snapped, her eyes ablaze with anger through the tears.

'I'm so sorry I've upset you.' Kate was about to abandon the conversation altogether when Adeline said, 'I couldn't *have* any more. How many times do I have to explain it? It wasn't *my* fault!'

Kate wondered if she dared say anything else. She wasn't sure if Adeline still had any violent tendencies, but at least there were no breadknives around. She took a deep breath. 'And then there was *Jenny*,' she said softly.

'A *whore*!' Adeline's eyes had taken on a strange light. 'A whore! That's what *she* was!' She turned her back on Kate. 'Are you *going* now? It's time you went.'

'Well…' Kate began.

'Please go! I'm busy, and I want you to *go*.'

Kate stepped back. 'Well, it's good to see you, Adeline.'

Adeline didn't reply but began to write again. After a moment, she looked up. 'I'll tell Freddy to show you out.'

Kate looked at Adeline, at her neat figure, her thick white hair carefully tied up in a scrunchie, her black jumper covered in brooches, and wondered. She wondered about her life, her childhood in Kenya, her marriage to Henry; so many things she'd love to know but probably never would. How had she come to be like this?

'Well, I'll be off then, Adeline.'

Adeline did not respond and didn't even look up from writing her letter to Henry. Kate closed the door quietly behind her.

As Kate got back into her car she broke down in tears. That poor woman! She still obviously recalled her little daughter – *and* Jenny. It would surely have been kinder if that part of her mind had been blanked out but instead poor Adeline had to live with the memory. And that remark she'd made: *I couldn't have any more after that… it wasn't my fault*. So she had definitely *not* given birth to Aaron – if that remark was true. The picture was slowly taking shape. No, *changing* shape would be more accurate. Well, Kate would get the final proof when Aaron's adoption certificate arrived. And that, apparently, could take weeks.

When Kate got home she found Angie on her phone asking an electrician to please, *please* come to sort out the electrics at the tea rooms.

'Like *yesterday*!' she shouted. 'I can't *wait* until next week!' As she came off the phone she said to Kate, 'Honestly, trying to find *anyone* to come and do *anything*…!'

'They are busy people,' Kate agreed. 'I should have thought next week would be fine. What's the hurry?'

'We can finally get into our cellar and work on the bar,' Angie said. 'The police have said they don't need to bother us further. There's an awful lot of clearing out to do and we're making a start in the main bar, or what will *be* the main bar.'

'That's great,' Kate said. 'How's Fergal getting on with the shower?'

'It's more or less finished, but we keep running it to make sure that we've really waterproofed the room and that there are no leaks anywhere. Do you want to come and have a look?'

Kate thought it might have been wise to have a plumber check it out, but decided not to say so. 'I'd love to have a look,' she said, eager to get another glimpse at the scene of the twenty-year-old crime.

An hour later she was being shown round the tiny upstairs apartment of The Locker Tea Rooms with a beaming Fergal in attendance. There was only room for two of them to squeeze comfortably into most of the rooms at once, so he hovered outside the doors while Angie gave a running commentary.

Eventually they squeezed into the wet room where the toilet was only a few feet away from the newly installed shower. 'No room for a hand-basin,' Angie said cheerfully, 'but we can use the sink.'

The bedroom was next door, painted white and filled almost to capacity with a large double bed and several stacks of boxes.

'We'll get it all sorted out eventually,' Angie said with a giggle. Kate hadn't seen her sister so happy in years, and was delighted that she seemed to have found something that fired her with such enthusiasm. Then she remembered that Angie had once been equally passionate about her paintings. Never mind, she thought, this could be the making of her. *I hope.*

They then proceeded to the living room where a small log-burner had been newly installed in the fireplace. There was one two-seater sofa and one armchair, and a small dining table with two folding chairs. Behind this was the mini kitchen where there was the sink, a small electric cooker, a few cupboards, a worktop, a microwave, kettle and toaster.

'Everything you could want,' Angie said happily, 'except space. But we're getting used to it, aren't we, Fergal?'

'Oh we are indeed,' Fergal agreed, 'and it's nice and compact so won't require much heating.'

'Or cleaning,' added Angie.

Kate decided not to mention the lack of a fridge, but assumed there would be several downstairs in the bar eventually. She knew that Angie had paid for everything; Fergal didn't even have the price of a pint much of the time, whereas Angie had inherited a large sum of money from her late mother-in-law. She had also been generous to Kate, who had now paid off all the outstanding household debts and had been able to squirrel some money away into her bank account. Despite their differences, they looked out for each other.

'I'm planning to be away for a few days next weekend, the eighth and ninth of February,' Kate said casually, 'and I was hoping you could look after the dog? If you can't I shall have to find kennels, but Barney won't like that.'

'No problem, he can be here with us,' Angie said airily, 'and I might even take him for a walk now and again. So where are you going?'

'Well, it's Woody's birthday and I thought I might treat him to a few days away somewhere.'

'That's a nice idea. Where were you thinking of going?'

'Don't know yet,' Kate lied, 'but I'm hoping to find somewhere interesting.'

CHAPTER NINETEEN

'I hope you don't mind,' Kate said the following day, as she sat down on the sofa beside her log-burner, having boosted her courage with a large gin and tonic, 'but I've booked us next weekend away for your birthday. *My* treat!'

Woody was sprawled in the armchair opposite reading his newspaper. '*What?*'

'A weekend away. For your birthday. I've found a lovely hotel.'

He dropped the newspaper onto the floor. 'Where?'

Kate cleared her throat. 'Liverpool.'

'*Liverpool?*'

'I've never been to Liverpool, and I thought it might be nice. Have you been?'

'No,' Woody replied, 'I haven't. And I never planned to go in February when it's even colder than here.'

'That won't matter, Woody. The hotel will be nice and warm, and we can wrap up well. You like The Beatles, don't you?'

'As far as I'm aware they don't live there any more,' he said.

'Yes, but you could go to The Beatles Museum and the Cavern Club! It'd be fun – take you back to your youth!' Kate met his eye nervously.

'Are you up to something?'

'Woody, I just want to take you away somewhere for your birthday. Drive up Friday, drive back Monday. I don't mind driving. I've always fancied visiting Liverpool.'

'Kate, this is a very generous gesture, but a bottle of Scotch for my birthday would have been fine. We don't have to go to *Liverpool*!'

'We need a break from here and—'

'We've only just recently got back from California! And we could have snow, so the roads would be icy. It's a long drive up there.'

'No, I've checked the weather forecast for the next couple of weeks and there's no snow forecast. I've booked the hotel, Woody! Oh, *please*! I so wanted to do something *different* for your birthday!'

Woody moved across and positioned himself beside her on the sofa. 'That's very sweet of you, Kate. OK, we'll go, but *I'll* do the driving. I don't fancy going all that way in your Fiat and, besides, my car could do with a nice long run.'

Woody had bought himself a sleek, one-year-old, white Mercedes at the end of the year to celebrate his retirement, and of which he was inordinately proud. Kate had hoped he'd offer to drive, but felt she'd had to make the gesture.

'We'll have a lovely time,' she assured him, snuggling up close.

All Kate's plans were falling into line.

The forecast was correct. There was no snow, just lashing rain, busy motorway traffic, and an excess of enormous trucks, one passing the other at a crawl and holding everyone up. There were the predictable hold-ups around the Birmingham area and there were roadworks every few miles. There was also a great deal of sighing from Woody.

'It's not that I don't appreciate your generosity,' he said to Kate, as they crawled along in the only lane that wasn't cordoned off somewhere near Stafford, 'but I kinda wish you'd chosen somewhere a little closer to home.' What made it even more infuriating was that, as usual, there appeared to be no one at all working in either of the two cordoned-off lanes.

'It's not too far now,' Kate said, as she watched the spray of mud, from the truck in front, slide down the windscreen where the wipers were working overtime.

'I'm going to have to find a car wash somewhere,' Woody muttered, as they edged forwards another few yards. Kate knew how proud he had been of the gleaming white bodywork of his nearly new car, which added to her guilt. She hoped and prayed that the weather would improve for their couple of days in the city; otherwise she had a feeling she was never going to be able to live this down.

*

It was late afternoon and already dark when they finally found the Belvedere Hotel, located in the city centre, after getting lost several times. Woody was tired and not in the best of moods, and Kate was worried that this weekend could be a complete disaster.

However, the hotel was beautiful, warm and friendly. The bedroom was large, modern and minimalist, with a great deal of taupe and off-white. There was an enormous flat-screen television and a well-stocked bar, which Woody was exploring before he'd even begun to unpack. His mood improved further when he found a bucket of ice, and he busied himself mixing two gin and tonics. There were even slices of lemon in a little container.

'Here we are!' he said, as he handed a glass to Kate. 'Let's sit down and relax.'

There were two taupe armchairs by the white-curtained window, looking out onto an attractive square, which bordered a tree-filled park and must have been lovely in spring and summer. As they sat down Kate said, 'Look, it's even stopped raining!'

Woody grinned as he took a sip of gin. 'Sorry if I was a bit cranky in the car,' he said, 'but it really was a pretty shitty journey.'

'It was,' Kate agreed, 'and it had me wishing I'd chosen Exeter, or Bristol or somewhere.'

'Why didn't you?' Woody asked, looking genuinely puzzled.

'Oh, I just thought about how much you liked The Beatles,' Kate said vaguely, 'and I didn't think there'd be too many tourists around at this time of year.'

'Well, sure, I liked The Beatles,' Woody said, 'but they're kinda history now.'

'And so are we,' said Kate with a nervous laugh. 'Anyway, we're going to have a lovely dinner tonight, a good sleep, and do lots of sightseeing tomorrow.'

'Sounds good,' Woody agreed.

Saturday morning dawned dry and sunny.

And Woody Forrest was sixty-two years old.

'Sixty-two!' he groaned. 'Who'd have thought it!'

'What do you mean?' Kate asked as she handed him a package wrapped in black-and-gold paper. 'Sixty-two's not old these days.'

'Maybe not, but I just never thought I'd get to be this old. Risks of the job and all that, and a few close shaves.'

'Well, I'm glad you did make it.' Kate watched as he carefully unwrapped his present and slowly withdrew a black wool dressing-gown. She had given up trying to persuade him to buy a new one to replace the tatty grey robe he was so attached to.

'Oh, wow! Thank you so much, darling!' He leaped out of bed and slipped the dressing-gown on over his naked body, and then did a couple of pirouettes in front of the full-length mirror. 'Who *is* this sexy guy I see in there?'

'No need to go overboard,' Kate said, pleased that he appeared to like it. 'It's got a tiny bit of cashmere in it too.'

'That would make it expensive,' Woody said, doing another couple of twirls. 'All this, and a luxury hotel! What have I done to deserve such treatment?'

Kate laughed. 'I'm collecting Brownie points. It's always good to be in credit!' I might need that credit tomorrow, she thought. 'But mainly I just wanted to see you draped in something worthy of your glorious body.'

'My glorious body is feeling extremely grateful,' Woody said, 'and in such a way that I fear we must get back into bed straight away.'

*

Two hours later, after a real northern full English breakfast, complete with black pudding and the American addition of home-made hash browns which pleased Woody no end, they emerged into the February sunshine complete with street map. The receptionist had given them a very detailed route, delivered at breakneck speed, and neither of them could remember a word of it.

'I'm so full that we're going to have to walk slowly,' Kate remarked, as they worked out their route.

'There was no need for you to have an extra portion of black pudding,' Woody said sternly.

'Or for *you* to have extra hash browns!' Kate retorted.

He grinned. 'OK, we'll walk slowly.'

It took fifteen minutes to get to the Royal Albert Dock, a complex of maritime buildings and warehouses, once dealing with cargoes of cotton, tea, oil, tobacco, ivory and much, much more, from all over the world. It was now a magnificent waterside development of bars and restaurants. There was also the famous Liver Building which, along with the Cunard Building and the Port of Liverpool Building, formed the Three Graces which lined the waterfront.

'The Liver Building was once the tallest in the city,' Woody said, reading from the guidebook.

Kate pointed skywards. 'Up there,' she said, 'are the two Liver Birds who watch over the city and the sea.'

They spent a long time in the Museum of Liverpool, with its recreations of The Casbah Coffee Club, the Cavern Club and Abbey Road Studios. There were even John Lennon's spectacles and George Harrison's first guitar, plus details of all their careers.

Kate found it interesting but was delighted to see that Woody was completely hooked. 'I'm reliving my youth,' he said happily, as she took pictures of him standing next to the bronze monument to the four icons. It had been a good choice.

They stopped only for a drink, and then both were amazed to find that it was late afternoon. The sky was visibly darkening as they headed back to their hotel.

'I think I'll be just about able to cope with dinner later,' Woody said, patting his stomach as they headed along the maze of corridors to their room.

'And dancing,' Kate added.

'*What?*'

'Dancing. It's a dinner-dance on Saturday nights.'

'Oh my God,' said Woody.

*

Woody turned out to be a good dancer, light on his feet and sure of step.

'Hey, you didn't tell me you could dance like that,' Kate said breathlessly as they returned to their table after a lively American jive.

'All thanks to my mom for insisting I went to dancing classes when I was only about seven years old,' Woody admitted. 'There were a few other guys there but the girls outnumbered us five to one. It's OK for a boy to go to dance lessons in California, though, because everyone wants to become Fred Astaire and be in show business. But I can still remember being petrified in case any of the guys in my school class saw me coming out of Francesca's Dance Studio.'

'You're a man of many talents,' Kate said as she picked up the dessert menu.

'You know far too much about me,' Woody sighed, 'and now you're going to forecast my choice of dessert.'

'Funny you should say that. How about apple pie and ice cream?'

'Bring it on!' said Woody.

CHAPTER TWENTY

The sunny weather couldn't last, of course. And it didn't; Sunday was wet and windy.

'What are we going to do today?' Woody asked, dipping his hash browns in egg.

Kate took a deep breath. 'I thought maybe we could part company for a couple of hours? Perhaps you go to the original Cavern Club and I'll go to the shops? We could meet up somewhere mid-afternoon?'

Woody laid down his fork. '*Shops?* On a *Sunday*?'

'Well, yes. They do open for a few hours on a Sunday and there were one or two things I wanted to look at.'

'Like what?'

'Well, I need some new bras and things, and I didn't think you'd relish trailing round M&S.' Kate knew she was on fairly safe ground here because he did not like shopping.

'You're right,' Woody confirmed.

'I've not had a chance to get to any decent shops for months,' Kate went on, visualising Demelza's Boutique in Middle Tinworthy, with its skimpy underwear and thongs.

'OK then, you hit the shops, I'll go to The Cavern, and we'll meet back here at...?'

'About 3 p.m.?' Kate suggested.

'As late as that? What is it with you women and shopping?' Woody asked, shaking his head in despair.

*

As soon as Woody set off for The Cavern, Kate grabbed a taxi from the front of the hotel. It was cold and wet, and the idea of working out the Sunday bus services, in an area she didn't know, did not appeal.

The taxi driver was grey, grizzled and had the world-weary look of someone who's seen it all, done it all. 'Where to?' he asked.

'Twenty-four Pretoria Road, please,' Kate said as she slid into the seat. 'That's in Sefton.'

'I know where it is,' he said, stifling a yawn.

They set off, the rain pounding noisily on the roof and windows, competing with the wailing of a pop group on the driver's radio, who were definitely not The Beatles. After some time the streets narrowed, jammed with parked cars. Pretoria Road was also narrow, with terraced Victorian houses either side. Some looked sad and neglected, grubby nets stretched across windows, while others had been gentrified with shiny new doors, some with shutters, and not a net curtain in sight. Number twenty-four had been revamped with a red-painted door and Roman blinds at the windows.

'Do you want me to wait?' asked the taxi driver, turning down the volume of the radio. 'How long you gonna be?'

'I honestly don't know,' Kate replied, 'but probably not very long. Can you hold on for a minute, please?'

He cut the engine and Kate got out, pulling up the hood on her raincoat as she walked up to the red door and rapped the smart brass knocker. A minute or so later a young, exhausted-looking woman came to the door, carrying a baby on her hip.

'I'm sorry to bother you,' Kate said, 'but I wondered if anyone called Jenny Jordan ever lived here? I'm trying to trace her.'

The woman looked at her blankly through an untidy blonde fringe and shook her head. 'No, don't know no Jenny Jordan,' she said, jiggling the baby, whose face was crumpling in preparation for a howl.

'Have you lived here long then?' Kate asked. 'Can you remember who sold your family the house? Could that have been a Jenny Jordan?' Kate knew from Jenny's death certificate that her name was Jordan then, but there was always the possibility that she *had* married after she left Cornwall and kept her maiden name. The baby opened his mouth and howled.

'We've been here three years,' the woman shouted over the din, 'and we didn't buy it from no Jenny Jordan.'

'Thanks. I'm sorry to have bothered you,' Kate repeated as she headed back dejectedly towards the taxi. She could still hear the baby wailing after the woman had closed the door. She was about to get into the taxi again when she saw an elderly woman, clad in long waterproofs, with a Yorkshire terrier on a lead, turning into the gate at number twenty-six next door.

She turned when she saw Kate approach. 'Were you lookin' for someone?' she asked.

'Oh, just someone who I thought might have lived next door once,' Kate replied. 'Have *you* lived here long?'

'Forty-eight years,' the woman replied in a broad Irish accent. 'Was nice round here in those days, people ever so friendly. But we got a lot of stuck-up newcomers here now. It's not the same.' She looked pointedly at the red door. Her own door was the original, and she had net curtains too, but the place looked clean and cared for.

Kate stopped in her tracks. 'I don't suppose you remember someone called Jenny Jordan who might have lived next door at one time?'

'Jenny? Oh yes, but that was a while back. She's not with us any more.'

'I know she died quite a long time ago,' Kate said, 'but I was hoping to find out something about her and about her twin boys.'

'Twin boys?' The woman frowned. 'I don't remember no twin boys.'

'Did you know her well?' Kate asked.

The woman stared at her for a moment, then opened her door and unclipped the dog's lead. 'It's cats and dogs out here; do you want to come in?'

'That's so kind of you,' Kate replied, 'but I have this taxi waiting…'

The woman snorted. 'That'll cost you a bomb. I should let him go. I'm Bridie, by the way.'

'Thank you so much, Bridie, I'd love to come in. I'm Kate.'

She paid off the taxi driver, shocked at the price. Bridie had left her door ajar and Kate hesitantly knocked as she entered.

'Come in, come in,' Bridie shouted above the yapping of the dog, which she was drying with a towel. 'I'll just dry Seamus and then I'll put the kettle on for a cup of tea. Hang your coat up on the hook there.'

'Thank you,' Kate said, following her into a cosy little sitting room with a smouldering coal fire. Bridie removed the fireguard and poked at the coals. 'It'll burn up again in a moment. I love an open fire although I had the gas heating put in last year, and what a difference that makes! Sit yourself down now!'

Kate sank into a chintz-covered armchair and took in her surroundings. It was a small room with a variety of floral patterns on the chairs, curtains and carpet. All was slightly faded but very clean.

Her hostess then disappeared and Kate could hear the filling of a kettle and the sound of it being positioned onto a hob. The dog was now sitting in front of the fire and, when Kate stretched out her hand to stroke him, he growled.

'Naughty boy, Seamus!' Bridie scolded as she re-entered the room. 'It's just the way he is,' she informed Kate.

'It's so kind of you to invite a perfect stranger into your house,' Kate remarked.

'Well, I don't get so many visitors these days and it's nice to have a bit of company. I didn't think you looked like the type to clobber me,' Bridie said. 'I've nothin' worth stealin' anyway. How d'you like your tea?'

A few minutes later, balancing a cup and saucer on her lap, Kate heard all about how Bridie, from Limerick, had been swept off her feet by a Liverpudlian called Ken O'Mara and come to live in Sefton. They'd had three daughters, 'all married with kids now and livin' all over the place.' And Ken had passed on some years ago, so now there was just herself and Seamus in the house. 'Why were you lookin' for Jenny?' Bridie asked.

'Well, I was doing some research on a family down in Cornwall, where I live,' Kate explained, 'and I think she worked for them there years ago.'

Bridie thought for a moment. 'Now, when would that have been?'

'Probably around forty-five years ago,' Kate replied, sipping her tea.

'Ah well now,' said Bridie, 'her mam lived next door. Old Mrs Jordan; she was a nice soul. The daughter, Jenny, was a nurse, wasn't she?'

'Yes, she was, and she worked for a family by the name of Hedgefield.'

Bridie shook her head. 'Don't know anythin' about that. But I do remember her comin' back here and movin' in with her mam again.'

'Was she pregnant by any chance?'

'Yes, I believe she was, but she didn't have the baby here. She went away someplace.'

'Baby?' Kate asked. 'So there was only one?'

'One? Yes, of course. A boy – Benjamin she called him, and a right little bugger he turned out to be!'

Kate thought for a moment. 'So she definitely didn't have twins?'

Bridie looked astonished. 'No, of course not. Unless one of them died or somethin' but then she would have been heartbroken, wouldn't she? And she'd have told her mam. And her mam would have told me.'

'So she and Benjamin stayed on next door?'

'Oh yes, for a good twenty years or so. The old lady looked after the boy when Jenny went to work. She had lots of gentlemen friends but she never married. And then the old lady died.'

'What about Benjamin?'

'Yes, a funny boy. We all knew him as Ben, because that's what his mam called him.'

'Funny? In what way?' Kate asked.

'Oh, you know, a bit moody, often rude to his mam. They seemed to argue a lot. I could hear them rowin' sometimes. No father, see. A boy should have a father.'

'You didn't know who the father was?'

'No idea. I never saw any sign of him. She never mentioned it and I never liked to ask. So, was it someone in Cornwall, do you think?'

'It may have been. I'm really enquiring on behalf of the family she worked for, as they wondered what had happened to her.'

Bridie sighed. 'She got cancer, poor lass. She must have died some twenty years back now, and then Ben disappeared and I've never heard anything of him since. Rumour has it he went down south somewhere. The house was rented, you see, so he wouldn't have had a roof over his head. I often wondered what happened to him.'

'That's rather a sad story,' Kate said. 'So he never came back?'

'No, he cleared out after his mother died and we never saw hide nor hair of him again. I suppose he didn't have any reason to stay, having no family here. Jenny had no brothers or sisters, you see, so there weren't any aunts or uncles or cousins. He was a lonely lad. I think that's what made him a bit moody.'

'You've been very kind and very helpful,' Kate said, glancing at her watch, 'but I really must be on my way now and I mustn't take up any more of your time.' She took her mobile out of her bag. 'I'd better phone for a taxi now; do you have any numbers?'

'A taxi?' Bridie sounded horrified. 'You've no need of a taxi! There's a bus stop right at the end of the road and a bus due in' – she consulted her watch – 'exactly nine minutes' time, and it'll take you directly into the city centre.'

Kate was relieved – she didn't want to pay another exorbitant taxi fare. 'Thanks, I'll do just that.' Kate stood up. 'I've enjoyed meeting you,' she said truthfully, 'and many thanks for the tea.'

Seamus, who'd been fast asleep in front of the fire, got to his feet and watched her putting on her raincoat, wagging his tail.

'I think he's pleased to see me go,' Kate said, tying her belt.

'He's not very sociable,' Bridie agreed, 'but he's a good friend to me.'

Kate pulled her coat securely around her and pulled on her hood as she trudged to the bus stop. She'd found out a fair bit about Jenny and her one son, Benjamin. But she *must* have had twins! It was interesting that she'd been 'away someplace' when she gave birth.

She was still deep in thought when the bus pulled up.

CHAPTER TWENTY-ONE

As Kate sat on the bus, which had arrived on the dot, she wondered what Woody would say when she confessed to him what she'd been up to. But she was glad she'd made the trip because she had located some useful pieces of the jigsaw. She knew where Ben had been for the first twenty years of his life – living with his mother, so there was a good chance he could have found out the identity of his father. Had he any idea he had a twin somewhere when he was growing up? Could that be what had caused the rows between Benjamin and Jenny? Perhaps his mother thought it kinder and safer to keep the truth from the son that she'd kept for her own?

Kate tried to imagine herself in Jenny Jordan's position; if Jenny hadn't told Benjamin that he had a twin brother when he was young, surely, once she knew she was dying and didn't have long left, it would be only natural for her to tell Benjamin who his father was and that he was one of twins. Given that he'd left Liverpool shortly after his mother died, wouldn't it make sense that Jenny had only broken the news to him *because* she was dying? It would certainly be understandable. After which it would seem that Benjamin had gone down to Cornwall to trace his father and brother. The dates fitted. Kate wondered whether Henry Hedgefield had ever known that he had another son. And had he rejected him? If Benjamin had arrived out of the blue – perhaps full of hatred for the rich man who apparently hadn't wanted him – Kate could well imagine that some sort of fight might have broken out. Perhaps Aaron's presumed version of events was right...

As she watched the rain lashing against the windows of the bus, Kate thought about how Benjamin might have reacted. Would he have resented his brother having all the advantages that money could provide? He may have felt cheated and angry. Kate felt sure that he probably had. The more she found out about Benjamin Jordan the sorrier she felt for him.

When she got off the bus in Church Street it was still only 11 o'clock. Should she have a wander round the shops? She didn't need to be back in the hotel until later in the afternoon, so there was still time to buy the underwear she'd told Woody she needed. She could always tell him about her visit to Pretoria Road another day – perhaps when they were driving back to Cornwall?

The more Kate thought about all that she had discovered, the more she wondered if she could manage to keep all this exciting information to herself. The shops didn't seem very enticing, and she couldn't see the point of buying things she didn't *really* need to keep up the subterfuge. She just wanted to get warm and dry. She'd go straight to the hotel and get dried off before Woody got back from The Cavern. Then she would fill him in on all the information she'd got. She could hardly wait to tell him. He'd be so surprised and impressed.

When Kate entered their hotel room she found Woody sprawled on the bed, watching television,

'You're back earlier than I thought,' he said. 'How was the shopping?'

'Ah, that's a long story,' said Kate. 'How was The Cavern?'

'Closed,' he said. 'A bit of a wasted journey and too wet really to go anywhere else.'

'Oh, I'm sorry about that,' Kate said as she hung her raincoat up in the bathroom.

'Just as well we went to the museum yesterday,' he remarked. 'So, no bras? No sexy underwear? No *thongs*?' He grinned, doubtless remembering her visit to Demelza's Boutique a few months back. Kate had gone there in the hope of finding some modest underwear and had come home with a thong with which to titillate Woody's fancy. It had certainly worked.

'No,' Kate agreed. 'No knickers, no bras, no thongs. Just some information.'

'What sort of information?' Woody asked, switching off the television.

Kate took a deep breath. 'Information about Jenny Jordan, the nurse who used to look after Adeline Hedgefield years ago, before she got sacked.'

Woody looked at her quizzically. 'Jenny Jordan? Who's Jenny Jordan?'

'I just told you – she's the nurse who used to—'

'Yes, I got that bit,' Woody said. 'How is it that you just happened to find this Jenny Jordan in amongst the bras in Marks and Spencer?'

'Of course I didn't. I went to where she used to live. I had an address for her, you see.'

'Where did you get that?' Woody asked.

'Well, I got chatting to Ida Tilley—'

'*Ida Tilley!*' Woody stared at her. 'How the hell did Ida know where she was?'

'Because Ida was great friends with her, years and years ago, when she was young. They went to dances together and all sorts of things! And Ida wrote to her for a while after she left Cornwall.'

Woody shook his head for a moment. 'So you came up here purely to try to find this Jenny Jordan?'

'No, of course not! We came up here because it was your birthday treat and—'

He raised a hand to stop her in mid-flow. 'You dragged me all the way up here just so you could try to find this woman?'

'No, no, Woody, but I knew you liked The Beatles and—'

'And it gave you an opportunity to stick your nose into somebody else's business *again*!'

'Woody, that wasn't the reason I—'

'Yes, it bloody well *was*!'

Kate had never seen Woody angry before, but there was no mistaking that he was angry now. 'My birthday was merely an excuse for you to do some nosing around. There was *no* need to come all this way otherwise, was there? Because you can't stop yourself getting involved, can you? After all the warnings I've given you! After all the times your life has been in danger!' He stood up and picked up his anorak, then headed towards the door. 'You didn't give a toss about my birthday!'

Kate could feel her eyes welling up. '*Of course* I cared about your birthday! It was just that I...'

She stopped talking as she saw Woody storm out and slam the door. Badly shaken, she sat down on a chair and stared miserably out of the window at the lashing rain. She'd ruined everything! Where had he gone? Would he get into his car, drive straight back to Cornwall and leave her right here? Was this the end of a beautiful relationship?

*

She *couldn't* let this happen! Kate grabbed her raincoat again and rushed along the corridor to find the lift, which was on the third floor and going up, and she was on the second. She couldn't wait. She looked around desperately and saw the door that led to the stairs. Kate hadn't run down sets of stairs in years, but somehow or the other she ran now, gasping when she got to the ground floor and emerged into the reception area.

There was no sign of him.

Kate rushed out to the car park and, sighing with relief, saw Woody's Mercedes parked exactly where he'd left it on Friday afternoon. At least he hadn't set off for home and left her behind, but where had he gone? Most probably he was walking in the rain, cooling off his anger.

What had she *done*? She'd only been trying to help to solve the mystery of Locker Man, who – after all – had been found in the middle of her sister's new business venture. Was it so awful that she wanted to find out what it was all about? She was doing it to help *him*! *He* was the one who had agreed to help his sailing buddy Aaron Hedgefield. And he *had* asked her to get involved, goddamn it! How dare he turn on her this way?

Kate looked out at the rain and at the deserted street for a moment before she turned and headed back up to the room.

She tried to read, to watch TV, to do a crossword, but she was unable to concentrate on anything at all. Had she wrecked everything? Yes, she had chosen Liverpool in the hope of tracing Jenny Jordan, but she'd also chosen it because she really did think Woody would like the association with The Beatles. And she'd wanted to take him *somewhere*. If she'd told him her main reason for choosing Liverpool he'd only have spouted that old cliché about not going looking for trouble. Of course he'd have had every right to say so when he'd had to literally rescue her from the jaws of death twice in a year. But still.

They'd never had a row before. She felt terrible for deceiving him, even if it was done with good intentions. What if she'd wrecked the relationship on account of one woman, no longer even alive, who might, just *might*, have been the mother of Aaron Hedgefield? Because she couldn't be certain yet. She had no absolute proof, a fact which Woody would doubtless point out to her. Perhaps it was all a horrible coincidence. What if a completely different family had adopted Aaron Jordan? What if she was wrong? What if she was following a completely false trail and in doing that she had jeopardised her relationship with the most wonderful man she'd ever known?

'Don't be ridiculous, Kate!' she scolded herself. 'You are *not* wrong. That skeleton in the tea rooms is the remains of Benjamin Jordan, an unhappy child who grew up into a lonely young man who went looking for his family and got himself killed for his pains. He didn't deserve to be unknown, unloved, grieved by no one. People should know his story and you, Kate Palmer, are the only one who can tell it.'

She knew in her heart of hearts that Woody would understand once she had the opportunity to explain everything to him properly. Well, she hoped he would…

Woody came back at five o'clock.

Kate continued pretending to read the newspaper. She wouldn't ask where he'd been, she'd wait to see if he said anything. Instead, he picked up the remote control, sat down in the other armchair, and proceeded to watch a recording of the previous day's Chelsea match. Nothing was said.

As six o'clock approached the football match ended and Woody stood up.

'I'm going to have a shower,' he said.

'Fine.' Kate had had a shower in the morning but needed to freshen up and change for dinner. Dinner? Would they even have dinner together? A terrible fear was nagging away deep inside her. What if he was just being icily polite until such time as they got back home, and then she'd never see him again?

That could not happen. She'd have to say something.

After about ten minutes Woody emerged from the bathroom in one of the white towelling robes provided by the hotel. Would he ever wear her birthday gift now?

Kate cleared her throat. 'Woody, I'm sorry.'

He glanced at her. 'Why? What have you done now?'

She was struggling not to cry. 'I'm sorry about the Jenny Jordan thing,' she said, 'but I was only trying to help.'

'They'll put that on your gravestone,' he said drily.

'I *was*! I didn't think you'd mind so much, and I wanted us to have a nice couple of days together, away from Tinworthy and everything.'

'Well, you've certainly got us away from Tinworthy,' he said. 'Probably around three hundred miles away from Tinworthy. But, sure as hell, we ain't away from *everything*! You've managed to bring along Locker Man with us. Three's a crowd, Kate.'

'I'm sorry, really I am. But I've come up with some interesting—'

Woody waved his hand. 'I do *not* want to hear it right now. We're going home tomorrow so you can tell me about it on the drive back. This is my birthday weekend until midnight tonight – OK?'

'OK, Woody.' Kate gave a sigh of relief. 'So we'll still be having dinner together tonight?'

He looked genuinely puzzled. 'Why wouldn't we?'

'I just thought maybe…'

'Maybe what?'

'Maybe you'd had enough of me?'

'Are you fishing for bloody compliments now on top of everything else?' he asked. There was a glimmer of a smile on his face.

'I'm sorry!'

'Quit apologising, woman! It's high time you got yourself glammed up to accompany me to dinner!'

'Yessir,' Kate said.

They were both subdued and extremely polite to each other over dinner. Woody complained about The Cavern being closed, they both complained about the rain, but at least the sun had shone for Woody's birthday.

'The sun shines on the righteous,' he remarked, as he licked his spoon after demolishing a huge portion of apple pie and ice cream.

'You should try the tiramisu,' Kate said. 'It was delicious. And you're part Italian.'

'I'm an all-American boy when it comes to dessert,' he said. 'Apple pie and ice cream every time.'

*

They adjourned to the bar and ordered a couple of liqueurs. It was still pouring rain outside, so there was no temptation to leave the comfort of the hotel and sample any nightlife but at least things were getting back to normal.

Several times Kate had almost said something about her earlier expedition, then just remembered in time. She'd bite her tongue until tomorrow.

They watched a late-night movie, lying together in bed. Kate wondered if he'd forgiven her sufficiently to make love, but as she glanced across at him saw that he'd fallen fast asleep. She'd tell him how the film ended tomorrow. She lay down and switched off the light with the day's events spinning in her mind.

CHAPTER TWENTY-TWO

They set off for home the next morning, directly after breakfast. The rain had cleared, the sun was doing its best to shine through swiftly moving clouds, and the roads were manically busy.

'Monday morning!' Woody muttered. 'The world goes back to work. We should have waited for another hour to let them all get there.'

'Bye, bye, Liverpool,' Kate said, glancing behind her.

'I *did* like what I saw of Liverpool,' Woody said, 'and I particularly liked the people, but I wasn't so keen on that rain we had yesterday.'

'We live in Cornwall,' Kate reminded him, 'so we should be used to it.'

'I guess I just don't expect to find it anywhere else, though,' said Woody, grinning, as they crawled along the motorway.

They drove for a couple of miles before Woody said, 'I *know* you're just bustin' a gut to tell me you've solved the whole Locker Man case.'

'I only wish I had,' Kate said ruefully. 'In fact, I think I may be adding to the mystery.'

'So, you found this Jarman woman?'

'*Jordan*. Jenny Jordan.'

'OK, tell me all you've got and let's see if we can unravel this mystery together.'

Kate told him all she'd discovered – about Ida telling her who Jenny Jordan was, about her visits to Adeline and how she firmly denied having a son but clearly remembered having a daughter which turned out to be true. She told him how she'd got the birth certificates for the twins and how on Aaron Jordan's certificate it said that he had been adopted. Woody listened without comment. Then, when Kate finished, he remained silent for a moment.

'So you found this Jenny Jordan?' he asked at last.

'No, I didn't find her because she died years ago. Didn't I tell you I got her death certificate?'

'You've told me so much I'm a bit hazy on the details. So if you didn't find her what did you find?'

'I found a next-door neighbour who lived there for years and years – Bridie was her name. She was great friends with Jenny's mother and recalled that Jenny came back to live with her mother after she left Cornwall. And yes, she did have a baby, a boy called Ben. But there was no indication whatsoever that Jenny had had twins. I've got proof from the birth certificates that the boys *were* twins, though. Jenny must have been determined to hide the fact. Apparently, she went away to give birth and stayed away for a few months.'

'Hmm,' Woody said, 'so this Jenny kept one of her sons.'

'Yes, his name was Benjamin and he disappeared after his mother died and – last Bridie heard – he'd gone down south somewhere.'

'So?'

'Well, he's never been heard of since. Perhaps Jenny told Benjamin all about the Hedgefields before she died – that Henry Hedgefield was his father and he had a twin brother. It would be understandable that Jenny might feel she had to tell him. It would be equally understandable that Benjamin would want to find his family after he'd lost his mother.'

Woody sucked his teeth. 'So, your theory is that this Benjamin appeared at Tremorron and threatened Henry in some way?'

'It's a possibility, isn't it? That is more or less what Eve says Aaron believes – that some man came to the house wanting something from his father, something that upset him badly; so badly that he later hanged himself. Perhaps Ben became violent and, in defending himself, Henry accidentally killed him.'

Woody sighed. 'Perhaps this, perhaps that! There's a lot of *perhaps*!' He patted her knee. 'And *perhaps* you're right, but we have no proof of any of this.'

'Has Bill Robson come up with anything better?'

'I don't know, Kate. Like I told you, he's refusing to give me any information. But I don't blame him. He's right. After all, he is the DI now, and I've familiarised him with the area as much as I can. Too much input from me now could be considered as interfering. I *am* a civilian these days.'

'There's no reason why you couldn't be a private detective,' Kate said with a giggle.

Woody snorted. 'Now why didn't *I* think of that! And then I'd need an assistant, would I not? I wonder where I could find someone like that?'

'You never take me seriously!' Kate was aware that he was being a little bit patronising, and not for the first time either. 'I'm not so bad at detective work, am I?'

'No,' he agreed, 'you're not. I'd go as far as to say you are becoming quite an accomplished investigator. But I think we should be careful not to step on Bill Robson's toes. On the other hand, I don't think you should go giving any of this information to him either. Let's leave the police to do their own investigation into this Locker business. See what he comes up with. After all, Bill Robson has to earn his money somehow.'

'But, Woody, remember that you agreed to help Aaron Hedgefield solve the mystery of the identical DNA, which I may have succeeded in doing…'

'Well, you haven't *exactly* proved it. All the evidence you've got is circumstantial.'

'What more do you need?'

'Well, for a start you can't even be certain that Henry Hedgefield adopted Jenny Jordan's baby or that he's the father of the child. You've got no proof he adopted a child at all.'

'Well, I've sent for Aaron Hedgefield's adoption certificate.'

'How do you even know he's got one?'

'I don't yet.'

'But you're absolutely certain he *is* adopted?'

'I'm as certain as I can be until I get that certificate. I really don't think there can be any doubt, taking into account Adeline's reaction as well. Anyway, I filled in all the details as far as I knew them for the adoption certificate, and if it arrives, and if the date of birth matches Aaron Jordan's date of birth, then surely that's absolute proof.'

'Maybe,' Woody conceded. 'For the time being I wouldn't go digging any deeper into this case. It seems to me that you're opening up quite a can of worms here.'

The road was finally clear and Woody got into the overtaking lane and put his foot down. They were silent again for a time. Woody was now making up for lost time and passing everything in sight. Then he said, 'Remind me – you checked Aaron's birth and his mother was recorded as Adeline and his father as Henry?'

'No – I couldn't find any trace of Aaron *Hedgefield*'s actual birth certificate, which is another indication that he was adopted. It doesn't make sense unless they were *Henry*'s babies and she gave one back to him.'

Woody appeared to be deep in thought. Then, 'OK, supposing your theory is right and Aaron does have a twin, does he *know* he has a twin? It doesn't seem likely, does it?'

'Aaron keeps insisting he doesn't have a twin, but if he doesn't even know he's adopted he wouldn't have any reason to think there was any possibility of that, would he?'

They were fast approaching Birmingham.

'Who else – apart from the old girl that you met yesterday – would have known this Jenny Jordan at that time?' Woody asked.

'Ida did. She told me that Adeline had found Jenny and Henry in bed together, which I don't suppose improved her mental condition. And Adeline did not give birth to Aaron, so who did if it wasn't Jenny Jordan?'

'I sure do wish I'd never let Aaron Hedgefield talk me into helping him over this DNA business.'

Kate grinned. 'From where I'm sitting it looks to me like I've done most of the helping.'

'Why the hell did he want us to get involved in the first place? Why wasn't he happy to leave it all to Bill Robson?'

'I think it's because he knows more about it than he's letting on,' Kate replied, 'or I suppose it could be that he doesn't know anything at all. Or it could be all to do with his father. Aaron probably knows that his father killed Locker Man, but he doesn't want him to be found guilty, even after all this time. Because he doesn't want the Hedgefield name sullied. Remember that Henry did hang himself shortly afterwards, so he probably couldn't live with the guilt.'

'Well, that's all very neat and tidy,' Woody said.

'So it could be true?'

'Yes,' Woody agreed, 'it could be true. But now we just have to prove it.'

'OK,' Kate said, 'but we won't talk about it any more now.'

'No,' Woody said, 'we won't.'

They arrived home in Lower Tinworthy just after half past four, having stopped off only briefly for a coffee and a comfort break. They had not spoken about the Hedgefields any more, and Kate was relieved that Woody was his usual self again and appeared to have forgiven her for the 'Liverpool incident' which was how she would always refer to this past weekend. He'd gone home to catch up with his mail and phone messages, and Kate wandered into the kitchen at Lavender Cottage to find a note from Angie saying not to worry, she was fine, Barney was fine, they'd gone for a walk and would be back later. A walk! Well, *that's* a first, Kate thought.

She checked the post but there was no sign of the much-anticipated adoption certificate. What if, as was likely, there wasn't one? After all, ordering the certificate had been a bit of a shot in the dark, but worth a try. As she was contemplating the possibilities, the door opened and in came a breathless Angie and a very excited Barney.

'We've been for a walk!' Angie exclaimed. 'We walked all the way up to the cliffs, didn't we, Barney? And you chased a rabbit, didn't you, Barney? My goodness, it was lovely up there today!'

Kate couldn't quite believe what she was hearing. 'I know it's lovely; I've been walking Barney up there more or less daily ever since we arrived in Cornwall,' she said, stroking the dog fondly. 'You should do it more often, Angie, it's brought colour to your cheeks.'

'I needed to get out of Fergal's way,' Angie said, sitting down opposite Kate, 'he's driving me nuts, hammering and sawing and making dust everywhere. So, how was Liverpool?'

'Liverpool was very interesting,' Kate said. 'I had my first row with Woody, but otherwise it was great.'

'What, you had a row on his *birthday*?'

'No, the day after.' Kate suddenly felt the need to confide in her sister. She glanced at her watch, six o'clock. 'I suppose you'll be wanting a gin? And, if you don't, I do!'

'My God, what's brought this on? Of course I fancy a gin! I thought you'd never ask! So, what's going on?'

As Kate ditched her cup of tea and poured out two hefty measures of gin she began to tell Angie about their trip, but leaving out any mention of her investigations into Jenny Jordan. It was delicate information. If Aaron Hedgefield *was* adopted but was completely unaware, the last thing Kate wanted was for him to find out about it because of conjecture and rumour.

'So what did you row about?' Angie asked with her first gulp of gin.

'Sorry, but I can't really tell you. It concerns some research I'm doing. I kind of got him to go up there on false pretences.'

'Well, no *wonder* you had a row. It was the poor bloke's birthday after all!' Angie stared at Kate. 'I thought you two did *everything* together? How come he didn't know about your research?'

'God knows why I didn't tell him. I think I was just trying to be smart,' Kate admitted.

'Well, you weren't *that* smart, were you? Anyway, you're OK now?'

'Yes, we're OK now,' Kate said with a sigh of relief and a large gulp of gin. But Kate still felt on edge. The Locker Man case was unsettling her… and she couldn't quite put her finger on why.

CHAPTER TWENTY-THREE

It had been a gamble, but a gamble worth taking, Kate considered. She'd sent for a copy of the adoption certificate for Aaron Hedgefield and would not have been in the least surprised to be informed that such a document did not exist. So when a manila envelope landed on the doormat two days later, sandwiched between a gaggle of leaflets offering double-glazing, chair-lifts and made-to-measure curtains, she'd almost popped it into the paper recycling container before spotting it.

Kate set it down on the kitchen table while she made herself a coffee, feeling excited and apprehensive as to what the contents might be. Then she sat down, took a deep breath, and slit open the envelope.

And there it was.

A copy of a certificate of adoption, neatly written out in little boxes:

Name of child: Aaron Christopher
Date of entry: 23 December 1975
Name, surname and address of adopters:
Henry Hedgefield, businessman and farmer
His wife: Adeline Annabelle Hedgefield
Both of Tremorron House, Tremorron, North Cornwall.
Date of birth of child: 25 March 1975

There followed details of the date of the adoption order and description of the court, plus the signature deputed by the Registrar General to attest the entry.

Nowhere did it say who his mother was or provide his original surname but, given the date of birth and the Christian names were the same, as far as Kate was concerned it was absolute proof.

Kate sat back feeling a mixture of shock with a sense of elation because her hunch had been right. Jenny Jordan *had* had twins, and *had* handed one over to Henry and Adeline, most probably because Henry was the natural father. If that was the case it was also probable that, after Jenny's death, Ben may have discovered that this twin was leading a privileged life in a large mansion on an estate in the Cornish countryside. And, most likely, he *wanted* some of that and came calling on Henry to secure his birth right, or for money, or for compensation for the years he'd lived on the breadline in Liverpool.

Kate could only stare at the certificate and wonder what she should do next. She knew of course.

She must phone Woody. 'Are you home? Good. Well, I have something of great interest to show you. Can I come over?'

Minutes later, with Barney on the lead, Kate was crossing the valley again.

'What have you got in this envelope then?' Woody asked as she sat down on the sofa.

Wordlessly Kate removed the certificate from the envelope and handed it to Woody.

He read it through carefully. 'Where did this come from?'

'I told you I applied for it. I just assumed Aaron *had* to be adopted,' she replied.

He blew out his breath. 'My God, you've excelled yourself here!'

'His natural mother was Jenny Jordan, who had twin boys,' Kate went on. 'She must have had an arrangement with Henry Hedgefield that she would hand over one of the babies to him – his natural father – and I wouldn't mind betting there was money involved. It wouldn't be surprising if Henry was prepared to pay a woman to give him the child he so desperately wanted and couldn't have with Adeline. After all, she had been having an affair with him, which was why Adeline attacked her and why it cost Jenny her job.'

'So why did he take only one of the twins?' Woody asked.

'Perhaps Henry only wanted one heir – he wouldn't have wanted to divide the estate. Anyway, that's assuming Jenny *knew* she was having twins when they struck their bargain, and perhaps Ben was an unexpected bonus. She got to give Henry the child he wanted, but was able to spare herself the pain of giving up both babies. He probably had no idea that she'd had twins.'

Woody was silent for a moment. 'Have you informed Bill Robson of this?'

'No,' Kate said firmly, 'and I'm not going to, not yet anyway. It's only right that Aaron should be the first person to be told about this, and besides, why should I rush to help Robson? I don't like the man, and he'll only have a go at me again for interfering with police procedures, and then he'll probably accept all the glory for finding out about Aaron being adopted and having a twin.'

'Hmm,' Woody said, 'you could be right, and I agree that Aaron Hedgefield should be told first. I mean we are supposed to be investigating who the man might have been and we've – sorry, *you've* – come up with an answer.'

'I think it has to be the only possible answer,' Kate said. 'Benjamin probably came to claim what he considered to be his share.'

'Wouldn't you have thought that Henry would have recognised him? I mean, they were *twins*, for God's sake!'

Kate sighed. 'I suppose yes, he must have recognised him but if he didn't know of his existence until then, seeing him suddenly must have been a terrible shock.'

'One way or the other, Aaron's got to be told,' Woody said.

*

Kate phoned Eve the following morning.

'Sorry to bother you, Eve, but we need to see Aaron and yourself quite urgently.'

'Have you found out something?' Eve asked.

'We think so. Could we pop in one afternoon?'

'Yes, of course. How about Saturday?'

Saturday afternoon, only a couple of days away, was agreed and when they arrived this time they were ushered straight into a large formal drawing room, stuffed with antiques. There was a log-burner in there too but it did little to warm the extremities of the room.

Kate sat down on a heavily carved mahogany chair with a seat upholstered in dark green velvet. It was like sitting on a rock, but at least she could feel a little warmth from the fire. Woody was huddled in his coat at the far end of the room. She stared at the portrait of a forbidding-looking ancestor (too early to be Henry) who glowered at her from above the fireplace within an elaborate gold frame.

'Coffee?' Eve asked.

'Coffee would be lovely,' Kate agreed, and Woody nodded.

'Unless you think I'm going to need a drink,' Aaron said jokingly as he chucked a log into the burner.

I think you are *indeed* going to need a drink, Kate thought, fingering the manila envelope nervously and contemplating how he was likely to react. She tried to imagine how *she* might feel if someone appeared out of the blue with proof that she had a twin and that she'd been adopted! Disbelief? Shock? Anger, maybe? She glanced at Woody, who appeared quite relaxed about the whole thing. Not for the first time she wondered if men really *did* worry about things as much as women did.

Once the weather had been discussed and the coffee poured, Aaron said, 'So what is it you have to tell me?'

Woody glanced at Kate. 'I'm going to let Kate tell you,' he said, 'because she's the one who's done the research.'

Kate saw two expectant faces swivel in her direction as she withdrew the document from the envelope.

She took a deep breath. 'This,' she said, 'would appear to be the final proof of what I've been working on.' She turned to Aaron. 'I don't know if you're aware of any of this, but you were adopted by the Hedgefields when you were a few months old.'

There was silence for a moment, the only sound being that of the roar of the fire in the log-burner.

Aaron swallowed as he finally broke the silence. 'You have *proof* of this?'

'Yes, I do.' With shaking fingers Kate passed the document to him. 'This is a copy of your adoption certificate.'

Aaron took the certificate while Eve stood up and moved across to stand behind him and look over his shoulder.

'Oh my God!' she exclaimed, putting a hand to her mouth.

Aaron said nothing for a long moment while he scanned the certificate, then finally lifted his head and glared at Kate. 'This, then, is the end product of your research?'

She looked him straight in the eye. 'Yes, it is.'

'So, tell me about this research of yours.' There was an edge to his voice.

'Well, it all began when I found out from an old lady that—'

'*What* old lady?' Aaron interrupted.

Kate did not want to get Ida Tilley into trouble so knew she had to tread carefully here.

Woody came to her rescue. 'Kate chats to all the oldies who visit the surgery with their aches and pains but, of course, their identities have to remain confidential.'

'Let me be clear about this,' Aaron said, 'some unidentified old lady came into your surgery and, out of the blue, began talking about *me*?'

Kate had foreseen some of the likely questions. 'No, of course not. This old lady wanted to tell me about how much she'd enjoyed dancing when she was young and used to go to the village hall with her friend, Jenny Jordan, who was the nurse looking after your mother – your adopted mother – at that time.'

'She gave you this information right out of the blue?' Eve asked.

'Only because she's stiff with arthritis now, and you know how old people like to reminisce,' Kate replied.

There was another short silence before Woody cut in. 'Not to put too fine a point on it,' he said, 'it appears that your father, Henry, may have been having an affair with this Jenny Jordan, the nurse, which may have resulted in a pregnancy.'

'Why on earth would Henry have an affair,' Eve asked, 'when he had such a beautiful wife?'

'I'm sure Adeline was beautiful,' Kate continued, 'but she appeared to have become increasingly unstable after losing her first child.'

'Her. First. Child.' Aaron spoke very slowly.

'Yes, she had a little girl who only lived for two days.'

'And you have proof of this?' Eve asked.

'I looked it up, for confirmation,' Kate said, 'because I knew she'd been called Emily.'

'I need a bloody drink,' Aaron said, standing up and heading towards a cluster of decanters arranged in a group on an enormous sideboard. 'Anyone else?'

Kate, Woody and Eve all shook their heads. 'I'll get us more coffee,' Eve said, heading back towards the kitchen.

Aaron sat down with a very large neat Scotch, and took a swig. 'How did you find out her name?' he asked.

'From your mother, Adeline,' Kate replied. She was not going to reveal any of the information she'd picked up in the surgery.

'*Adeline!*' Aaron shouted. 'Adeline is daft as a bloody brush! That's why she's in The Cedars, for God's sake!'

'She has some lucid moments,' Kate went on, trying to remain calm, 'and she was very clear about this.'

'You went to visit Adeline then,' Aaron stated; it was not a question.

'You did ask us to investigate,' Woody put in defensively, 'and so we did.'

Aaron took another huge swig of his drink. 'What I want to know is – what any of this has to do with some strange bloke coming to pester my father or the body in the tea rooms?'

Woody took over. 'The strange bloke, whose DNA was identical to yours, was your twin.'

Aaron exploded. 'My *twin*! Don't be so bloody ridiculous!'

Eve came in with the coffee pot and refilled their cups. 'Don't get upset, darling,' she said, laying a comforting hand on Aaron's shoulder, 'hear them out.'

'Jenny Jordan gave birth to two boys, Benjamin and Aaron, seven months after leaving your parents' employment,' Woody continued, 'and you, Aaron, were born Aaron Christopher Jordan and later adopted by Henry and Adeline Hedgefield.'

'What about this Benjamin then?' Eve asked, anxiously eyeing her husband, who was now heading back across the room for a refill.

'It seems likely that Jenny may have kept one twin and handed over the other,' Kate said. 'It would seem, in the circumstances, that Henry was most likely their natural father. Perhaps he had no idea that Jenny had had twins, perhaps he only wanted one, perhaps he badly wanted a son; who knows?'

There was silence again before Kate added, 'It would appear that you, Aaron, were very much wanted by the Hedgefields.'

'But *not* by my natural mother,' snapped Aaron, downing half of his second Scotch.

Eve stroked her husband's shoulder. 'We don't know that, darling. It may well have broken her heart.' She turned to Kate. 'What happened to the other twin – this Benjamin?'

'That,' said Woody, 'is the million-dollar question.'

'Yes, it's not entirely clear,' Kate agreed. 'We've only been able to find out where he lived with his mother until she died.' She saw Aaron flinch. 'We understand that Benjamin was a' – she struggled for a diplomatic adjective – '*withdrawn* youngster and may have gone off the rails—'

'How do you know this?' Aaron interrupted.

'I spoke to the lady who lived next door to them,' Kate said. Here we go, she thought, he'll probably go ballistic in a moment.

'Next *door*? You had the *address*?' Aaron gulped back the remainder of his glass. 'Where the hell did you get *that* from?'

'From my patient,' Kate explained. 'She corresponded with Jenny for several years before she died. Naturally, she wanted to know what happened to her.'

Aaron snorted. 'And where *exactly* did this twin of mine, and this woman-next-door live?'

Here we go, Kate thought. 'Liverpool.'

'*What!*' Aaron stood up clutching his empty glass and glared at Kate. 'You went to *Liverpool*?'

'We both did,' Woody said calmly, 'but Kate did most of the research because it's mainly been women who were involved and Kate's good at chatting to women.'

Aaron made his way back to the decanter.

'I'll have one too,' said Eve, looking less composed than usual.

As Aaron sat down with his third large Scotch, and Eve added soda to hers, he said, 'Next thing is I expect you'll be looking to me to pay all your expenses.'

Kate and Woody exchanged glances. 'I told you we did not want payment,' Woody said, 'and we were going to Liverpool anyway.'

'Why?' Eve asked, gulping her drink.

'Well, it was Woody's birthday,' Kate said, 'and he was always a great Beatles fan, so it was his birthday treat.' She cleared her throat. 'And I hoped it would help with my research.'

'I just *bet* you did,' Aaron said rather nastily between gulps of alcohol. His normally fresh complexion was turning a worrying shade of puce.

'So,' Eve said, 'your theory is…?'

Woody turned to Aaron. 'We think that your twin, Ben, found out about you being here, and probably thought he was entitled to some compensation for his fatherless life and living on the breadline.'

'For being the twin that *hadn't* been handed over,' Kate added.

'And you think that this Ben came to Henry asking for money or something,' Eve said, looking at her husband with concern.

Aaron's voice was slurred as he turned to glare at Woody. 'Surely my father would have recognised his own son, my so-called twin?'

'Obviously he must have done,' Woody said, 'but it still must have come as a terrible shock to him.'

'Are you saying that they got angry and blows were exchanged?' Eve said, draining her glass.

'That would be understandable,' Woody replied.

'And then poor Henry probably killed him accidentally in self-defence,' Eve said.

'At the moment, that would appear to be the likely explanation,' Woody confirmed.

'Have you told the police?' Aaron asked as he got unsteadily onto his feet and headed back to the decanter once more.

'Not yet,' Woody said, signalling to Kate, with a nod towards the door, that it was time to be leaving. 'We thought we should tell you first.' He and Kate both stood up. 'I realise there is a lot of very personal information for you to absorb and come to terms with, so we'll leave you in peace.'

Aaron had sat down again with his refilled glass and appeared to be having a problem finding his lips.

Eve stood up. 'I'll see you out,' she said.

As they got to the front door Eve said, 'Aaron doesn't normally drink like this, but I'm sure you appreciate he's had the most enormous shock.

I don't want him to become sick with worry if this case is given much further publicity. Hedgefield is *such* a respected name round here.'

'Surely Henry would only have been *defending* himself if he killed Ben?' Kate said.

'Defined as manslaughter,' Woody added.

'I still don't think Aaron would consider that to be acceptable,' Eve said. 'I *really* think we should leave this inquiry alone now. No need for the police to know all these details, or for you to do any more digging, is there?'

As Woody unlocked his car he said, 'Even though Henry went on to commit suicide?'

'Henry plainly took his own life while the balance of his mind was upset by the dreadful incident,' Eve said, 'which is a different thing altogether. I'm sure the police would agree once you have given them the information.'

*

'Will they?' Kate asked quietly as she slipped into the passenger seat, out of earshot. 'I doubt that somehow.'

'You and me both,' Woody agreed after he'd shut the door.

Then, with a wave of their hands to Eve, who was still standing in the doorway, they drove away.

'Well,' said Kate, 'wasn't *that* interesting!'

'It certainly was. I don't think Aaron's going to be doing much for the rest of the day.'

Kate sighed. 'No, he isn't. But what did you make of that little scenario?'

'I get a strong impression that he's hiding something,' Woody replied, 'but I'm damned if I know what it is.'

'Nor do I,' Kate said, gazing out at the Atlantic rollers crashing onto the rocks below.

CHAPTER TWENTY-FOUR

'Let's go back to my place,' Woody said as they drove down into Lower Tinworthy, 'because we need to chat.'

'Good idea,' Kate agreed knowing that, on a late Saturday afternoon at Lavender Cottage, Angie was very likely luxuriating in a scented bath to offset a week of cleaning and painting at The Locker Tea Rooms.

'Something to eat?' Woody asked as they wandered indoors.

Kate glanced at her watch. 'A sandwich would be great.' She followed Woody into the kitchen.

'I've got some bagels,' he said and then, peering into the fridge, 'with cream cheese and ham?'

'Perfect,' Kate said. 'I'll make some tea. I imagine Aaron will be having a lie-down now,' she added.

'He's certainly got a headache coming,' Woody agreed, cutting the bagels. 'What I'd like to know is, what bothered him most: finding out he was adopted, finding out he had a twin or the likelihood that the twin met his fate when he came visiting?'

'Do you think he already knew any of that?' Kate asked as Woody carried their sandwiches through to the coffee table in the sitting room. He opened the air vent on the wood burner and tossed another log into the flames.

'No idea,' he said, sitting down opposite Kate, who'd placed two mugs of tea on the table. 'He might just be a bloody good actor. They both seem very keen to pin the blame on Henry.'

Kate sipped her tea. 'Do you think Henry *did* kill him? You don't think it's anything to do with Aaron, do you? I mean, Henry committed suicide because our theory is he couldn't live with what he'd done, and why would he take his own life otherwise?'

'And then there's Adeline,' Woody added.

'What – you think Adeline might have had something to do with it?' Kate hadn't even considered Adeline.

'Well, if she attacked Jenny Jordan with a knife then she'd most likely be quite capable of having a go at anyone she didn't much like the look of.'

'I suppose so, but Locker Man had his head bashed in, did he not? I don't see her being capable of that. But that would have been shortly before Adeline was dispatched to The Cedars, of course. Perhaps we're looking at the wrong Hedgefield...'

Woody stared into the fire. 'I get the impression that Eve's hoping the whole thing will blow over. She plainly doesn't want all the details of the incident publicised again.'

'Is that really to protect the saintly reputation of the Hedgefields?' Kate asked.

'Or is it to protect Aaron?'

Kate gave a deep sigh. 'Should we be telling Robson of our findings?'

'Not yet, Kate. He's not been particularly communicative with me recently so I don't feel inclined to share this information. Yet, anyway. It's not as if we have definite proof of who it was that murdered Locker Man. I think, left to his own devices, Robson might eventually just close the case.'

'That would make Aaron and Eve happy. But surely Benjamin Jordan deserves some justice?'

Woody nodded. 'Yes, but I think we need to find out a little more about that particular period, and who else might have been on the scene.'

'Well, there was Mark Edderley, and Freddy, of course, but he's no longer with us.'

'Exactly,' said Woody. 'There must have been others, though, servants or whatever.'

'I have an idea,' Kate said, 'I'll pay another visit to Ida Tilley. After all, I did promise to let her know if I found out anything about Jenny, so that gives me an excuse to call. Ida just *might* be able to remember who else worked up there at the time. I got the impression that she's not a great fan of the Hedgefields and she definitely insinuated that Freddy's accident may have been rigged, presumably because he knew something that he shouldn't. We certainly need to get her on our side.'

'That's your department,' Woody said. 'Now, can we talk about something else?'

'Like, what are we having for supper tonight?' Kate suggested with a grin. 'Why don't we go back to Lavender Cottage and I'll do us a nice curry.'

'Sounds good,' Woody agreed.

'I was just going to call you,' Angie said when they arrived back. 'Fergal and I fancy a Chinese and wondered if you might like to join us?'

'That would be nice,' Kate said, 'but we thought we'd have a curry here and a quiet night in.'

'OK, just thought I'd ask. What have you two been up to this afternoon?'

'Oh, this and that,' Kate replied casually. 'Where's Fergal?'

'He'll be here in a minute. He's having a shower,' Angie said.

'A shower?'

'Yes, he's finally finished the wet room and he's trying it out. We fancy doing a bit of celebrating, not *just* the shower but the fact that our licence has been granted and so we can open at Easter.'

'Well, that's good news,' Kate said, pleased to see a sparkle in Angie's eye.

Just then Fergal appeared. 'Oh, hello,' he said and then, turning to Angie, 'have you told them yet?'

'Yes, I believe you've finished the shower room,' Kate said.

'Ah yes,' said Fergal, 'we have indeed. But you and I are going on a little holiday, aren't we, Angela?'

Angie beamed. 'Yes, we're going to Venice for three days.'

Kate stared at her sister. '*Venice?*'

'Venice,' Angie confirmed.

'*Venezia*,' said Fergal, a wide smile on his face.

'Very nice too,' said Woody, exchanging glances with Kate.

'It was a really good deal,' Angie went on, 'although we'll have to fly out from Bristol, but never mind. We've found a hotel right on the Grand Canal!'

'Well, good for you.' Kate was well aware that Angie's new-found wealth would be footing the bill.

'We should be there for the carnival, or some of it,' Angie went on.

'And we'll be having a drink in Harry's Bar,' added Fergal.

'And one in Florian, too,' said Angie happily.

Kate poured herself some wine. 'You do know, don't you, that a drink in either of those places is going to cost you almost as much as the holiday itself?'

'We don't care, do we, Fergal?' said Angie.

'Not one bit,' said Fergal cheerfully. 'Anyway, we must be off now. See you later!'

With a lot of waving and kiss-blowing they left.

'I don't believe this!' Kate stuttered. Angie appeared to have regained the spontaneity of her youth when she used to do this type of thing all the time. Yet again Kate wondered if they could really trust Fergal. After all, they still didn't know a lot about him…

'Oh, let them get on with it,' Woody said dismissively. 'We'll go to Venice one day, Kate, and I might even treat *you* to a drink in Café Florian!'

'That would be nice,' Kate said wistfully. 'It's many years since I visited Venice. But it's not that, Woody. It's what it's *costing*. This money of hers isn't going to last long at the rate she's spending it. She's paying for all the work at the tea rooms, and now this holiday. And very likely the Chinese tonight. I'm worried Fergal is taking advantage of her.'

'Stop worrying about her, Kate. She's old enough to know what she's doing, and it seems to give her pleasure. Besides, you have plenty more important things to occupy your mind!'

'We said we weren't going to talk about that any more,' Kate said. Then, after a moment, added, 'I *will* go up to see Ida again!'

CHAPTER TWENTY-FIVE

Nevertheless, as Kate drove up to see Ida at Pendorian Manor the next day, she did think about Angie. Angie did not have a limitless amount of money, and what she did have she was spending at an alarming rate. But Woody was right, of course, she certainly was old enough to know what she was doing and, hopefully, The Locker Tea Rooms might prove to be a lucrative investment once the transformation into a bar was complete. But, Venice…? Kate sighed at the thought of herself and Woody gliding along in a gondola, under the Rialto Bridge. She'd been there once before, and always wanted to go back.

As she parked at Pendorian she cleared her mind of such matters and concentrated on what she was going to say to Ida. She'd have no further excuse, after today, to come back here, so she needed to find out as much as she could.

'Oh, it's you,' Ida said as she opened the door, accompanied by two wildly excited Labradors.

'I just thought I'd pop in to let you know what I found out about Jenny,' Kate said, stroking the dogs, who were leaping up in frantic welcome.

'Better come in then,' said Ida, leading the way into the kitchen where – as on Kate's previous visit – one cat was dozing on the table and the other in the fireside chair.

'Chuck that cat off the chair,' ordered Ida as she filled up the kettle.

'Don't worry, this is fine,' said Kate, hurriedly pulling out a chair from the table. She had no wish to antagonise that cat again.

'So,' said Ida, placing the kettle on the Aga, 'did you find her?'

'Unfortunately not,' Kate said ruefully. 'You were right when you reckoned Jenny might have died at the time the letters stopped.'

'Thought as much,' said Ida, with a sniff.

'I found her house in Liverpool—'

'What – you went all the way to Liverpool?'

'Well, I had other reasons for going there, Ida. Anyway, I found the address but she'd long gone. However, the woman next door remembered her well. Jenny had lived there until she died, of cancer. Did you know she had a son?'

'A *son*? No, I don't think so, dear. She'd surely have told me.'

Kate cleared her throat. 'She had a son called Benjamin, seven months after she left here.'

Ida was visibly shocked. 'She never told me, she didn't. Why did she never tell me?' She thought for a moment. 'Of *course* I know why! That'd be Henry Hedgefield's son! I'd put money on it!'

'It does seem quite likely,' Kate agreed.

'So, what happened to the son?'

'We don't know for sure,' Kate said carefully, thinking of Locker Man. 'Last we know of him he was on his own, in and around Liverpool.'

'Poor boy!' Ida murmured.

'Well, he'll be a man now, around forty-five or so,' Kate said, being careful to use the present tense. She waited to see if there was any reaction from Ida. Everyone now knew that Locker Man had been holed up for more than twenty years and that the body was that of a man in his twenties. Ida did not seem to be putting twenty-two and twenty-two together. Then again, why should she?

'I wonder if Mr Henry ever knew he might have had another son?' Ida had a faraway look in her eye as she poured out the tea.

'I don't know,' Kate said casually, 'but perhaps some of the staff might have had some idea. I expect there were other people working for the Hedgefields back then, as well as your Freddy?'

'Oh, there was!' Ida said, gazing out of the window for a moment. Then she turned to Kate and handed her a mug of tea. 'I remember Mrs Carne, God bless her. Mary Carne. You've never tasted Eccles cakes like she used to make!'

'Mary Carne,' Kate repeated. 'I'm guessing she was the cook?'

'She was, for years and years. She must have worked up there until she was nearly eighty. Probably dead now. Knew everythin' that went on, did Mrs Carne. Everythin'! Her pastries would melt in your mouth! Melt in your mouth, they would! She'd put a couple of sweet pastries in a brown paper bag and give them to Freddy, and he'd bring them to me and we'd sit in the park and eat them, along with a thermos of tea. Lovely they were, them pastries.'

'What happened to Mary Carne?' Kate asked.

'Last I heard her went down to live with a sister in Falmouth. Always meant to go and see her, but it's a bit of a way to go, is Falmouth.'

How could she possibly find out the sister's name? Kate wondered.

'Mary Carne never married, then?'

'No, dear, her never married. Always known as "Mrs" Carne though, cos in them days if you was a cook or a housekeeper they always called you "Mrs". Same as the sister; her was Mrs Carne too and was housekeeper to Lord Dorman down in Penzance for years.'

Two Mrs Carnes, Kate thought. Probably ancient, or in care. Or dead. Worth a try, though.

'The other person I remember was Lenny Bush, the gardener,' Ida said. She chuckled again. '*Bush*, the gardener! Good name for a gardener, ain't it? Bush!'

'Yes, very suitable,' Kate concurred. 'So, what happened to Mr Bush?'

'Still lives round here, he does. Got a flat on the estate, he has. On the estate. His wife passed away years ago.'

'You have a good memory, Ida. Can you remember any others? I find it very fascinating, a bit like *Downton Abbey*!'

'Oh, they weren't gentry like that,' Ida retorted, 'not like Lord-Whatever-His-Name-Was!'

'Even so, I daresay there were other servants,' Kate prompted.

'Yes, there was, but they came and they went. Didn't stay long. Didn't stay long, they didn't. My Freddy didn't agree with all that comin' and goin', he didn't. Always said you should stay with your job if you got a good one. And Mr Henry was a fine man to work for, a fine man.'

'I've no doubt he was,' Kate said.

Ida drained her mug of tea. 'Have you heard any more about that body they found in the old fishermen's house?' she asked out of the blue. 'Haven't heard any more about it lately, I haven't.'

'No, no idea who he was.'

Ida sniffed. 'I thought maybe you'd heard somethin', what with you knowin' that policeman and everythin'…?'

'No, he's not a policeman any more, Ida. He's retired now. I know no more than you do.'

'Oh well, never mind,' said Ida. 'More tea?'

'No thanks, Ida.' Kate placed her mug on the table and stood up. 'I should be on my way.'

'Well, thanks for stoppin' by. Sorry to hear about Jenny, though.' Ida got to her feet and, with a more pronounced limp than Kate ever remembered before, accompanied her across the hallway to the front door.

'Sorry I'm bad on me feet,' she said, giving Kate a sideways look, 'but it's me knees. I'm countin' on you puttin' in a word for me. I'm goin' to be needin' new knees.'

Not as much as I needed that information, Kate thought, feeling excited as she drove away.

CHAPTER TWENTY-SIX

As Kate unlocked the front door the phone started ringing. She hurried into the hallway to pick it up.

'Kate?'

'Yes…'

'It's Eve Hedgefield.'

'Oh, hi, Eve!' Kate said, wondering why she was being contacted so soon after their visit.

'Aaron's off sailing with Mark Edderley, making the most of this nice clear weather,' Eve said, 'and I wondered if you'd like to come up for a coffee?'

The weather had turned colder and frosty after the spell of rain, and there was little wind. For a moment Kate wondered why you'd want to go sailing when there was no wind, but she knew nothing about sailing and, knowing Aaron, he probably had a state-of-the-art engine on board.

'That would be nice, Eve, when did you have in mind?'

'Well, what about now?'

'Yes, OK, I'll be with you in about half an hour.'

As Kate replaced the receiver, she felt sure that Eve must have an ulterior motive. Might she be trying to find out if Woody had passed on the information about Aaron's adoption to the police? Or, perhaps, Kate thought, she just *likes* me?

Kate climbed out of the Fiat clutching a tiny pot of hyacinths. In preparation for the visit she had also donned a couple of warm sweaters and some thermal socks.

She was pleasantly surprised when Eve ushered her into a small sitting room, which led off the kitchen and felt cosy and welcoming with its large wood burner.

'This is the snug,' Eve explained, 'where we sit most of the time. Unless we have visitors, when Aaron likes to show off.'

'Well, this is very nice,' Kate said, looking round at the comfy sofa and chair and the cluster of family photos on the dresser.

'Make yourself comfortable,' Eve said, 'while I go and sort out the coffee.'

Kate sank into the sofa and looked round the little room. It was homely and very warm, so much so that she wondered if she might have to remove one of her sweaters. She studied the framed photographs with interest. They were mainly of Aaron and Eve: their wedding, their daughters and some of a young Eve with what was almost certainly *her* family. Kate hoped she might see one of Henry or Adeline or, better still, one of Henry and Adeline together. But there were none.

'Here we are!' Eve had reappeared with a tray of coffee things.

Kate confirmed that she liked hers strong, with just a dash of milk, and accepted a piece of shortbread.

'This is a delightful little room,' she remarked.

'It's the only room in the house I really like,' Eve admitted with a rueful grin. 'Aaron's never going to move so I spend most of my time in here.'

'I was admiring your photographs,' Kate said. Then, feeling bolder, added, 'I don't see one of Aaron's parents, though.'

Eve sighed. 'They don't feature much round here. It's sad really because it was Aaron's dad, grandfather and great-grandfather who built this house. But Aaron doesn't seem to want to be reminded of them.'

Kate thought this seemed odd. 'Really?' she said. 'Knowing how proud Aaron is of the house you'd think he'd want to show off the family who built it and bequeathed it to him.'

Eve's face had an odd expression – she seemed slightly cross and flustered. 'I suppose you can love a place and be proud of it but not necessarily feel the same way about the people who built it.'

Kate could think of nothing appropriate to say so concentrated on her coffee.

'I don't know if your friend Woody's found out anything yet,' Eve continued, 'but I felt I should tell you that Aaron's become quite neurotic about the whole thing.' She took a deep breath. 'I think he's afraid what the truth might reveal. You see, like we were saying, he thinks that his father might have got into an altercation with whoever it was who called that day, who must have been the mysterious twin you've discovered. Henry might have got into a fight and killed him accidentally. He still had keys to the old fishermen's place, so it's possible he could have buried the man in the cellar. It was of course completely out of character, but the news would have been a shock. There's probably no other explanation.'

'It certainly seems that way,' Kate said. 'Aaron must have found the news we brought him incredibly upsetting.'

'He did,' Eve agreed. 'That's why I suggested he take the boat out today. I thought it might soothe his nerves a little.'

'Good idea,' Kate said, 'I hope Aaron's enjoying his sail although there's not much wind.'

Eve glanced out of the window. 'No, there isn't,' she agreed. 'He tried to get out of going when he heard the forecast, but I was determined he should get out into the fresh air and try to blow some cobwebs away. I told him he didn't want to disappoint Mark – Mark Edderley, that is. Mark loves being out on the water. They won't be marooned because Aaron's had a brand-new engine installed in the boat. I know he's planning on taking Woody out for a sail sometime soon.'

'Woody would love that,' Kate said truthfully. 'And I met Mark when he came to the surgery recently.'

'Mark told us you'd taken out his stitches.' Eve pulled a face. 'That was Aaron's fault really, plying him with drinks in the pub. Anyway, I've told him to come straight home today and I'm expecting him back any time now.' She glanced at her watch. 'It begins to get dark so early at this time of year.'

They went on to discuss books they liked, TV programmes, their offspring and general topics before Kate took her leave. She liked the woman well enough but there was something about Eve that was slightly off-putting. She seemed distracted at times and a little distant. Kate suspected that might be because Eve was none too happy in the marriage.

Again, as Eve escorted Kate to the door, she said, 'Honestly, Kate, we appreciate what you've found out, but Aaron's finding it very hard to come to terms with everything. I'm so afraid he'll have a breakdown or something, like he did after his father died. Can I appeal to you to let this matter drop? He's so concerned about the family name and reputation, and we both think we should leave well alone. We obviously have no idea what the police have come up with, but we'd be very grateful if you didn't pass on this adoption information to them. After all, it is personal family information and it's a very delicate matter. Woody did say that the new detective wasn't confiding in him, so what's the point?'

'Well, they won't hear it from me and I'm sure Woody will be very discreet,' Kate said, heading towards her car. 'Thanks so much for the coffee.'

CHAPTER TWENTY-SEVEN

'All chaos has broken out down at Plymouth,' Woody said, 'Aaron has just rung me because the coastguard has been called out to look for Mark Edderley, who's gone overboard.'

'*Mark?*' Kate exclaimed. 'He was sailing with Aaron!'

'He *was*,' Woody said, 'until he fell overboard sometime after midday and hasn't been seen since.'

'He fell *overboard*?'

'Seemingly. It doesn't make sense,' Woody said, 'because he was an experienced sailor, a strong swimmer and the sea was like a millpond. He must have hit his head or passed out or something. Anyway, how did *you* know that he'd gone sailing with Aaron?'

'Because I had coffee with Eve this afternoon. This is *dreadful*! Surely they'll find him? I mean, there can't have been many boats out and about at this time of year and, if the sea's so calm, surely it must be easy to spot him?'

'We can only hope so,' Woody agreed. 'Now, do you fancy a drink at The Gull? Because I could certainly do with one. And, if we're likely to get more information anywhere, we'll get it there.'

'I've just heard about poor Mark Edderley,' Des said sadly as he passed their drinks across the counter. He shook his head. 'Don't understand it at all; he's been out on that boat before and he swims like a bleedin' fish. It's cold all right, but calm as can be out there.'

'What I don't understand,' Kate said, 'is what Aaron was doing when Mark fell over. Couldn't he have dived in and rescued him? Or thrown him a lifebelt or something?'

'Well, perhaps Aaron was below deck when Mark fell,' Des suggested.

'We have no idea yet what happened,' Woody said. 'They've probably found him by now anyway.' He turned to Kate. 'So, what's this about you having coffee with Eve Hedgefield?'

'She phoned to ask me.'

Woody took a sip of his beer. 'Why would she do that?'

'Couldn't it possibly be that she *likes* me?'

'Yes, it could be. It could also be that she wanted something.'

Kate nodded. 'She did. She emphasised how shattered Aaron was at finding out about his adoption and having a twin.'

'Well, that's understandable,' Woody remarked. 'So, what did she want?'

'She wants us to forget the whole thing. Say nothing to the police. Leave well alone.'

Woody sucked his teeth. 'That doesn't make sense, because the police are on to it anyway.'

'Yes, but the police don't know about Jenny Jordan or the adoption and all that. I suppose they could find out, but are they likely to?' Kate asked.

'Possibly not,' Woody said. 'I got the feeling that Robson wanted the whole thing done and dusted. But then there's the DNA so I don't suppose he can ignore that…'

'So they'll *have* to investigate. The Hedgefields seem convinced that Henry accidentally killed Locker Man.'

Woody pondered this for a moment. 'Let's try to picture the scene: Henry is at home when this stranger appears and introduces himself as the other son he never knew he had. Perhaps he started making demands. Perhaps he threatened to tell the whole village and expose the fact that the oh-so-respectable Hedgefield family had been living a lie for the past twenty years; that Aaron Hedgefield was not only adopted but illegitimate as well. You could well imagine that Henry was driven to coming to blows in an effort to defend the family honour.'

'That's possible,' Kate said, 'but don't forget Adeline may have had a part in all of this. When I mentioned Aaron to her she said, "Evil", so she obviously never loved him. How would she have felt if, suddenly, another son of her husband's dalliance had appeared out of the blue? I'm wondering if it would be a good idea to pay another visit to Adeline.'

'Adeline? What on earth for? I doubt she knows what day it is,' Woody said. 'What possible information could Adeline give you?'

'I don't have to be going just to get information,' Kate said crossly. 'First of all, Adeline doesn't get many visitors, not even from her own family, I'm told. I feel sorry for her, so why shouldn't I visit? Just imagine, how must she have felt having to accept a baby that wasn't hers? I can't help feeling sorry for her.'

'I'm sure you mean it kindly,' Woody said, 'but it might seem a bit strange if Aaron found out about another visit.'

'Aaron won't find out because he never goes there,' Kate said. 'But Adeline did remember having a daughter, and she did remember not having a son, so she's still got some memory, and who knows what else she may be able to recall.'

'As far as I know, she's been in one institution or another for years, so I honestly don't know how she could help,' Woody remarked.

'Leave it with me,' Kate said.

She took a sip of her wine finding herself wondering about what had happened to Mark Edderley.

'Is Mark married?' Kate asked.

Woody nodded. 'His wife's a hairdresser at Heaven's Above, next to the old furniture shop up in Middle Tee, near the boutique.'

Kate knew where the salon was but hadn't been inside it because she'd been recommended a hairdresser in Launceston when she first arrived.

'I don't think I've ever met her,' Kate said.

'You've probably seen her; she has a big standard poodle and she often walks him up on the Downs and the coast path before and after work.'

Kate thought for a moment. 'Yes, I think I have seen her,' she said, 'but had no idea who she was. Poor woman! Is there a family?'

'I think so, but I'm not sure how many, or if they're still at home,' Woody replied.

'This doesn't bode well for Aaron, does it?'

'No, it doesn't,' Woody agreed.

'That would be the second death that looks like an accident,' Kate added.

'Do you mean the old boy driving into the tree?'

'Yes – Ida hinted that might have been no accident.'

Woody sighed. 'Ida had a helluva lot to say!'

'Yes, but she was right about Jenny Jordan and her address in Liverpool. Ida may be elderly and a bit cranky, but she's still got all her marbles.'

Mark Edderley's body was found washed up on the beach at Cawsand. Woody said that the injuries to his head were such that a post-mortem might have to be done. Once again Tinworthy could speak of little else but the unexpected death of one of their own. The demise of Mark Edderley was on everyone's lips. Everyone liked Mark. Everyone knew he was an experienced sailor and a strong swimmer, so how on earth could this happen? Plainly he must have knocked his head on something as he toppled from the boat. Aaron was reputedly devastated and inconsolable.

Apparently, he hadn't noticed Mark falling overboard. He'd thought Mark had gone down below deck because he'd made some remark about being cold and needing an extra sweater. It was ten or fifteen minutes before Aaron became aware of his absence. He then turned the boat around and retraced his route as far as possible, but there was no sign of Mark. He'd called the coastguard at twenty minutes past one.

Kate went back to work the following morning to find the surgery buzzing with rumours and gossip yet again.

'Apparently,' Denise said in a stage whisper, 'they found Mark Edderley with half his brains knocked out!'

'How do you know that?' Kate asked as she picked up her list of patients. 'We haven't had the result of the post-mortem yet.'

'Well, you see, my cousin Edie – that's the one who lives in Saltash and breeds corgis – her husband's friend is with the Lifeboats down there and he was at Cawsand when Mark was brought in. Horrible it was, he said.'

Sue, picking up her list, said, 'So he must have hit something really hard when he fell into the water.'

'Like what?' said Denise. 'There was nothing anywhere around, either on the side of the boat or in the water that could have damaged him like that.'

'There must have been something in the water,' Kate said, 'like an old boat that's sunk or a wreck…?'

'There's nothing like that round that bit of the coast,' Denise went on. 'Everyone down there knows exactly where there's any wrecks or anything.'

'So, what are you suggesting, Denise?' Sue asked.

'I'm not suggesting anything, just stating a fact. The type of injuries Mark sustained were more than would be expected from just hitting his head on something.'

'So, you think he was clobbered then?' Sue asked.

'I'm just telling you what Edie's hubby's friend reckons,' Denise said firmly as she turned to deal with the first patient waiting at the desk.

Sue grimaced at Kate. 'Denise does love a bit of gossip,' she said.

'It does seem strange, though,' Kate said. 'I wonder if there was anyone else on Aaron's boat?'

'Watch this space!' Sue said. 'No doubt Denise has another cousin somewhere who's an authority on what happened!'

In the course of the day Kate was told by her patients that Aaron Hedgefield kept a load of booze on his boat and doubtless they were both pissed as newts, that they were the best of friends and Aaron was too traumatised to answer questions, and that Aaron didn't like Mark that much and they probably had a fight, that they were lovers and Aaron had got jealous because Mark fancied someone else. She heard all sorts.

Nevertheless, something strange had happened, and Aaron was involved. Had the police down there checked the boat? And why would Aaron want Mark killed? They were supposedly friends and often sailed together so that didn't make sense. It would be interesting, to say the least, to see what the post-mortem came up with.

CHAPTER TWENTY-EIGHT

Another unexplained death linked to Aaron Hedgefield made Kate feel her investigations were more important than ever. She needed to find out more about Aaron and his past life to discover whether there was anything in his character that might indicate if he could be capable of murder. Aaron had admitted himself that he had been in trouble with the police in his youth. As had Mark. Was there a connection there? And had Robson interviewed Mark about the old school tie business? He certainly couldn't have been arrested if he'd been out sailing, but he *could* have been murdered. What the hell was going on?

Kate was beginning to wonder whether Eve's insistence that Henry had accidentally killed Benjamin in some sort of altercation was just a bit too convenient. After all, Henry wasn't around to defend himself. Could it be that Aaron was the guilty one? It made sense; Aaron was the one who would lose out most if Henry Hedgefield had welcomed his unknown son into the fold. What if Henry was planning to divide his fortune between Aaron and Ben? Might not Aaron want this intruder out of the way? If Aaron had killed Ben out of greed, would that be reason enough for Henry Hedgefield to kill himself? Had Mark Edderley been involved and, if not, how did he know about the tie? And was his death really an accident? Kate needed to get some more information from people who were around at the time. She would seek out the gardener and the cook that Ida had told her about, and see if they could tell her more about the young Aaron Hedgefield.

*

Kate discovered that Lenny Bush lived in Flat 7, Firwood House, which was a three-storey block of retirement flats at the far end of the housing estate in Middle Tinworthy. She spent Tuesday morning wondering what possible excuse she could invent to call on him out of the blue. He was obviously a healthy individual – probably due to all that gardening – as he hadn't visited the surgery in the past couple of years.

She'd never approved of cold calling, but Kate reckoned there seemed to be little option other than doing just that. Still unsure how she was going to introduce herself, Kate drove along to the estate at the end of her shift.

Firwood House was a rendered building painted in a type of sage green, and boasted a Warden's Office just inside the door. The warden, a bald, middle-aged man with an artificial eye, appeared as Kate entered. One eye or not, he didn't miss much.

'I've come to see Mr Lenny Bush,' she said, 'in Flat 7.'

'Oh, is he not well then? Why didn't he tell me?' The man seemed very anxious.

'No, no,' Kate assured him, 'this is a private visit.' She'd completely forgotten she was still in uniform. 'I've just come straight from work.'

'All right,' he said, 'first floor, turn right, down to the end of the corridor.' With that he headed back into his little office.

Kate obeyed his instructions and headed upstairs. The treads were covered in blue-and-grey striped carpeting, and there were wooden handrails on both sides. Everything was spotlessly clean. Outside the door of number 7 Kate hesitated for a moment, wondering what on earth she was going to say. Finally, she gathered courage and knocked.

After a moment she could hear someone inside muttering, 'I'm coming, I'm coming, what do you want *this* time?' Then the door opened to reveal a tall, thin elderly man with a luxuriant thatch of white hair with eyebrows to match.

'Oh,' he said, 'I thought it was that woman in number 5. She's never done borrowing stuff.' He had very bright, clear blue eyes which now focussed on Kate. 'You don't want to borrow anything, do you?'

'No, no,' Kate said hastily. 'I'm Kate Palmer and I'm assuming you're Mr Lenny Bush?'

'That's me.'

'I wondered if I could have a chat with you about when you worked for the Hedgefields?'

He looked shocked for a moment. 'The Hedgefields? Why would anyone want to talk about *them*?'

'It's just for some research I'm doing,' Kate said.

'What, medical stuff?'

'No, no, sorry! I've just come straight from work, but it's nothing to do with medicine. It's because I'm interested in eminent local families and the Hedgefields in particular. I'm thinking of writing a book about the history of the Tinworthys because I'm fascinated by local history.' Kate knew she was telling something of a white lie, but it wasn't too far from the truth because she was interested in local history. 'I wondered if you could spare me a few minutes of your time?'

He stared at her for a moment and then said, 'Well, I suppose you'd better come in then.'

She followed him across a tiny hallway into a small sitting-cum-dining-room. There was a mock fireplace with an electric heater with two easy chairs on either side and a small sofa opposite.

'Have a seat,' he said, 'although I've no idea how I can possibly be of any use to you.'

Kate sat down on one of the chairs and withdrew a pen and notepad from her bag. 'I'm interested in knowing what it must have been like working for the Hedgefield family years ago. I understand you were the gardener?'

'I were that,' he said proudly, 'for sixty years. I were fifteen years old when I started up there.'

'Well, that's a long time,' Kate said. 'You must have seen many comings and goings.'

'I were only the gardener,' he said, 'so I were outside most of the time except when I went into the kitchen for me meals. What was it you wanted to know?'

'I'm interested in how those big country houses operated,' Kate said, 'and how people like the Hedgefields treated their staff.'

'You writin' a book, you say?'

'I might one day,' Kate said vaguely.

Lenny sat down in the chair opposite and dug down the side to retrieve a pipe, which he began to fill with tobacco from a pouch in his pocket.

'Don't mind if I smoke?'

'Of course not, it's your home.' Kate hoped he wasn't going to contaminate the air with anything too noxious, with memories of one of her uncles getting them all coughing with something called Black Twist. 'Did you enjoy working up there?'

He finished filling his pipe, then struck a match and, with a great deal of puffing, finally got the thing going to his satisfaction. 'It were all right,' he said. 'Her were barmy, of course, but Mr Henry were all right. A proper gentleman.'

Kate was scribbling *Adeline – barmy, Henry – all right, gentleman.*

'Oh good,' she said, 'and did they have any other staff, Lenny?'

'Oh yeah, plenty of 'em comin' and goin'. There were just the three of us there what never left: meself, Freddy Parr and Mrs Carne.'

'Did you all get on well with the Hedgefields?' Kate asked.

He scratched his head and puffed his pipe. 'Daresay they did. Poor Freddy got killed some years back,' he said, 'but Mary Carne's still goin' strong, far as I know.'

'It must have been a terrific shock to everyone when Henry took his own life?' Kate prompted.

Lenny narrowed his eyes against the smoke. 'Funny enough I'd just been mowin' round them apple trees in the orchard just the day before,' he said. ''Twas Mr Aaron what found him. Nasty business.'

'The poor man must have been very depressed about something,' Kate said.

'He weren't a man to get depressed,' Lenny said. 'Never known him to be down in the dumps or to lose his temper.'

'There must have been *something* bothering him,' Kate stated.

'Freddy reckoned there was more to it than that. Some dirty business goin' on there.'

'Really?' Kate stopped scribbling for a moment.

'You ain't some friend of them Hedgefields, are you?' Lenny asked suddenly, removing the pipe from his mouth and giving her a steady stare.

'Oh no, but I just love bits of gossip about what went on in those places back then. I'm a great *Downton Abbey* fan – below stairs and all that! For my book. I'm a newcomer round here, you see.'

'Hmm, well.' Freddy reinserted the pipe and puffed for a moment. 'I've seen you somewhere before, though, haven't I?'

Kate sighed. Her involvement in the previous year's murders could prove to be a liability at times.

'You're that *nurse*!' he exclaimed. 'The one who nearly got—'

'That's me!' Kate interrupted.

'Fancy that,' he said. 'Would you like a cup of tea?'

'That's kind of you, but…'

'I'll just boil up the kettle,' he said, getting up and heading towards the tiny kitchenette which led off the dining area.

'This is a very nice little flat,' Kate said truthfully.

'Suits me fine,' he said. 'One bedroom, one bathroom, warden on duty all day, panic button if I need it during the night. You take milk and sugar?'

'Just milk, please.' Kate wondered how to get him back onto the subject of Freddy and the Hedgefields.

He reappeared with two china mugs of tea and set one down on the table beside her chair. He then solved the problem by saying, 'Yeah, Freddy didn't reckon Mr Henry did himself in.'

'He didn't? Why?'

Lenny tapped his nose and shook his head. 'Never did find out. Freddy says to me, on the Monday mornin', I think it were. "Lenny," he says, "I don't reckon for one moment that Mr Henry hanged himself." "Oh," I says, "so what do you think happened?" "I'll tell you tomorrow," he says, "cos I got to go to the police in Launceston now." And off he goes – and never comes back. Drove into a tree.' He glanced at Kate and shook his head. 'Freddy were a good driver. More to it than that, I reckon.' He puffed away for a moment. 'Probably shouldn't have told you none of that.'

'Please don't worry, you haven't said anything out of place.' Kate cleared her throat. 'What did you think of Aaron Hedgefield?'

Lenny sniffed. 'He were a bit wild as a lad. Got in trouble with the law a couple of times. He went a bit peculiar after his father died, a bit strange. No surprise there though when you remember his mother. Her's up in The Cedars now, you know, nutty as a fruitcake.'

'Unfortunate family,' Kate agreed. 'I'd rather like to have a word with Mrs Carne. I understand she lives down in Falmouth now?'

'Yeah, her's in Pattertown, down near Falmouth, with her sister. Both in their eighties.'

'You wouldn't have the address, would you?' Kate asked hopefully.

'No, dear. I just remember the Pattertown. Funny name, ain't it?'

'Pattertown,' Kate repeated, scribbling in her notebook.

'That's it,' said Lenny. 'More tea?'

'No, thanks,' Kate said, draining her cup. 'I must be off. It's been really interesting talking to you, Lenny, and thanks for the tea.'

'Sorry I didn't have nothin' much to tell you,' Lenny said as he accompanied Kate to the door, 'but I were outside most of the time. Just a pity Freddy's not still around cos I bet he could tell you a thing or two!'

'I'm sure he could,' Kate said wistfully.

'Terrible news about Mark Edderley,' he said, opening the door. 'Don't know if you knew him?'

'Yes, I did meet him once.'

'I hear he fell off Aaron Hedgefield's boat, and they found his body washed up on some beach or other.'

'So I believe,' Kate said. Obviously Lenny was not aware of Mark's injuries.

'Can't understand it. That lad knew how to handle a boat, and he were a good swimmer. Don't make no sense.' He shook his head sadly.

'It's tragic,' Kate said sincerely.

'Him and Aaron was always thick as thieves when they was younger. Makes you wonder, don't it?'

'Wonder what?' Kate asked.

'A lot of things,' said Lenny enigmatically. 'Nice to have met you. Mind how you go.' With that he shut the door.

Kate was none the wiser what he might have been wondering.

CHAPTER TWENTY-NINE

Kate got home and was in her bedroom changing out of her uniform when Angie burst in.

'Could I borrow your black cashmere sweater?' she asked wheedlingly. '*Please!* It'll be chilly in Venice.'

'You should buy one for yourself,' Kate said.

'There's no *time*! We're off to Bristol tonight because the flight leaves early tomorrow morning and we've found some accommodation near the airport.'

'You're leaving *tonight*?'

Angie looked at her watch. 'I'll be out of here in less than two hours' time. Fergal went to get the remainder of his stuff out of the caravan in Plymouth, but he should be back any minute. We haven't packed yet. Oh, and the tan ankle boots, could I borrow them too, Kate? *Please!*'

'Angie—'

'Oh, you're such an angel, Kate! Honestly, as soon as we get back I'll be off to the shops to update my wardrobe. There just hasn't been time when we've been so busy. Oh, *thank* you, Kate!'

Kate stood open-mouthed as Angie grabbed the sweater and the boots and disappeared into her own room. There followed much crashing and swearing as Angie got the suitcase down from the top of her wardrobe.

Kate pulled on a sweater and jeans and went downstairs to phone Woody.

'Looks like I've got a few nights on my own,' she said. 'Angie's off to Venice so would you like to come over here for a change?'

'Yeah, let me get my toothbrush and a few bits and pieces together and I'll be over around half past seven, OK?'

'Yes, good. I have some interesting stuff to tell you.'

Angie changed her mind three times about which coat she should wear for her trip.

'I think the black is the smartest, don't you?' Angie asked Fergal, who was already booted and spurred and reading the paper while he was waiting. 'Yes, fine,' he said, without looking up.

'But the check one is warmer,' Angie went on, looking perplexed. She turned to Kate. 'Or is it a bit country bumpkin?'

'Well, you are a country bumpkin now,' Kate said.

'Maybe the black would be better then. Or what about my trench coat? It rains a lot in Venice at this time of year, doesn't it?'

Finally Fergal looked up from his newspaper. 'What the feck does it matter, Angela? Get a move on because we're leaving here in *five* minutes.'

The black coat won. Kate breathed a sigh of relief as she hugged them both and wished them a great time. 'Have a Bellini for me!' she said wistfully, and then waved them off as they drove away.

Woody arrived half an hour later. 'They've gone?'

'Yes, with half my wardrobe. Glass of wine?'

'Please.' Woody looked tired as he sat down by the fire. 'I've spent most of the day repairing that damned fence at the back of my garden,' he said. 'It was worse than I thought. Some sheep got in a couple of nights ago and ate everything still green. Anyway, now I've had a shave and a shower and I've slathered on the aftershave so you should find me irresistible.'

'Since there's no decent competition around, I suppose you'll have to do,' Kate said with a sigh. 'Now, let me tell you about my visit to Lenny Bush, the Hedgefields' old gardener.'

'What did he have to say?'

Kate told him in as much detail as she could remember. 'He was definite about the fact that Henry was not the suicide sort – if there is such a thing – and that Freddy Parr appeared to have some sort of proof that he *didn't* hang himself, but then had the "accident" before he had an opportunity to tell the police or tell Lenny.'

'Hinting that Henry was perhaps strangled and dangled?' Woody suggested.

'That's one way of putting it,' Kate said with a grimace.

'It was Aaron who found him, wasn't it?'

'Yes, Aaron found him.'

Woody scratched his chin. 'So, if your friend Lenny's suspicions are correct, then who might have wanted rid of Henry?'

Kate sipped her wine. 'Who, indeed?'

'Are you thinking what I'm thinking?'

'Very likely.'

Neither spoke for a moment. Then Kate asked, 'Why would Aaron want to kill his father?'

'I don't know. But it would tie up with Freddy's demise, and Mark…'

'You don't think *Mark*…?'

'I'm beginning to wonder. I guess it's time we told the police what we know, Kate. They may have already found out about Aaron being a twin and adopted, though I doubt it.'

'Probably not, because they – Robson – won't know about Jenny Jordan. How could he? And, without knowing about Jenny Jordan, there's no way they could check out the information,' Kate reminded him.

'I'll go up there tomorrow and fill them in on all this,' Woody said.

'And I shall go to Pattertown to see Mrs Carne on Thursday,' Kate said. 'I wonder if she comes up with the same suspicions. Women see things that men don't and she was working inside, closer to the family. So it should be interesting.'

CHAPTER THIRTY

Pattertown was little more than a cluster of houses on each side of a B road, some five miles from Falmouth. It did however have a sign saying, 'Welcome to Pattertown', and boasted a church, a pub and a shop. A few yards after that was a sign saying, 'Thank you for driving carefully through Pattertown', when Kate realised that was the end of the village. It was one of those places that, if you blinked, you missed it, so she had to reverse and drive back to the village shop. Inside two elderly ladies were engaged in conversation with the equally aged shopkeeper who was crowned with some very unlikely red curls. There was a slight whiff of paraffin or something similar, but the shop was better illuminated and better stocked than Bobby's Best Buys in Lower Tinworthy. Some attempt had been made at making the place self-service, but the main counter with weighing machine, till and Old Redhead were at the very back of the shop. Kate wondered if they ever had problems with shoplifters. All three stopped talking and turned round as she entered.

'Excuse me,' Kate said, 'but I wonder if you could tell me where Mrs Carne lives?'

'Now, which Mrs Carne would that be?' asked the old redhead. 'Cos we got two of them!' This was accompanied by much chuckling from the two customers.

Kate was puzzled. 'Don't they live together?'

'That they do. Which one you be wantin'?'

Does it matter? Kate wondered. 'Mrs Mary Carne.'

'Ah, Mary Carne,' said the redhead, brushing some curls off her forehead.

'Ah, yes, Mary,' echoed the customer wearing a pixie-hood.

'Yes,' said Kate, 'so could you tell me where she lives, please?'

'Well, she be livin' in Pear Tree Cottage,' the other customer said.

'There ain't no sign up or anythin',' said Redhead.

'So how can I find it?' Kate asked.

'Well,' said Redhead, ''Twill be three cottages past the church.'

'No, the fourth past,' corrected Pixie-Hood.

'And there's a big apple tree in the front garden,' said the other.

'No pear tree?' Kate quipped.

They looked at each other in astonishment.

'Oh no, dear, they ain't got no pear tree,' Redhead said, 'but they got some fancy nets on their windows.'

'What could do with a wash,' added Pixie-Hood.

'Thank you, I'm sure I'll find it,' Kate said, preparing to make a hasty retreat. As she went out of the door she could hear one of them saying, 'Wonder who *she* is?'

Another replied, 'Looks like that woman from the postcode lottery, don't she? Wonder if Mary's won some money?'

Kate found the old stone cottage with what looked like an apple tree, in its leafless state, in the front garden. The net curtains appeared to be perfectly clean.

Here we go, she thought, as she rapped on the well-polished brass knocker.

The little woman who opened the door was elderly, stout, but surprisingly pretty with bright blue eyes and short, curly white hair.

'I'm sorry to bother you,' Kate said, 'but I'd like to talk to Mrs Mary Carne for a moment, please.'

The woman turned round and called back into the house, 'Mary! There's somebody here to see you!' She turned to Kate. 'Come into the porch, dear, cos it's bitterly cold out there.'

Kate stepped inside and waited hopefully.

The woman who appeared was slightly taller, much chubbier, and with the same blue eyes and white hair. Kate was amused to see both ladies wore floral overalls, which crossed at the front and tied at the waist. She hadn't seen these 'pinnies' in years. Kate remembered from her childhood how women of a certain generation would wear them all day to do the housework and only remove them in company to reveal the immaculate jumper and skirt underneath.

'Can I help you, dear?'

Kate introduced herself and reeled off her well-practised opener about doing some research about local Cornish families, in this case the Hedgefields, and, in particular, about the days when they had a full quota of staff.

'Lenny Bush thought you might be able to help me,' she added.

'Ah, Lenny,' said Mary Carne. 'He made a lovely job of the gardens, he did. I was only the cook, dear, so don't suppose I can help you much. But come in.'

She led the way into a sitting room with a low-beamed ceiling and a huge inglenook with an open fire. There was a wonderful smell of baking, mixed with polish.

'Janet's just doin' a bit of polishin',' she added, indicating the other Mrs Carne, who'd sat down at the oak dining table at the far end of the room with a mountain of brass and copper pots, and a tin of Brasso. She was polishing like her life depended on it.

'Let me take your coat, dear, and I'll put on the kettle.'

Kate was bowled over by the friendliness of the two sisters as she plonked herself down on a chintz-covered settee. There were some pretty watercolours on the white-painted stone walls, and a huge Turkish rug covered most of the slate floor. An old dog – some kind of terrier with one brown eye and one blue eye – climbed up beside her, tail wagging.

'Get down, Derek!' ordered Mary as she reappeared.

Kate laughed. 'I've never known a dog called Derek before!'

'Well dear, when he was just a tiny pup, we saw them funny coloured eyes, just like the postman we used to have when we were girls. Isn't that right, Janet?'

'Yes, Derek the postman had different coloured eyes,' Janet agreed.

Mary giggled. 'We tried callin' him other names, but it didn't work, did it?'

'No,' said Janet, 'we tried Rufus, didn't we, and Bob, but we – the both of us – just kept comin' back to Derek.'

They both laughed heartily and Kate knew she was going to like these two old ladies very much.

Tea was produced along with an array of cakes and pastries.

'I've heard about your delicious pastries,' Kate said, thinking of Ida, as she helped herself.

'These are cinnamon. They were Master Aaron's favourite, they were,' Mary said, 'poor little mite.'

'You must have known him from the time he was born?' Kate asked, relieved that Mary had brought the subject up.

'Well, no, not exactly, cos he was born in Switzerland, see,' Mary replied, 'so he was a couple of months old before any of us saw him.'

Kate decided to plead ignorance. 'Really? Why on earth was he born in Switzerland, Mary?' The cinnamon pastry she'd chosen was delicious.

'That's a long story,' said Mary, chucking a log into the fire. 'Miss Adeline, the mother, was having a difficult time.' She tapped her forehead. 'Mr Henry sent her over there to some fancy treatment place or other, and that's where she had Aaron.'

'I had heard,' Kate prompted, 'that Adeline had lost a little girl a year or two before.'

Mary shook her head. 'So sad, that was so sad. Miss Adeline was never quite the full shilling, you understand, but she went properly round the bend after that.'

At this point Janet replaced a gleaming copper kettle and warming pan on what was obviously their normal positions on each side of the inglenook. 'Only four more to do,' she said cheerfully, returning to her table.

'She was taken away a few times, Miss Adeline was,' Mary continued sadly. 'And she never showed interest in that poor little boy. Do you know, he spent more time in the kitchen with me than he ever did with his own mother? Isn't that terrible?'

'Yes, it is,' Kate agreed, 'but he was fortunate to have you. I bet you spoiled him rotten?'

'Oh, just a bit,' Mary said with a giggle, 'but he grew up to be a fine young man. Well, he was a bit naughty in his youth, but he got over that. And that Mark fellow – I've forgot his other name now – was a right bad influence, but it was his father dyin' like that what changed him.'

'I understand his father hanged himself in the orchard?' Kate said.

Mary was quiet for a moment. 'So they say. But I'll tell you somethin', dear, Mr Henry was not the type to take his own life. No, not at all.'

'He must have been very depressed about something, surely?'

Mary shook her head. 'He had a visit from some man or other shortly before that, and he was never the same afterwards.' She refilled Kate's tea cup. 'Somethin' funny happened there.'

'Such an unfortunate family,' Kate said.

'Aaron changed after that. He went away for a bit, but' – Mary gazed into the fire – 'he was affected real bad by it all.'

Kate told her about how they'd met Aaron when he gave them a lift from Heathrow back to Cornwall. She decided not to mention any further meetings.

Mary nodded. 'He became a bit showy, if you know what I mean. He had the house done up, all posh like. I was glad to be retirin', truth be known. All them fancy clothes and cars – he never used to be like that.'

'Perhaps he was compensating himself for the loss of his father?' Kate suggested.

'Hmm. Either that or trying to please that wife of his. She was always wanting this and that.'

'Really?' Kate said, feeling a little surprised.

'Oh yes! She came from a poor farming family, see, so I suppose once she married Aaron, she wanted all the stuff she couldn't have before.' Mary sniffed. 'At least he pays my pension, but he never comes to visit, does he, Janet?'

Janet stopped polishing to confirm that he certainly didn't.

'Janet worked for proper gentry,' Mary added, 'and they pop in now and again. They send birthday cards and that. No, Mr Aaron's become very hoity-toity if you ask me. Not the sweet little boy he used to be.'

Kate badly wanted to comfort her. 'Still, I'm sure he thinks of you though, particularly as you were so important to him as a child. I expect he thinks of you all, Freddy as well.' She was determined to bring Freddy into the conversation.

'Poor Freddy,' said Mary. 'He was a hard worker. He knew more about that family than any of us.'

'I believe he died in a car accident?'

'That was a bit of a coincidence…'

'What do you mean? Coincidence?'

'We all thought he'd found out somethin' that was goin' on, somethin' he was goin' to tell us about, but he never got a chance.'

'You don't think…?'

'I'll say no more on that subject. Would you like another pastry, dear?'

'No, thank you, Mary. You've been very kind and very helpful, but I really must be on my way.' Kate stood up and had one last try. 'What made you think Freddy had found out something? Did he hint at anything?'

Mary shook her head. 'Not really, dear. But I do know that he was heading to the police station in Launceston that day. He said he wanted to talk to the police before he told us anything.'

'Did you consider telling the police after he was killed?' Kate asked.

'Tell them what? I knew nothin'.' Mary patted Kate's arm. 'Would you like some of them recipes I used to do? I could write some out and send them to you if you like?'

'That's incredibly kind of you, and I'd love the one for those delicious cinnamon pastries.'

'Well, I won't keep you now, but you just write down your address on here' – she produced a pad – 'and I'll send it on.'

Kate produced a card. 'Here you are, my address is on there. You have been so lovely. Thanks again for the chat.'

Kate thought it highly unlikely she'd ever get round to making the pastries and, even if she did, doubted they'd taste anything like as delicious as those made with Mary's magic touch.

'You call in anytime you're passin',' said Mary Carne, 'cos it's lovely to have a visitor.'

'I will,' said Kate, wishing she lived nearer. There had to be some perks to all this investigating.

CHAPTER THIRTY-ONE

'Those ladies,' Kate told Woody the following day, 'were absolutely lovely.'

'Did the chef lady throw any light on the Hedgefields' murky past?' Woody asked.

'She more or less confirmed what Lenny Bush had said, or *insinuated*, anyway. And she was adamant that Henry Hedgefield was not the suicidal type at all. She also said that Freddy Parr had wanted to tell them something of interest but he'd said he wanted to tell the police first. Then he met his demise before he was able to tell anyone what it was. Again, echoing what Lenny said.'

'Trouble is,' Woody said, 'there's no way now, at this late date, to prove or disprove if Freddy's car was tampered with or not. It was probably crushed into razor blades long ago.'

'And now there's Mark,' Kate added.

'Yes, now there's Mark. According to one of my old mates in the Plymouth police, he was definitely killed by a blow to the head with – or by – something blunt. All very inconclusive at the moment. The boat's been detained for examination in case he hit his head on the boom or the rudder or something. Bearing in mind it was a good half hour before Aaron called the coastguard to report him missing, there was plenty time for any marks to have been washed off.'

'Will we ever know for sure?'

Woody shrugged. 'I believe Mark's wife – widow – is devastated, as you can imagine. She's got three teenagers and very little income. I hear she's been counselled by Penelope Bowen.'

'Penelope Bowen?' Kate scratched her head. 'I've heard the name but never met her.'

'She's one of those women who likes to be in everything,' Woody said. 'She took over the Women's Institute after Fenella Barker-Jones's death, she runs a hundred and one committees, and she's recently trained as some sort of counsellor.'

'Sounds very worthy,' Kate remarked.

Woody snorted.

'You don't like her?'

'I've only met her a handful of times,' Woody said. 'Bossy, snobby, not my kind of person. Mind you,' he added with a sideways glance at Kate, 'she hasn't yet got involved in crime-solving.'

He ducked to avoid the tangerine Kate threw at him.

'So, tell me,' she said, 'how you got on with Robson.'

Woody shook his head. 'I get the feeling that, unless he does things in his own way, he doesn't much appreciate any input from outsiders. Either that, or he won't entertain any theory that might have come from you.'

'I don't understand,' Kate said. 'Surely he needs all the information he can get? What did he say?'

'Well, I told him that we – and I emphasised the *we* because I thought it would make him more amenable than if I'd just said your name – that *we* had found out the name of the nurse who'd been employed by Henry Hedgefield to look after his wife. I said that we had it from a good source that they were having an affair, that the nurse was sacked and then she gave birth to twin boys seven months later. I told him we were convinced that she'd kept one twin and given the other one, Aaron, to Henry. The other twin appeared twenty years later, that there was some sort of fracas, and that he must almost certainly be the body in The Locker. I also told him we had copies of all the relevant birth and adoption certificates, and that there was a chance that both

Freddy Parr's and Mark Edderley's deaths could be connected in some way.'

'Surely he thought that was relevant?' Kate asked. 'Surely it explains the DNA match?'

'He made notes,' Woody said drily. 'He said it was a possibility and he'd look into it.'

'He didn't exactly have a eureka moment?'

'Funnily enough he didn't.'

'Tell me something,' Kate said, 'if you were still the DI and you were investigating this case, and someone came in with information like that, wouldn't you be delighted?'

'I'd be more than delighted,' Woody replied. 'I'd be checking it all out straight away and hotfooting it up to Tremorron.'

Kate was puzzled. 'So why do you think he's so reluctant to accept what is plainly very relevant information? Is it partly because I came up with that proof of poisoning last year and he can't get his head round the fact that a mere woman might have found something he'd missed?'

Woody shrugged. 'Possibly. Either that or he's under the impression that we're some sort of competing force.'

'Even if he doesn't like me, surely he'd listen to *you*, Woody? You've done the job, you've helped him settle in and I helped him solve the poisoning case. I just do not understand him.'

'I guess he's got some kind of complex, Kate. He's divorced, so maybe he's had reason to go off women in general; I don't know.'

'Hmm. Well, if he spoke to his wife in the condescending way he spoke to me, I'm not in the least bit surprised he's divorced,' Kate said. 'And, if he's not prepared to confront Aaron about it all, then I think we should.'

'That could be dangerous, Kate. I know, I've said it before, many times, but it's not wise to get too deeply involved. Leave it to the police. I think Bill Robson will do something about this. Give it a few days.'

'Could it be that Aaron Hedgefield's best of friends with Robson's boss? Could they both be Masons, or something? Golfing partners maybe, or another one of his sailing pals?'

'No, because I'd know if that was the case. He was my boss for a long time too.'

'Well, you *think* you know, but if they are connected in some way…'

Three days passed and Kate heard nothing. Woody had said that Robson was 'looking into it', which was all Robson ever seemed to do. But it was perfectly evident to Kate that, when Robson was 'looking into it', he refused to see what was right in front of him.

It was early evening on the Sunday when Angie arrived home, hugged Kate and said, 'I'm totally in love!'

Kate looked at Fergal, following in her wake and lugging two suitcases.

'Not with me,' he muttered.

'For God's sake, what have you been up to?' Kate asked.

'I'm in love with Venice, with Italy, with those gorgeous, handsome gondoliers…' Angie looked starry-eyed.

'Yes, well, that'll soon wear off,' Kate said, knowing Angie and her passions only too well. She turned to Fergal. 'Did *you* enjoy the trip, Fergal?'

Fergal nodded as he set down the suitcases. 'I did, Kate. We had a lovely time and Venice is beautiful, if crowded.' He glanced at Angie. 'Herself went a bit over the top about everything.'

'Herself is inclined to do that,' Kate agreed. She turned to Angie. 'You've been there before, haven't you?'

Angie was heading into the kitchen. 'Only once, with George.' She grimaced as she dug out the bottle of gin. 'Are you having one with us?'

'No, thanks. Has Venice improved then?' Kate asked.

'It's always lovely, but maybe it's because I'm older now that I appreciate everything that much more.' Angie sighed.

Fergal rolled his eyes. 'She terrified a fecking gondolier!'

'You can't terrify gondoliers,' Angie snapped, 'because they're quite accustomed to women falling in love with them. It's all part of the glory of Venice.' She handed Fergal a glass, and they both collapsed onto the sofa with their drinks. 'It's a long journey so we need this. I think maybe we should offer Bellinis in The Locker, and maybe have a mural of Venice above the bar, and I could do Prosecco cream teas.'

Fergal groaned. 'For God's sake, Angela, we're supposed to be promoting Cornwall, not Venice.'

'She'll get over it in a couple of days,' Kate assured him, sitting down opposite with a glass of wine. 'Anyway, I gather you enjoyed it?'

Angie sighed. 'This gondolier was called Francesco, and he had the deepest brown eyes you've ever seen. I think he really did fancy me.' She smiled coquettishly. 'He told me I was *bellissima*!'

'Like he tells every other daft woman who pays a feckin' fortune to hire him and his bloody gondola,' said Fergal, taking a healthy swig of his drink.

'I paid to go again, the next day, didn't I, Fergal?'

'You bloody well did. I went off exploring, Kate, and left her to it.'

'Very wise,' Kate agreed.

'You were just jealous,' Angie retorted, 'particularly as Francesco asked me to go out with him in the evening. If I hadn't been with Fergal…'

'You'd have had a one-night stand with an oversexed lothario who was young enough to be your son,' Fergal said.

Kate had heard enough. 'For God's sake, grow up, Angie! You're acting like a silly teenager!'

'It's because I'm young at heart,' Angie explained, patting her chest. 'I only feel about thirty inside *here*!'

Fergal drained his glass. 'I'll be off then,' he said, 'to my lonely bed in The Locker.'

'I'll pop over later,' Angie said, with a wave of her hand.

Fergal grunted as he picked up his suitcase and headed towards the door.

'You'll lose that man by being so silly,' Kate said when he was out of earshot. 'Don't forget he's a free spirit, and an attractive man. He could easily find some other daft woman to subsidise him and take him to Venice, or New York, or Hong Kong even.'

'Just because you've got Wonderboy Woody under your thumb, don't go denying me a little fun. Those Italians are *hot*!'

'I'm aware of that,' Kate said, 'and don't forget that Woody is half Italian.'

'Which half would that be?' Angie asked before breaking into raucous laughter.

Kate ignored her.

'So, what's been happening while we've been away?' Angie asked. 'Has Miss Marple managed to solve the mystery of Locker Man?'

'I might just have done that,' Kate said. 'I may be paying a visit to Tremorron soon to have a little word in Aaron's shell-like, and ask a few questions.'

'Can I come with you?'

Kate stared at Angie in astonishment. 'Why on earth would you want to come with me?'

Angie shrugged. 'I just feel that I'm buying a little piece of Tinworthy history and he is part of that history, if he owned it or leased it, or whatever he did once. I wondered if he could tell me a thing or two? After all, he might have heard all sorts of smugglers' stories when *he* took it over, don't you think? Perhaps he's got some interesting old photographs he might let me do copies of, so I could do a display on the wall.'

'I very much doubt it. In any case I'm not sure that this is going to be a particularly friendly visit, so it's definitely not a good idea.'

'Well, I'll just have to go on my own then,' Angie said, 'before you go upsetting them, or whatever it is you're planning to do.'

'That's an even worse idea,' Kate said. 'Stay away from there, Angie!'

'You've become very bossy in your old age,' Angie snapped.

Bossy or not, Kate thought, the last thing I need is Angie visiting the Hedgefields just when I'm about to confront them.

'Aaron won't know anything,' Kate said, 'because don't forget he's younger than us.'

'Yes, but his father might have told him some interesting stuff, or he might even have records of The Locker dating back from years ago.'

'Surely anything of great interest will be in your own deeds,' Kate said. 'As far as I know, the place was used as a general dumping ground for the fishermen's and builders' gear before that, so you'd have more luck chatting to one of those old boys, if any of them are still alive.'

'Hmm,' said Angie.

Kate had a feeling her warnings were falling on deaf ears, but the last thing she needed at the moment was Angie poking around up at Tremorron.

'Just stay away from the Hedgefields,' she said, 'because this is a rather delicate time in our dealings with the family. Don't forget that he would have liked to have bought The Locker, so you might not be too popular.'

'I will bear it in mind,' Angie said huffily.

CHAPTER THIRTY-TWO

On the Tuesday evening, Elaine, whose home visiting duties Kate had inherited, finally got round to retiring. In the evening, after the surgery had closed, Dr Ross, Dr Baxter, Dr Smith, Denise, Sue, Elaine and Kate all stayed on to sip champagne (thanks to the doctors), to nibble canapés (thanks to Sue and Kate) and to have a slice of the cake which depicted, in multi-coloured icing, the image of a surprised-looking nurse, in full uniform, alongside 'Good luck, Elaine' (made by Denise).

'I don't have wonky black legs like that,' Elaine muttered.

'Nor are you squint-eyed,' added Sue, 'but Denise did her best.'

Around eight o'clock the three doctors departed, and Denise suggested that they continue their celebrations at The Tinners' Arms, which was just a few yards along the road. Elaine, Sue and Denise could all walk home, but Kate had her car, so she made her excuses and left too.

These days she never quite knew if Angie would be at home in the evenings or at the tea rooms with Fergal. Not only was Angie at home, but she was in a state of high excitement.

'You'll never guess where I've been this afternoon,' she said before Kate had even got her coat off.

'No idea,' Kate said truthfully as she headed into the kitchen to make some coffee.

'*I've* been up to Tremorron!'

Kate froze. '*What?*'

'You heard. I went up to Tremorron to introduce myself to the Hedgefields. I don't know why you've got a thing about them because they are absolutely *charming*!'

Kate took a deep breath. 'Honestly, Angie, you don't know half of it!'

'I don't need to know half of whatever it is you're on about. I take people as I find them, Kate and, quite honestly, they're a lovely couple, particularly Eve. Aaron was OK too, but not as friendly as *she* was.'

'Did you tell them you were my sister?'

'Well, of course I did, but they knew anyway. I told them I was the proud new owner of The Locker Tea Rooms, and that I was planning to revamp and re-open with some alcohol on the menu. I also told them about the shock I got when we discovered that body in the cellar. They seemed *fascinated*.'

'Yes, I daresay they were,' Kate said through gritted teeth.

'Eve went out of her way to look for anything that might be of interest. She even went up to the attic and found some tarnished old candlesticks and an ancient lantern, which I think will clean up well. Aaron found some old photographs going back to the 1800s, when the building was little more than a hovel. In one photo, there's a line-up of fishermen in caps and droopy moustaches all standing in a row outside the door. It was fascinating.'

'I'm glad they were helpful,' Kate said, wondering what the Hedgefields had really thought. They might possibly have wondered if Angie knew about the DNA and even if she knew that Woody and herself had been asked to look into it. Perhaps they didn't, but who knew?

'Not only that,' Angie continued, 'but Eve has promised to have a really good scout around and if she finds anything interesting which could be displayed in The Locker, she'll call me straight away. Isn't that nice of her? I can see us becoming great friends!'

'Don't get too carried away,' Kate warned, 'because they might not be quite as delightful as they'd have you believe.'

Angie glared at Kate. 'What *is* it with you?' she asked. 'Why are you so bloody suspicious of everyone?'

'I seem to recall,' Kate said, 'that, when we were going up there for our second dinner in five days or so, *you* were the one who said they must have wanted something. Remember?'

'Well, they must have liked you, I suppose,' Angie retorted dismissively.

'In fact, they did want something,' Kate went on, 'which I may be able to tell you about in a few days' time. We have reason to believe that there's a little more to Aaron than meets the eye.'

Angie shook her head. 'Ever since we came to live down here you really have fancied yourself as some sort of private investigator, haven't you? *You're* not a policewoman, and have never shown any inclination to become one. It's all down to Wonderboy Woody, isn't it? Him being a detective and everything?'

'It may have escaped your notice, Angie, but I didn't ask to get involved in any of the murders last year. You know yourself that I just happened to be in the wrong place at the wrong time.'

'But you couldn't leave it to the police, though, could you? You meddled away, making your wonderful lists and God-knows-what, and nearly getting yourself killed in the process.'

'It's only that I'm interested in people, Angie. You hear things when you're a nurse because patients like to gossip and some of it can be quite useful!' She thought of Ida Tilley.

'I'm just saying that you need to be careful. You're the only sister I've got and I don't want to lose you.'

Much to Kate's surprise Angie gave her a bear hug.

'Oh Angie, that's such a nice thing to say. I promise to be careful.'

'At least I don't have to worry about you as far as the Hedgefields are concerned,' Angie said. 'Such a lovely couple!'

CHAPTER THIRTY-THREE

Kate's first patient on Wednesday morning was George Pearson, a thirty-five-year-old ex-soldier who'd lost a leg in Afghanistan, and had recently come to live in a mobile home on the fringes of Higher Tinworthy. He arrived at the surgery with a deep gash on his forearm.

'Damn stupid of me,' he said to Kate, 'I was changing a pane of glass when it slipped and…'

'Thank goodness it missed your artery,' Kate said. 'I'll give you a jab and then we'll see about stitching that up. Was the glass for your window or something?'

'Yeah,' he said. 'My wife, myself and our two kids came down here in the hope of finding a plot of land and building some sort of home for ourselves. We bought the old caravan so that we could live in it while we were building. Then Charlie, my seven-year-old, only goes and kicks a ball through the main big window, so I was trying to replace it. And it's *cold*,' he added.

'I bet it is,' Kate said. 'The wind knows how to blow up there. Any luck with finding a building plot?'

George sighed. 'We've just missed out on one,' he said. 'There was a really nice one going up there on Hedgefield's land with lovely views, planning permission, the lot. But apparently some policeman or other has bought it.'

'Policeman?' Kate asked, as she withdrew the syringe.

'Yeah, something like that. I think he might be a detective.'

'Can you remember his name?' Kate asked casually as she cleaned the wound.

He thought for a moment. 'Could be Roberts, Robertson, something like that…'

'Robson?'

'Yeah, that's it, Robson. Apparently, he's only been down here a few months too, but he seems to know the right people.'

'Really?' Kate straightened up. 'So, this Robson is buying a building plot from Aaron Hedgefield?'

'That's about it. Do you know either of them?'

'Yes, I have met them both at various times.' Kate was having to concentrate very hard on her suturing.

'Thing is, Robson got it for a rock bottom price. I offered more but Hedgefield would not be moved. I'm desperate to start building a roof over our heads, particularly for the kids, so, if you hear of anything going…'

'I'll certainly let you know,' Kate promised.

After she'd bandaged him up and sent him on his way, Kate grabbed a quick drink. As she warmed her hands around the mug, she mulled over what she'd just heard: Bill Robson was buying a piece of land from Aaron Hedgefield! He was doing a deal with someone he was supposed to be investigating! Who was doing who a favour here? Was Aaron buying Robson's silence with a cheap building plot? Was that why Robson seemed to be in no hurry to investigate Aaron – for a piece of land?

As the morning progressed, Kate became angrier and angrier just thinking about it.

Armed with this knowledge she was going to have to confront Bill Robson.

*

Kate drove straight over to Launceston Police Station as soon as she'd finished work. There was the usual palaver about getting an appointment with the wretched man. Was it urgent? Didn't she know that Detective Inspector Robson was a very busy man?

'I am a very busy woman,' Kate told the young constable on the front desk. 'I need to see him now, or else please arrange an appointment for as soon as possible.'

The policeman scratched a lurid spot on his cheek. 'He should be back in the station about four o'clock tomorrow,' he said, shuffling through a large appointment book. 'I'll ask him if he can spare you a few minutes before his five o'clock meeting.'

'I shall need more than a few minutes,' Kate said. 'I finish work at four so I shall come straight here. Kate Palmer's the name.'

On previous occasions Kate had always felt nervous and anxious in Robson's presence, but today she felt so angry she couldn't care less.

Kate arrived at Launceston Police Station shortly after four o'clock the following day. She'd seen Robson enter the building as she parked her car, so knew he was in there. He'll keep me waiting, though, Kate thought, just to show who's boss around here.

He kept her waiting for fifteen minutes before she was summoned into his stuffy little office. She wondered what had happened to the nice, big, airy office that Woody used to occupy.

Robson was poking around in a filing cabinet when Kate was finally ushered in.

'Mrs Palmer,' he said without enthusiasm, and without looking round, 'do sit down.'

Nasty, rude little man, Kate thought as she sat on the uncomfortable metal chair, which was not designed to make you feel comfortable or relaxed.

Finally, he turned round, sat down with a sigh, and rubbed his belly, which was one of his many less endearing habits. Kate noted with pleasure that he had a stain on the front of his shirt which looked like tomato sauce.

'So, what can I do for you *this* time?' he asked, abandoning his belly for a pen which he tapped up and down impatiently on his desk.

'You can *do* nothing whatsoever for me,' Kate said, 'but I was hoping you could *tell* me a thing or two.'

He removed his glasses, gave them a polish with a tissue and then replaced them. 'Like what exactly, Mrs Palmer?'

'Where shall I start?' Kate was determined not to get ruffled. 'Let me see; how about the fact that you were given some very relevant information about Aaron Hedgefield, which relates to the body of the man found in The Locker Tea Rooms, and yet you appear to be doing nothing about it?'

He rubbed his chin and glared at her. 'I fail to see,' he said, 'what business this is of yours?'

'Then I will tell you what business it is of mine. I found out about Jenny Jordan being the mother of Aaron and his twin brother, Benjamin. I found out where she'd lived and got first-hand information from a neighbour. It was after Jenny Jordan died that this mysterious stranger appeared at Tremorron, which initiated a chain of events, beginning with Henry Hedgefield hanging himself and culminating, twenty years later, in a body being found with exactly the same DNA as Aaron Hedgefield. This would indicate that the body could only be that of Aaron's twin, Benjamin. Someone killed Benjamin and, since we believe that he was the most probable person to be threatening Henry Hedgefield, might it not be entirely possible that he killed Benjamin? Or, considering that Aaron Hedgefield's credit card was found on Benjamin's body, isn't it also possible that Aaron and Ben got into a fight about the theft and Aaron killed his twin? That scenario seems an even greater possibility to me since the suspicious death of Mark Edderley.'

'So now you think Aaron Hedgefield killed Mark Edderley?'

'All I'm saying is that it's possible.'

'This is all possibilities, mights and maybes; there's no proof of anything.'

'Isn't it strong circumstantial evidence given that Henry Hedgefield killed himself not long afterwards?'

'It's circumstantial, but it's hardly evidence,' Robson said.

'Well, I believe he did,' Kate said, 'and I believe Aaron Hedgefield has been covering up for his father ever since.'

There was silence for a moment. Then Robson leaned forward. 'Your friend, Woody Forrest, has already given me this information and I told him, as I'm telling you, that we are looking into it.'

'In what way?' Kate asked.

'What do you mean?'

'In what way are you looking into it? Have you brought him in for questioning?'

Kate could see a red flush spreading from his collar upwards.

'It is none of your business,' he snapped. 'This is a police investigation and we have our way of dealing with things. Furthermore, I do not need to be interrogated by a member of the public who frequently pokes her nose into police procedures. *Frequently!*'

Kate knew she had the upper hand here. 'Without me poking this nose of mine into police procedures you'd probably never have come up with the person who was dishing out the poison last autumn.'

'Are you looking for some kind of medal, Mrs Palmer?'

'No, Detective Inspector Robson, I am not. I am looking for some sort of justice for the poor man who was murdered twenty years ago.'

'And we are looking into it. How many times do I have to tell you that this is a police matter and – not to put too fine a point on it – none of your damned business!'

'It just made me wonder,' Kate said slowly, 'if your apparent reluctance to make any progress investigating this case could have anything at all to do with the fact that I hear you're buying a plot of land from Aaron Hedgefield? Is that entirely ethical?'

She could tell from his face that she'd definitely caught him unawares.

'Who told you that?' he asked sharply.

'I have my contacts, but I'm not at liberty to say who.'

He leaned forward again and narrowed his eyes. 'What I do in my private life has got nothing whatsoever to do with you!'

'You're absolutely right, of course,' Kate said, 'but it has everything to do with this case. Aaron Hedgefield is a prime suspect and – from the little I know from a civilian point of view – policemen do not do business with their suspects.'

Robson's face went a shade of puce. 'Please get out of my office.'

Kate stood up. 'I'll be glad to. It's very claustrophobic in here.' She turned and walked out of his office with as much dignity as she could muster. She was aware that she was trembling and was relieved to sink into the driving seat of the Fiat.

She sat for a few minutes regaining her composure. She'd said what needed saying and the next move had to be his. With a great sense of relief Kate reversed out of her parking spot and set off home to Lower Tinworthy.

Kate had stopped off at the supermarket on the way home and bought the ingredients for a cream tea, which she felt they both deserved. Diet be damned! She placed the tray with the warmed scones, the thick Cornish cream and the strawberry jam on the table beside Woody, who was warming his stockinged feet in front of the wood burner.

'Wow!' he exclaimed. 'What a treat! I'm feeling like a tourist!'

'While you're pretending to be a tourist,' Kate said, 'let me tell you some very interesting facts.' She then related the day's findings.

Woody was astounded. 'I knew he was planning to have a house built,' he said, 'but Robson never indicated where he had a plot or even *if* he had a plot. This is crazy, Kate! I'm going to go to Bodmin in the morning and check with the planning office to confirm that he has put in for permission to build, and to find out exactly where the plot is.'

'I wonder why he wanted to build?'

'I think he might have got himself a girlfriend and wants to make a new start,' Woody said with a grin. 'I overheard him a couple of times on the phone talking to who could only be a woman, and certainly not his mother!'

'Can any woman be that desperate?' Kate met Woody's eye and they both giggled. 'But, really, Woody, this is not ethical, is it?'

'If this is true then it certainly isn't ethical, but I shall find out tomorrow. Thank goodness that poor guy cut his arm, otherwise we'd never have known – at least not for a while. It does explain why Robson's not keen on investigating Aaron, because Aaron is plainly buying him off.'

'And,' Kate said, 'you'll never believe this!'

'Try me,' said Woody.

'Angie's only gone up to Tremorron and introduced herself to the Hedgefields.'

'Why on earth did she do that?'

'She thought Aaron might have some history about The Locker Tea Rooms because she's dead keen on finding bits and pieces from years ago.'

'I doubt Aaron would be of much help,' Woody said. 'She'd be better off chatting to some of the old guys playing dominoes up in The Tinners'.'

'Nevertheless, apparently they unearthed a lantern or something, and she thinks Eve is the bee's knees.'

Woody frowned. 'You don't suppose they think *we* sent her up there, do you?'

'What do you mean?'

'Well, she's your sister and you know all about Aaron's history, so maybe they think *she* knows too, and that perhaps she went up there to snoop around or something?'

Kate frowned. 'That doesn't make sense.'

'Probably not. Then again there's a lot about this inquiry that doesn't make sense,' Woody said. 'In the meantime, I shall check with Bodmin.'

'Will you phone and let me know if you find out anything?' Kate asked. 'I'm home all day tomorrow.'

'OK,' said Woody. 'Will do.'

It was late on Friday morning before Woody phoned, by which time Kate was beside herself with curiosity.

'Yes,' said Woody, 'Bill Robson bought a half-acre plot, on the far side of the orchard at Tremorron, on the twentieth of January, from Aaron Hedgefield.'

'We've *got* him now!' Kate said triumphantly.

'Yes, but tread carefully. I'm going to call into the police station on my way back from Bodmin, so leave him to me.'

'I certainly don't want to go anywhere near him again,' Kate said with a sigh. 'He must surely be reported because isn't there a conflict of interests, or whatever you call it?'

'I'll deal with that side of things, Kate. Just take it easy and I'll see you this evening.'

As she ended the call Kate felt invigorated. Woody was going to deal with Bill Robson and she had a long afternoon stretching ahead of her. Perhaps she'd call on Angie to see how they were getting on down at the tea rooms. She put the lead on Barney and down the road they went.

There was no sign of Angie as she wandered into the bar. She was probably upstairs. Kate still felt great sadness as she looked down at the trapdoor, wondering again how someone could die and never be missed. She could hear banging and knocking upstairs so she headed up to the little landing.

'Angie!' she called. No reply. She called again. This time Fergal, covered in dust, emerged from the main room. 'Just putting up some shelves,' he said cheerfully.

'Is Angie there?' Kate asked.

Fergal shook his head. 'No, she left a couple of hours ago; said something about Eve Hedgefield having some stuff for her, and something about clay pigeon shooting.'

Kate began to get a bad feeling in the pit of her stomach. Surely Angie hadn't been so stupid as to go up to Tremorron again, pestering the Hedgefields? Perhaps it was time for *her* to visit Tremorron.

Kate went home to Lavender Cottage to see if her sister was there. But Angie wasn't there – and there were no signs of her having recently been at home. The bad feeling increased and Kate reached for her phone to call Woody. But after a moment's hesitation she decided she couldn't delay; she needed to get up to Tremorron quickly. If Angie was with Aaron Hedgefield, she could be in danger. Aaron was now at the top of Kate's list of suspects and she wouldn't rest easy until she saw with her own eyes that Angie was unharmed. Kate pulled on her coat, shut the dog indoors, and headed out to her car.

CHAPTER THIRTY-FOUR

It was mid-afternoon when Kate, on her way up to Tremorron, pulled in by a farm gate to watch some tiny lambs frolicking in the sunshine while their mothers munched placidly at the grass. It gave Kate a moment to calm her nerves. She was worried sick about her sister being anywhere near Aaron Hedgefield, who could well be responsible for several deaths. She had no proof of this, only a strong gut feeling. She knew she should really have waited for Woody to accompany her but Angie could be in great danger and she wanted to find her as soon as possible. And, if she turned out to be wrong, she still wanted to question Aaron. Perhaps she was extremely naïve to imagine he'd open up more to her on her own. God, she thought, why would he open up to *me*? Am I crazy?

She stood at the gate watching as some of the lambs ran back to their mothers, to latch on for milk, their tiny tails wagging frantically. Spring comes early in Cornwall. It might only be the end of February but the daffodils were in full bloom in everyone's gardens, and in golden clumps along the roadsides. Some of the trees had that look they got when the sap began to rise and their leaves were preparing to burst forth.

With a final look at this pastoral scene and the sea in the distance, Kate got into her car and sped off towards Tremorron. The first thing she saw when she got there was Angie's car. So, her suspicions confirmed, Kate now began to worry about what, if anything, might be happening to Angie.

Aaron opened the door.

'Hello, Kate! Are you looking for Angie? She went to the barn with Eve to look at some bits and pieces she might want, and then they were going clay pigeon shooting.'

'Clay pigeon shooting? *Angie?*'

'Well, I imagine she's releasing the pigeons for Eve to shoot at. They should be back soon. Have you any news for us?'

Kate felt a surge of relief. Angie was with Eve. Thank goodness, she'd be safe. Even Aaron appeared calm and rational and a very unlike a cold-blooded killer! Had her assumptions been wrong? Should she be here at all?

'Not news exactly; would this be a convenient time for us to have a little chat? There's something I want to talk to you about. It's just you I wanted to see.'

'Oh, OK, you'd better come in. Can I get you a drink?'

'Just a glass of water, please.'

She was led into the little snug, where she sat down by the fire while Aaron went to get drinks. Her courage was already waning but there was no escape now. She could hardly say 'I just called in to say hello' or something equally inane. Furthermore, if Angie was safely with Eve, she needn't worry about her sister.

It was around five minutes before Aaron came back in with a glass of water, but it felt like a whole lot longer. Kate drank thirstily, grateful for the water because her mouth had become very dry.

'I would never have imagined Eve was into shooting,' Kate said.

'Oh, she learned when she was young on her father's farm. She's a really good shot, wins championships and things, and she goes out any chance she gets. And today is such lovely weather!'

'Yes, it's a beautiful day,' Kate agreed.

'Coming up to my favourite time of year, the spring,' Aaron said.

'Yes, mine too,' Kate said.

'Well,' said Aaron, 'I'm intrigued! What can you possibly want to speak to me about?' He smiled disarmingly.

'Well, I'm sure you can guess that this has something to do with the body in The Locker: your twin.' Kate took a gulp of water. 'I know this is a difficult subject,' she said, wondering again if she should have come with Woody for support.

'I wanted to talk to you about that, Kate. I want to apologise for my behaviour that day when you came to impart the news about my being adopted and that I had a twin. I realise it must have been very difficult for you. I know that it was me who asked you to find out what you could. I shouldn't have been so accusatory about the way you came up with the results. It's just that I was never expecting you'd find out what you did.'

'It must have come as a dreadful shock to you,' Kate replied, relieved he wasn't angry with her about this. Perhaps she was misjudging him after all...

Aaron gave her a glimpse of a smile and seemed about to speak, then hesitated for a moment. 'You haven't told anyone in the village about it, have you?'

'No, of course not.' Kate felt a pang of guilt as she recalled her conversation with Bill Robson.

'I'd like to keep that information private and, after all, Henry was my real father, so I am a member of the family. And the heir to the estate.' He gave a strange sort of half shrug. 'OK then – if you've got something to ask me you'd better fire away!' There was a forced note of cheerfulness in his voice.

Kate cleared her throat. 'I understand you've sold a building plot to Detective Inspector Robson?'

'Oh, I wasn't expecting that.' Aaron looked genuinely surprised. 'Word gets around fast.'

'With all due respect, he is the officer in charge of the investigation in which you are a suspect.'

'Ah well, the police have been known to sail close to the wind at times,' he said.

'And I believe he got it for a rock bottom price,' Kate said, raising her chin and trying to muster the confidence to continue.

'Now, who would have told you *that*?' He sounded a little less confident now and Kate could see a worried look in his eye.

'Someone who was prepared to pay considerably more,' Kate replied.

'Ah, George Pearson, I expect. I didn't really want young kids running around up here, you see. I've no doubt you've really come up here to ask me if I'm buying Robson's silence?'

Kate swallowed. 'Yes.'

'Why would I do that?'

'Because I think that your father might have deliberately murdered your twin brother, Ben, when he came to claim some of what he considered to be rightly his. Either that or it was you, because you didn't want to share the Tremorron empire with him.' Kate took a large gulp of water to counteract more dryness in her mouth. 'And you've been covering up ever since.' There now, she'd said it, and there was no going back.

'Is that so?' Aaron had a strange, faraway look in his eyes.

'I don't think you'd have had any qualms about finishing off anyone who might have found out.' As she spoke, Kate could hear some movement from behind the door and wondered if anyone else was in the house. At least it couldn't be Eve. Her confidence was waning fast and she was beginning to feel a cold fear coursing through her body. She looked at Aaron, who was staring into the fire with a strange expression on his face.

Kate cleared her throat. 'I just want to see some justice done for Ben. As far as I can see he's been lying in that cellar for twenty years with, presumably, no one to mourn him, and no one apprehended for what they did to him. I find that incredibly sad and unjust.'

Still Aaron didn't speak but continued to stare into the flames. Finally, he looked up and met her eye. 'You've got it wrong, Kate.'

'What have I got wrong, Aaron?'

He took a deep breath. 'I'm not Aaron. I'm Ben.'

CHAPTER THIRTY-FIVE

Kate stared at him in total disbelief. For a second she could think of nothing to say. The man she knew as Aaron Hedgefield was now sitting forwards with his head in his hands. Only a clock chiming somewhere in the house broke the silence.

Finally, he spoke. 'I've lived this lie for precisely twenty years and seven months, and I don't want to live like this any longer. The pressure's been mounting and mounting. Ever since the DNA, I knew that, sooner or later, I'd have to confess.' He rubbed his head, shuddered and, when he looked up, Kate could see tears welling up in his eyes.

'Do you want to tell me about it?' she asked gently.

'I don't know where to start.' His voice was wobbly.

'Start at the beginning,' Kate encouraged, 'which was, presumably, Liverpool?' There was that sound again outside the door. Did they have a cat?

'I was born in London,' he said, 'as was Aaron, of course. I knew nothing of any of this until my mother, when she was dying of cancer, explained everything to me. I couldn't bloody well believe what I was hearing.'

'So, what exactly did she tell you?'

'She told me I had a twin brother and that our father was Henry Hedgefield. She'd worked for him in Cornwall and he wanted an heir, so when Mum told him she was pregnant, he was over the moon. She didn't tell him she was having *twins*. He paid her a sum of money, and footed the bill for her to have the birth, privately, in London, just so he could have the baby when it was born. He was delighted that it was a boy, apparently.'

'He had no idea your mother was expecting twins?' Kate asked.

'No, and apparently he never even set eyes on her while she was pregnant. He could have had two for the price of one, but he had no idea.' He snorted.

'Did she never tell him?'

'Never. She handed one over – Aaron – and kept one – me. I've sometimes tortured myself as to why she handed over Aaron and not me; did she toss a coin, for God's sake? Apparently, we were identical but perhaps he was slightly better looking. Maybe I was a grizzly baby and he wasn't.'

'Aaron – sorry, Ben – did you never think that *you* might have been her favourite and that's why she kept you?' Kate suggested.

He shook his head. 'Don't get me wrong. I loved my mum dearly but never knew who my father was until she was on her deathbed. Before that she'd just say, "Oh, someone I met, can't remember much about him" and stuff like that. So I grew up thinking I was the result of a brief encounter with some passing stranger.'

'Did that bother you?'

'Yeah, it did, particularly in school. You know what kids are like. I used to make up stuff: my father was an officer in the army and got killed before he could marry my mother. By the time I'd finished describing him I'd elevated him to such a heroic level that I almost believed it myself. It didn't quite tally, though, with us living in a rented two-up, two-down, and a mother who worked every hour God sent in a home for the mentally ill. She'd blown the money she got from Henry. I don't know how much that was, but she had a few years when I was tiny living it up.'

Kate was trying hard to come to terms with the fact that this was *Ben*. The man she'd thought had been buried deep in The Locker

Tea Rooms for all those years, and realising that the man in cellar could only be Aaron.

'So you *knew* all this already when Woody and I came up to tell you that you had a twin?'

He nodded. 'Yes, I knew, but what shocked me was that *you* knew. I realised then that it could only be a matter of time before my secret had to come out.'

'What I'm struggling to understand,' Kate said, 'is why you asked us to investigate?'

He shrugged. 'I didn't think you'd be so damned thorough. I never thought anyone would work it all out. I hoped the whole thing might blow over but, in the meantime, I wanted to make friends with the right people and be in the know if the police really planned to investigate further.'

There was another silence for a few minutes before Kate asked, 'So, what happened when you left school?'

'I kind of drifted, I guess. I'd hated school although I was a bright kid, but there was no question of going on to university because there wasn't the money. I'd got no idea what I wanted to do anyway. I worked in a bookie's, in a supermarket, I worked on building sites as a labourer, all over the place, and managed to save enough to buy a campervan because I did not want to stay in Liverpool. When Mum told me who my father was, and where he lived, she said, "You go tell him who you are, because you're entitled to some of that."' He snorted. 'It didn't quite work out the way she hoped, though.'

'Can you tell me what happened?'

'I came down to Cornwall in my campervan and parked up on the moorland roads most of the time, just to have a recce around. I grew a beard and wore a beanie hat well down over my head so that, as I wandered around, people might not notice any resemblance to my twin. It gave me a chance to study Aaron and my father from a distance while I slept in the van and had the occasional drink in The Tinners'.'

'How long did you live like this?' Kate asked, still reeling from the information.

'Oh, for around a month. I saw the life that Aaron had: the beautiful house, the acres of land, the smart car, even a bloody yacht! I got chatting in the pub and asked about the Hedgefields. Lotsa money, fingers in every pie, I was told. And Aaron hadn't gone to the village school, of course. Not him, oh no, he was educated *privately*.'

'Did you feel jealous?'

Ben thought for a moment. 'It wasn't so much jealousy as resentment. He had all this without ever having to get his hands dirty. And that could have been *me*!'

He crossed the room to the pretty corner cupboard and withdrew a bottle of Glenfiddich and a large tumbler, which he carried across to where he was sitting. Having poured himself a generous measure, he sat down again and took a large swig.

'When did you decide to approach your father?' Kate asked.

'It was after several weeks. One day I waited until I saw Aaron setting off in his fancy sports car, and then I wandered up to Tremorron. Henry was outside chopping up logs, and I have to say I felt a bit nervous when I saw the axe!' He gave a glimmer of a smile. 'It took some courage to start a conversation like that in broad daylight, dogs chasing around everywhere and barking away.'

Kate was intrigued. 'How on earth did you start the conversation?'

'I'd rehearsed it well beforehand, although I can't remember the exact words I used now. What I can remember is the disbelief on his face at first, and then how he kept staring at me.'

'You managed to finally persuade him?' Kate prompted.

'He invited me inside. I had no birth certificate or anything to prove who I was, but I had photos of myself with my mother. He could see anyway, because we were identical. The poor man was badly shaken, I can tell you.'

'I'm not surprised.' Kate tried to imagine herself in Henry's position, with a carbon copy of his son appearing out of the blue.

'He said he needed time to digest the information and that I was to come back in a couple of days' time. I don't think I slept a wink those two nights wondering how he was likely to react.' He gulped his whisky. 'He could well have told me to get lost, I suppose, and then I don't know what I'd have done. But he was a decent man.'

'You went back?'

'I did. I'll never forget it. I was ushered into this very room. I can remember thinking that, if this place was mine, I'd be ushering my guests into one of the large reception rooms. But then I don't suppose I was considered to be a guest!' Ben snorted. 'And, standing there, stiff as a poker, was Aaron, my twin.

'I shall never forget it; it was like looking into a mirror, except I'd got a beard. I can remember pulling off my hat and even our hair was exactly the same!'

'How did Aaron react? He must have had a massive shock, surely?'

'It sounds crazy now, but I really wanted to hug him. He was my long-lost twin, for God's sake! I felt really emotional but he didn't like it. I could tell that straight away. He kept staring at me and making polite noises, but he wasn't happy. He certainly didn't welcome me with open arms.'

Kate frowned. 'You'd have thought he'd have been thrilled to discover he had a twin, wouldn't you?'

'No,' Ben continued, 'he wasn't that kind of man. He was the apple of his father's eye and, of course, sole heir to the whole estate.'

'And Henry was presumably now considering you as an heir, too?'

'Something like that.' Ben took another swig of his whisky. 'I showed Aaron all my photographs, and even he could see how much we both resembled our mother.'

'Who was *not* Adeline Hedgefield,' Kate put in.

'Henry seemed very accepting of me, as opposed to Aaron, and he actually told me about Adeline and how she couldn't, or wouldn't, have any more children after she lost the baby girl. That had put paid to any chance of Henry having an heir, and so he couldn't believe his luck when my mother became pregnant. She'd kept her part of the bargain and given him an heir who, as far as the community was concerned, was Adeline's. She'd supposedly given birth in Switzerland while she was being treated for her mental condition. She came back via London, where she picked up Aaron, who was then two months old, and passed him off as her own.'

'And your mother went back to Liverpool?'

'Yes, she went back to Liverpool with me.'

Kate blew out her breath. 'So how did Aaron react to all this?'

'He was strangely silent. Then, just when I was leaving, Aaron asked me to meet him the following day at the old boat house, now known as The Locker Tea Rooms. He said he wanted to talk to me privately, without our father being around.' Ben shrugged. 'Seemed like a reasonable idea at the time.'

'And you went?'

'I went. Aaron was waiting for me. He began by saying that I should go back to where I came from, that I should forget the whole thing, that I was not wanted at Tremorron. I argued that our father thought otherwise, that I'd lived on the breadline for most of my life and that it was time I had a share in the Hedgefield empire. It got nasty then. I couldn't believe that my own brother – my identical twin – could say the things he did.' Ben shuddered and drank some more. 'He had a gun, Kate, and he was pointing it at me. He said that if I didn't leave and forget the whole thing, he'd shoot me and bury me in the cellar. He even showed me where he planned to bury me!'

'Oh my God!' Kate exclaimed.

'He meant business. I tackled him. I had no intention of killing him, Kate, none at all. I tackled him because I had to. He had the gun, but I was more streetwise and I got him down on the floor. He was like a man possessed, and he was strong, but finally I managed to kick the gun away and grab it from the floor. He was coming at me with a hammer which had been lying around somewhere so I smacked him on the head with the butt of the gun. I only wanted to knock him out and get away from this hellish place. Liverpool had never seemed so inviting.'

Kate wished she wasn't driving because she could certainly do with some of that whisky.

'I killed him, Kate. I had no idea you could kill someone that easily. I only meant to stun him.' With that Ben broke down, his head in his hands, his body wracked with sobs.

Kate sat absolutely still, unsure if she should comfort him or not.

Ben looked up, tears streaming down his face. 'I killed him, Kate. I killed my own brother. My twin brother!'

CHAPTER THIRTY-SIX

Kate couldn't move and couldn't speak for a moment or two. 'What did you do then?' she asked when she finally found her voice.

'God help me, I buried him in the cellar! I buried him in the spot he'd planned for me, and then I bricked up the wall.'

'After that?'

'After that I went up to Tremorron, shaved off my beard and decided to be Aaron. To be lord of the manor. But, you know what?' He leaned towards Kate. 'I got it wrong. I got it badly wrong.'

'What happened?' Kate was agog.

'I realised I hadn't got the first clue about Aaron's life: what he did, where he went, who his friends were, how he got on with his father. I didn't know which way to turn. In retrospect, I suppose I should have gone straight back to my van and driven off at high speed. But a little voice inside kept telling me that all this could be mine, *should* be mine, that I was now the rightful heir.'

Kate could not imagine how it must feel to literally step into somebody else's shoes and pretend to be that person without knowing anything about them. 'How on earth did you manage to fool everyone?'

'A strange thing happened then, that very day. An attractive woman arrived on the doorstep and begged me to "take her back". Take her back? Back to where? I must have looked panic-stricken because she said, "Aaron? Why are you looking at me like that?" She kept staring at me. Then she said, "You're different somehow. What's going on? Have you lost your memory or something?"'

Kate was mesmerised. 'One of Aaron's girlfriends?'

'His ex-fiancée. *Eve*.'

'*Eve?*'

'Yes, Aaron had called off their engagement after some massive row or other. Said he never wanted to lay eyes on her again, which he didn't, of course. She'd come begging him to take her back.'

Kate had read books about stolen identities but had never been able to believe it possible to carry it off in real life. Now here it was – fact stranger than fiction. 'Surely she must soon have realised you weren't Aaron?'

'She knew almost straight away. I had no option but to tell her everything and, as you can imagine, she was completely shocked. But, when she recovered, we made a deal. She'd been in love with Aaron, wanted to marry him, have his children and live in this house. She would keep my secret if I married her. I needed her to guide me through the inevitable minefield of friends, relatives, what Aaron liked, what Aaron didn't like, the whole bit.'

'My God! She could just as easily have gone to the police and—'

'You don't know Eve!' Ben interrupted. 'She came from a poor farming family and her ambition was to marry well. Having said that, I think she genuinely did love Aaron. But she'd been hurt by their breakup. She saw an opportunity to start afresh with me. She was definitely as keen to be the lady of the manor as I was to be the lord! I realised too that I couldn't take Aaron's place without Eve to guide me. Even then it was hell at times.'

'But what about your father? Didn't he realise or even guess that something was going on?'

'Not for some time. Aaron had his own part of the house so our paths didn't cross as often as you might think. Adeline was still at home at that point and I think he spent a fair bit of time keeping an eye on her. She used to do some crazy things, you know. He and Aaron weren't all that close. Also, Aaron had been a bit of a naughty boy in his youth. He'd got into drunken brawls, been in trouble with the police, and all that stuff. Henry, apparently, had been horrified and humiliated by it all, so perhaps that's when he and Aaron had drifted apart somewhat. Anyway, Eve moved in with me and, for a while, I was able to cope. In fact, the first person to become suspicious was Freddy. He looked after my father and the house in general. Don't ask me how he knew, but he did. Freddy was no fool.'

Kate couldn't bring herself to ask the question uppermost in her mind: had he tampered with the brakes on Freddy's car?

'No, before you ask, I didn't kill him,' he said flatly, then changed the subject. 'Eve and I got married and, somehow or other, managed to cope with all the hordes of friends and relations who appeared out of the woodwork. I'd have been happy to nip down to the local registry office, but both Eve and Henry insisted we had the full works. Henry was a stickler for tradition and Eve wanted everyone to know she was marrying well.'

Kate cleared her throat. She needed to ask. 'One thing you haven't told me, Ben. Did you love Eve?'

He didn't answer for a moment, then shrugged. 'Like I said, she was a very attractive lady. Still is. Not sure about love…'

'That's sad. Do you think she loved you?'

He shrugged again. 'I was a replica of the man she loved. She *said* she loved me, I *said* I loved her, but who knows? Anyhow, we've had a good enough marriage and two lovely daughters, although God only knows what'll happen now. Thank God the girls are at boarding school and university.'

'And your father? Did he find out? Is that why he hanged himself?'

This time Ben looked her straight in the eye. 'He *didn't* hang himself.'

'He didn't?'

'He was strangled, dragged out to the orchard and it was made to look like suicide.'

'Why, Ben?'

'He realised I wasn't Aaron. He'd caught me out several times. Once he actually asked me if I was suffering from amnesia. Then he twigged, and said that he was going straight to the police.'

Kate was horrified. 'You strangled your own *father*?'

He shook his head sadly. 'No, Kate, I didn't strangle him. Eve did.'

CHAPTER THIRTY-SEVEN

'*Eve?*'

Ben nodded.

'*Eve* killed your father?'

'I couldn't do it. In spite of what you may think of me, I couldn't kill anyone in cold blood.'

'But Eve *could*?' Kate was beginning to feel quite faint as a result of these incredible revelations. Now she did wish that Woody was with her. For one thing, she was in very dangerous territory here – and so was Angie because Angie was with Eve…

'Oh yes, Eve could do it.'

'How ever did she manage to murder him and then string him up?'

'My father was in a terrible state once he'd made up his mind to go to the police. Eve could always wrap him round her little finger, and she convinced him that he should wait until the morning. She was always able to charm anyone into doing exactly what she wanted, except Aaron perhaps. Anyway, she sat up with Henry trying to persuade him to change his mind, all the time plying him with whisky. He was so drunk that I had to put him to bed. About an hour afterwards she came into our room, woke me up and told me what she'd done. She seemed to relish telling me. She'd gone and got some rope from the garage, tied it round his neck, then looped it round the post at the head of the bed and pulled on it until she was sure he was dead. "He didn't suffer," she said, as if that made it all OK. I helped her stage the hanging because he was a heavy man and she couldn't lift him or carry him on her own. I had to do it; I had no choice.' His voice broke for a moment, and then he composed himself. 'After she killed my father I had to go away for six months. Everyone thought I'd had a nervous breakdown, which I very nearly did, but that wasn't the real reason. It was because I had so much to learn. Sailing, skiing, golf – I'd never done any of those things in my life. I had to learn to appreciate good food and fine wines, all of which Aaron would have taken for granted.'

Kate knew she had to ask. 'What about Freddy Parr?'

Ben nodded again.

'*What?* She killed Freddy *too*?'

He took a deep breath. 'She knew a thing or two about mechanics, having learned on the farm tractor and their rickety old Land Rover. Her farm upbringing made her tough and she can turn her hand to most things. But, at the same time, she can charm the birds out of the trees, just so long as they don't cross her in any way. Eve Hedgefield is a dangerous woman. She's envied and respected by the local community, the mistress of Tremorron and the Hedgefield Estates – the whole works. She's not about to give up any of that, Kate, and she certainly has no intention of being arrested.'

Kate was dumbfounded. *Eve!* Eve, who was so friendly and down to earth, so protective of her husband or, more likely, of herself! Eve, who was a crack shot and who, at this very minute, was with *Angie*! She took a deep breath, trying to control her fears. Kate needed to keep Ben talking, to give her time to figure out what to do next, so she asked, 'What about Mark Edderley?'

Ben refilled his glass. 'I'd got friendly with Mark when I first arrived and was drinking at The Tinners'. He saw the resemblance straight away and, more fool me, I told him my story. All of it. I was desperate to confide in someone. He warned me that Aaron was "a cold fish", and that he'd bullied Mark when they were kids. It was pure coincidence that he came into the hut just as I was disposing of Aaron's body. He said nothing except something about wasn't it typical of Aaron to be wearing his old school tie? He helped me brick up the wall. He swore to keep my secret, but I always worried.'

'So, you killed *him*?'

'That was a genuine accident. I was really fond of Mark and he was invaluable when it came to the boat because my crash sailing course didn't begin to cover all the stuff Aaron would have known.' His voice wobbled again. 'I honestly didn't see Mark falling overboard, and I am bloody gutted because he was one of the few genuine friends I've made since I became Aaron Hedgefield.'

Kate took a deep breath. 'So, what on earth happens now?'

Ben looked directly at her. 'You'll be the judge of that. Doubtless you'll go straight back and tell your friend, Woody, everything I've told you. Then the police will come calling, won't they?' He looked at his watch. 'Eve should be back shortly so, if I were you, I'd be out of here. Pronto. But you'll want to wait for Angie…?'

In spite of the alarm bells ringing in her system, there were still some details that Kate badly wanted to know. Could she *believe* him? Was he *really* innocent of those murders? Could he not be blaming Eve as an act of desperation?

'Before we go,' Kate said, keen to get away soon, 'tell me why Eve is like this. Why is she so obsessive about you and about Tremorron? So obsessive that she'd *kill*?'

He took another huge gulp of his whisky.

'Eve,' he said, 'is the youngest of the four daughters of an impoverished local dairy farmer. Nice guy but he was more of a drinker than a farmer. Eve spent her life in her sisters' hand-me-downs and was determined, from an early age, to do well for herself, which was why she made a play for Aaron. I've never found out exactly why she and Aaron had the big bust-up, but I suspect it may have been because Aaron found out what a social climber and money-grabber she was.'

'But *you* went ahead and married her?'

'I had no choice. She knew I'd killed Aaron and taken on his identity. So we both had to pay the price to become the owners of the Hedgefield Estates.'

While he'd been speaking Kate was aware of a commotion taking place somewhere in the house. She looked at Ben in alarm.

'You should have gone when I told you to,' he said calmly, taking another long swig of his drink.

Kate was aware of an icy chill creeping up her spine, and fear forming in the pit of her stomach. Oh God, she thought, what the hell is going on now?

The commotion was coming ever closer, raised female voices, one very familiar indeed. Kate stood up and looked nervously towards the door, knowing now that there was no means of escape.

Then the door burst open and Angie stumbled in, ashen-faced, her eyes wide with terror. Behind her, holding a shotgun, which was jabbed into Angie's back, was Eve Hedgefield.

CHAPTER THIRTY-EIGHT

For a split second it seemed as if the world stood still.

Kate took a step back in horror. She couldn't believe Angie had got caught up in all of this.

'Sit down!' Eve snarled at Kate. 'And take a good look at your stupid sister because you're not going to be seeing her for much longer, unless you both do exactly as I tell you.'

'Don't go to the police, Kate, or she'll kill me!' Angie wailed, her face frozen in terror.

Ben stood up and faced his wife. 'What the hell do you think you're doing, Eve?' He appeared to be genuinely shocked.

'I'm preparing to leave,' she shouted, 'and you should be doing the same. Now you've told this bloody woman everything we've no choice but to get out of here! I've checked that the plane is ready and waiting at Newquay.'

'What are you talking about?' Ben roared back. 'We are *not* going anywhere! You're insane, *insane*!'

Eve laughed as she prodded the gun further into Angie's spine. 'Then I'll have no choice but to kill the three of you!'

As she spoke, Kate, shivering, realised that this woman was indeed insane.

'What about the girls?' Ben was edging slowly closer to his crazed wife. She was now waving the gun at him before pushing it back again into Angie.

'Where do you think you're going to go? How do you plan to get there if you kill me? *You* can't fly the bloody plane!' Ben's eyes never left her face. 'What about Amber and Jade, for God's sake?'

Kate, shivering, could only stare mutely at her terrified sister and wonder yet again how on earth had Angie got herself involved in this mess.

'They can join us afterwards,' Eve rambled on, 'at Easter. We haven't time to collect them now, darling. Angie, dear Angie, I'm glad you decided to call today, because you are coming with us, locked in the boot of our car, and there you will stay until we've got safely away!' With that she stared straight at Kate with narrowed eyes. 'Because, if you even *think* about going anywhere near the bloody police, you'll never see this sister of yours again!'

At this, Angie dissolved into noisy tears.

'Put that gun down, Eve,' Ben said quietly, inching closer. 'You – we – can't get away with this. Where the hell are we supposed to be *going*? I'm going *nowhere* without our girls!'

'We've got offshore accounts, so we can start again!' There was a strange light in Eve's eyes that Kate had never seen before. She looked back at Angie, shaking with terror, and longed to hold and comfort her, but knew it would be folly to move.

'Put the gun down,' Ben repeated.

'I'm prepared to kill you *all* if I have to!' Eve ranted. Then, turning to Ben, 'Are you coming with me or are you not?'

'I am not leaving our daughters, Eve, and neither are you.'

For a fleeting moment some doubt replaced the fury on Eve's face. Then Ben, with the speed of light, was flying across the room, flinging himself on Eve, who'd been aiming the gun directly at him. There was a shout, a shot, and a scream, followed by a loud crash. Now, temporarily free of the gun in her back, Angie had staggered forwards towards Kate, tears streaming down her face. Kate, still terrified, couldn't make out who had shot who as Eve and Ben wrestled across the floor.

'Angie, quick, *down*!' Kate grabbed her sister by the arm and pulled her roughly to the floor where, on all fours, they both crawled round behind the sofa, while the wrestling and swearing continued in the doorway. Afterwards Kate would always remember the impressive volley of swear words emanating from Eve Hedgefield. She had never heard so many, and spat out with such venom.

There was a loud crash as the gun fell onto the floor. Kate looked cautiously round the corner of the sofa to see Ben, still wrestling, kicking the gun away. Eve, doubled up, was clutching her stomach, blood trickling through her fingers, while Ben picked up the gun and, turning to Kate, said, 'Would one of you please call for the police and an ambulance?'

Kate stood up shakily, found her bag alongside the chair where she'd been sitting and, with trembling fingers, managed to unearth her phone. As she called 999 she kept a wary eye on Eve, who was now rolling around on the floor, moaning.

'We need police and ambulance,' Kate said into the phone. 'There's been an incident at Tremorron House. Please come quickly!' She watched Ben pick up the gun, remove the cartridges and completely ignore Eve, who'd begun to snarl some more obscenities in his direction.

Kate advanced slowly towards the door. 'I should have a look at that wound,' she said to Ben, 'because she's losing a lot of blood.'

Ben looked at her as if she was crazy. 'Don't *touch* her!' he snapped.

'Ben, I have to. You don't want another death on your conscience if it can be avoided. Now, go into the kitchen and fetch me as many clean tea towels as you can find.'

Kate knelt down beside Eve, who was now losing consciousness, and examined the wound. It was in her hip rather than her stomach, so hopefully it wouldn't be fatal. Ben came back into the room and handed Kate a handful of clean, pressed tea towels which she packed into the wound. Whatever Eve had done, Kate was not about to let her die.

'Will she live?' Ben asked, as if he didn't much care what the answer was.

'With any luck,' Kate said, as she applied pressure to the wound.

Ben walked back to his seat, sank into it and put his head in his hands.

Kate looked back at Angie, who had sunk into one of the armchairs.

'Do you think I could have some of that whisky?' she asked no one in particular. Then, seeing that she was being completely ignored, Angie picked up the Glenfiddich bottle and took an enormous gulp. And then another. And then another.

Kate was overwhelmingly relieved when she finally heard the wailing of the sirens was becoming louder and louder.

CHAPTER THIRTY-NINE

Angie was on her second large gin. 'How was *I* to know?' she bleated for the umpteenth time. 'Eve phoned and said I must come up because she had something of great interest to show me and which would be ideal for my bar.' She looked helplessly from one to the other. '*How was I to know what she was planning*? How was I to know I was going to be taken at gunpoint into that *horrible* barn, and tied up with *horrible* baler twine or something, and locked in by that *horrible, horrible* woman. I have never been so terrified, *never*!'

'You weren't to know,' Kate said, chucking another log into the burner.

'I thought she was so *nice*,' Angie went on. 'I couldn't believe it when she stuck a gun in my back and locked me in there. She said I was their "insurance" as they'd be leaving the country later in the day. She must have been eavesdropping, I suppose, before she came back to get me and march me through the house. And then, when she kicked that door open, and there was *Kate* standing there…' She shuddered.

'Try to put it out of your mind, Angela,' soothed Fergal, his arm round her shoulders.

'It's not that easy, Fergal. It's giving me nightmares, and the very thought of that body in The Locker Tea Rooms has put me off the place a bit.'

'But you knew about that before,' Fergal reasoned. 'What difference does it make whether it was Aaron or Ben down there?'

'Yes, but it's more *personal* now.' Angie took a large swig of her gin.

Woody sighed. 'I'm beginning to think I can't trust either of you two gals to behave yourselves when you're out of my sight! Whatever possessed you to go up there alone, Kate? You *know* I'd have come with you.'

'I'm not sure what difference that would have made,' Kate said, sipping her wine. 'There'd just have been an extra person in the room for her to shoot at.'

'Didn't you suspect she might have been listening at the door?' Woody asked Kate.

'Well, yes, I did wonder when I heard some movement out there. But then it went quiet again and I didn't think much more about it. Anyway, Eve was supposed to be clay pigeon shooting.'

'And apparently she's a crack shot,' Woody said with a wry grin. 'She's won championships and all sorts, so I wouldn't have given a lot for your chances if Ben hadn't been on the ball.'

'I'll never forget how she turned from being this nice, sweet person to being such an evil cow,' Angie said. 'I have *never* been more terrified.'

'She fooled us all,' Kate said sadly.

Angie drained her glass. 'I'm going to need another one of these, Fergal.' Fergal obediently got to his feet. 'I do feel sorry for poor Aaron,' she added.

'He's not Aaron, he's *Ben*,' Kate reminded her.

'I'm still having problems getting my head round that,' Woody admitted. 'And we thought *he* was the controlling partner in that marriage.'

'They put on a good show,' Kate agreed. 'When I think I used to feel sorry for her being stuck in that big house where she had us believe she didn't want to be.'

'It was exactly where she *did* want to be,' Woody added.

Fergal had replenished Angie's glass and was now topping up everyone's wine. 'So, what happens now?' he asked.

'Well,' said Woody, 'Eve is in custody, accused of two murders – Henry Hedgefield and Freddy Parr. Two innocent old men whose only crime was not to be fooled by her and Ben.'

'What about Ben?' Kate asked anxiously. 'You know, I did believe him when he said he killed Aaron in self-defence. But how can they prove that after all those years?'

Woody shrugged. 'Fact is, they probably can't. It's unlikely to be able to be proven one way or the other. He can, of course, be charged as an accessory and for keeping the murders secret. But, boy, won't the press and the media have a field day! Stolen identity, murders, bit of blackmail on Eve's behalf, wow! And all on the edge of a sleepy Cornish village!'

'Not so sleepy these days,' said Kate. 'It's the two daughters I feel sorry for.'

'Hopefully Ben will still be around, or his sentence won't be as long as Eve's at least,' Woody said, 'but unfortunately the girls are going to have to live with the Hedgefield scandal, and the fact that their mother and father are both killers.'

'He insists he didn't kill Mark Edderley,' Kate said. 'He seemed really upset about that.'

'Well, he couldn't blame that one on Eve, could he?' Woody said. 'It looks as if the evidence for Mark's death is inconclusive, and that it's possible he did hit his head on the front of the boat when he fell into the water.'

'So we may never know?' Kate asked.

'We may never know,' Woody confirmed.

'Well,' Angie said, 'it'll all be good for tourism, won't it? I bet there'll be thousands of visitors queuing up to get into the tea rooms, and to see where the body was found – and to see *me*, too, because I was a *hostage*! Eve was so obsessed with getting away, convinced the police would arrive any minute and *I* was their guarantee!' She was looking more and more pleased with herself.

'We'll have some plaques made to fix on the wall and explain everything,' Fergal added happily. 'And we,' he said, squeezing Angie's shoulders, 'are going to make a fecking fortune!'

Kate and Woody exchanged glances. Then Woody, taking Kate's hand, said, 'I've given up telling you not to get involved. I know when I'm beaten! But, Kate, you don't need me to tell you that you can only flirt with death so many times…'

'I know,' Kate admitted. 'I'm going to be good from now on and keep my nose out of trouble.'

'That'll be the day!' Angie snorted.

'I have some more news,' Woody said. They all looked at him expectantly. 'Bill Robson's gone!'

'*What?*' Kate could hardly believe what she was hearing.

'His handling of the case left a lot to be desired,' Woody continued, 'and he knew it. In spite of the fact he's got himself some new woman, it's apparent he doesn't like women in general.'

'I can confirm that,' said Kate with feeling.

'Several women complained about his attitude,' Woody said. 'Added to the fact that he was buying a piece of land at a silly price from a suspect, and you get the picture. He's *out*!'

'Sacked?'

'Not exactly. Because he's retiring age and they've given him the chance to resign. Which is more than he deserves.'

'What'll he do now?' Kate asked.

'He's going back to the Midlands. At least he's done one decent thing: he has agreed that George Pearson can have the plot of land for the low price. Because Bill can't get out of Cornwall fast enough!'

'Good riddance!' said Kate. 'He was the most charmless man I've ever met!' She thought for a moment. 'I wonder who we'll get in his place? You'll have to initiate him into the job yet again, Woody.'

Woody beamed. 'Here's the thing – it's a *woman*! From all accounts she's in her early fifties, blonde and a real looker!'

'You're kidding!' Kate felt her elation rapidly dissipating.

'Nope!' Woody said. '*That's* what they tell me.'

'Well, don't sound so pleased about it,' said Kate, draining her glass.

Woody said nothing but continued beaming.

'I suspect,' said Fergal, standing up again, 'that we might all be ready for another drink?'

CHAPTER FORTY

The little nurse named Fran appeared just as Kate was signing in at The Cedars.

'Nice to see you here again,' she said.

Kate smiled. 'I thought Adeline might tolerate a visitor.' She fingered the little cameo brooch in her coat pocket.

'Well, you know your way to Primrose Wing by now,' Fran said with a smile as she disappeared into the office.

As Kate tapped on the door of Room 15 and gently pushed it open, she was relieved that she didn't need to question Adeline any more; no further grilling about babies, about Henry, about Aaron.

Adeline was sitting at the table again, covered in brooches and writing furiously. She looked up briefly as Kate entered and said, 'Oh, it's *you*.'

That's an improvement, Kate thought, because at least she must realise that she's seen me before.

'Yes, it's me. How are you, Adeline?'

'I'm busy,' said Adeline.

'Who are you writing to today?' Kate asked. 'Henry?'

Adeline laid down her pen and looked Kate straight in the eye. 'Henry's dead,' she said flatly.

'Oh, I'm sorry,' Kate said, taken aback for a moment.

'I'm not,' Adeline said vehemently. 'He sent me away, you know. You can't trust men.'

Kate decided it wise to change the subject and channel Adeline's interest elsewhere. She dug out the little oval cameo brooch with the insert – a picture of a tiny girl with golden curls.

'I've brought you a brooch, Adeline,' she said.

Adeline looked down doubtfully at her laden chest. 'I don't know where we're going to put it,' she said.

'We'll find a place somewhere,' Kate said, setting down the brooch on the table in front of her.

Adeline stared down at it for what seemed like a long time. Eventually she lifted her head and Kate saw that she had tears in her eyes. 'It's Emily,' she said at last.

Kate nodded. 'I thought that too. Isn't it a nice picture?'

'It's Emily,' Adeline repeated, and then she smiled broadly. 'She'd look just like that.'

Kate had never seen her smile before and was struck by how it lifted up her face, put a sparkle in her eye, and made her look quite beautiful.

'Thank you,' Adeline said, smiling at Kate, 'for bringing me Emily.' She kissed the little brooch. 'Will you come again?'

'Yes,' Kate said, squeezing her shoulder briefly, 'I will.'

The Locker Tea Rooms, The Locker Bar, The Smuggler's Cabin – whatever it was going to be called – was looking normal again in the late-afternoon sunshine. The police had gone, the tape had gone and Kate could actually hear Angie humming as she made her way into the bar area. Angie was varnishing the shelves behind the counter which would eventually hold the rows of bottles.

'Hi!' she called out cheerily. 'What have you been up to?'

Kate sat down on the one and only bar stool. 'I've just been up to see Adeline Hedgefield.'

Angie stopped varnishing for a moment. 'That was beyond the call of duty, surely?'

'I didn't do it out of duty. And I wasn't being saintly. I just feel sorry for the poor woman. She's never had many visitors, and she'll have even fewer now.'

'You look tired,' Angie said, as she resumed varnishing.

'I am tired, Angie. This Hedgefield business has exhausted me. I'm getting too old for all this detective work.'

'Then don't go stirring up hornets' nests,' said Angie. 'Get Woody to take you out for a nice meal or something.'

'He's taking me up to The Edge of the Moor tonight,' Kate said. 'It's sort of become "our place" and it always makes me feel relaxed.'

'Good. Leave the detective work to the sexy new lady-in-charge!'

'You certainly know how to ruin my mood!' Kate retorted.

Angie laughed. 'You've nothing to fear there, Kate. That stupid bloke is mad about you!'

'Woody? Do you really think so?'

'I think it's obvious to everyone except yourself. Aren't you two ever going to get married?'

Kate was astounded. 'Married? Why would we do that? We like things the way they are.'

'Hmm.'

'What does that mean – *hmm*?' Kate asked.

'Work it out for yourself,' said Angie, grinning.

As she was about to leave, Kate turned round and hugged her sister. Was Woody really mad about her? she wondered. She felt a little glow of happiness, and also a great sense of relief and gratitude that both she and Angie had survived this latest escapade.

'Still, I wouldn't go buying a hat if I were you,' Kate called as she went out of the door.

A LETTER FROM DEE

Dear Reader,

Thank you for reading *A Body at the Tea Rooms*, and I hope you enjoyed meeting Kate Palmer, amateur super-sleuth, and her friend, Woody. I assure you that Cornwall is really a very peaceful place, so don't let these crimes put you off coming down here; just avoid Tinworthy!

To keep up with Kate's escapades, or any of my other books, you can sign up on the following link:

www.bookouture.com/dee-macdonald

Your email address will never be shared and you can unsubscribe at any time.

If you enjoyed the book, I'd very much appreciate if you could write a review. I love to know what my readers think, and your feedback is invaluable.

You can also get in touch via Facebook and Twitter.

Dee x

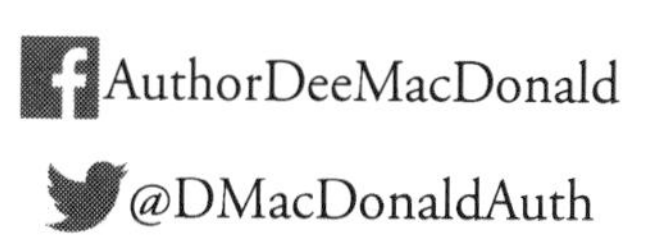

ACKNOWLEDGEMENTS

A huge thank you to my editor, Natasha Harding, without whose expertise and patience this book would not have taken shape. She has guided and encouraged me, as always.

Thanks also to my supportive agent, Amanda Preston at LBA Books. I shall forever be grateful to her for introducing me to Natasha, and to Bookouture, who I think is the nicest and most supportive publisher in the world!

Again, heartfelt thanks to Rosemary Brown, my friend and mentor, whose eagle eyes miss nothing! She straightens up my rambling plots and sorts out my timelines, which are inclined to straggle all over the place.

Thanks to my husband, Stan, for his support, and to my son, Dan, and family, who keep a close watch on my reviews and my place in the charts.

Printed in Great Britain
by Amazon

61161217R00140